THE GENTLEMAN'S CLUB
by
John Angus

Bonus Pages

THE GENTLEMAN'S CLUB by John Angus

1

Sir Edward Rawlins stared eagerly out the window of the helicopter as the island came into view. There was little to see, for the aircraft approach lane was designed to minimize sightseeing from the air. All he could catch sight of was the lush tropical greenery, the long white sanded beaches, and the red tiled roof of the large and beautiful main residence building.

His chest was gripped by an anxious tightness as the helicopter came into land, and he still found it hard to believe the fanciful tales which had been told him about the Viceroy Club, the gentleman's association of which he was now a probationary member.

The helicopter landed perfectly and he, its only passenger, stepped out to be greeted by a thin faced older man in a smart suit. If the warmth bothered the man he gave no sign as he bowed, actually bowed to Sir Edward before directing two other men in ties and tails into the helicopter for his bags.

"Sir Edward, my name is Anthony. On behalf of the staff let me be the first to greet you and welcome you to the Viceroy."

"Um, er, well, thank you," Edward said, licking his lips a trifle nervously.

His particular, well, preferences had been a long held secret, and he was uncomfortable with anyone knowing about them. He was still far from certain how the Viceroy had come to be aware of them.

"I'm at your disposal, Sir, if you'd like a tour of the facilities. Or I'll show you to your suite if you'd like to relax."

"I'd, er, rather like a quick tour actually," Edward said hesitantly.

"Of course, sir. Your bags will be taken to your suite and your things made ready for you. In the meantime, if you would come this way please, sir?"

Edward smiled as the man bowed again and swept his arm towards a Rolls sitting a few yards away. He was happy that this place, at least, had help which knew its place. That was something of a rarity even in London's better shops and clubs. He walked to the Rolls, where a Chauffeur bowed and held the door for him. Anthony got in beside him and the chauffeur pulled away from the helicopter.

The ride was a brief one, ending at a small garage set amongst the trees. The chauffeur hopped out and opened the door on his side, bowing again as Anthony got out. Edward preened at this respect, for he seldom experienced it back home, where, despite his wealth and undeniable physical attractiveness he was something of an outcast, the butt of jokes amongst his peers and even in the mass media.

Edward was in his early thirties, yet his boyish, handsome face was far from the only thing about him which was immature. He had a tendency to sulk when he didn't get his way, was a well-known coward and bully, and had a cruel streak which made him such a tyrant to his servants that it had proved almost impossible to keep any, even at triple wages.

Anthony led him down a winding, flower-lined path and thence into another building, where they were met by a small, gruff man in working clothes.

"A carriage for two, in Sir Edward's name," Anthony said.

"Right away, Sir Edward," the man said respectfully, bowing and tipping his hat before hurrying away.

Anthony and Edward followed, and Edward suddenly halted, brought up short in astonishment as the man opened what appeared to be cages and brought out two women.

The women were both quite tall, and muscular, and entirely nude. Their bodies gleamed darkly, heavily tanned, and each had a sort of harness about her upper torso.

The leather harness was composed of straps over their shoulders and around their chests. Both women had their arms bound in leather sleeves which pulled them behind their backs and then up high, the tops of the sleeves, obviously containing their hands, bound to collars at the back of their necks.

Neither woman struggled or made any effort to protest as they were led towards a small, low-slung carriage and their harnesses attached to the front. As Edward's wide-eyed stare took in every detail he watched the man attach lead lines to small rings in their nipples. These lines led under their arms and back to the carriage.

"Step aboard, Sir Edward," Anthony said, bowing and motioning him towards the carriage.

Edward obeyed in a daze, climbing up and taking his place on a heavily padded seat while Anthony got aboard next to him.

"These are their reins, of course," Anthony said.

Edward took them, staring at them, then ahead at the tight, firm buttocks of the two women now attached to the carriage.

"And that's for encouragement," Anthony said, pointing at the buggy whip protruding from a small holder next to Edward's seat.

"How, I mean to say, how um -"

"As you would horses or oxen," Anthony smiled.

Edward swallowed then snapped the reins. The two women started walking forward, then began to jog, leading them along a paved, cobblestone path through the grounds.

"My God," he said, shaking his head.

"Our membership prefers a civilized mode of transportation rather than smelly cars or unsightly golf carts," Anthony said with a smile.

The carriage took them to the edge of a rolling eighteen hole golf course, where Anthony explained a few of the finer points, then to a large, beautiful pool of water below a waterfall, then down to the beaches before turning towards what he called the barn.

"We're quite proud of the barn, really," Anthony said. "Our breeding program is well underway now. Our ambition is to be self-sustaining. That's not to say occasional new blood won't added into the mix, but we won't need the constant recruitment we now require to satisfy our members' needs."

"How do you er, uh, get your new recruits?"

"Oh we have a number of ways. We have contacts out there, people who recruit for us, who are on the watch for just the right kind of girl for the Viceroy. Usually these are young ladies with little if any family who will not really cause much of a stir when they disappear. Sometimes, of course, we recruit what we call special girls."

"Special?"

"Oh, certain young ladies whom a member or members considers especially deserving of such treatment, if you know what I mean."

"So I could have a particular girl, er, imported then if I wanted?"

"Certainly, for a price."

"I have just the one in mind," he said. He licked his lips at the thought of Amanda...

2

"Have you ever done any bondage?"

The words hit her with a sudden jarring burst of excitement, and Lisa could feel her chest tightening as butterflies took flight in her stomach.

"I - no," she all but whispered.

David smiled roguishly and quirked his lip at her.

"Would you like to be my little slave girl?" he breathed, sliding his fingers through her hair.

Excitement warred with caution inside her. She'd only known David for two weeks now, and they'd only made love on two occasions. He was a stunningly attractive man with a deeply sensuous and exciting personality, but she had already come to realize that he had a cruel streak.

Yet the idea was so erotic, and though she'd had fantasies about bondage before she'd not dared voice them to any of her former lovers for fear of being seen as a tramp, or worse yet, pathetically unbalanced.

"Come on," he teased, his fingers easing down along her ribs then up her front, cupping her breasts and lifting them upwards as his lips brushed the top of her head.

God, he was so sexy! She nodded her head shakily. Surely David wouldn't do anything that would hurt her. After all, what was there to fear? It wasn't like he could, well, rape her, not when she'd already given herself to him.

He smiled and she felt an instant wave of delight at having pleased him, at the same time feeling a nagging doubt that she'd opened herself up to something she wasn't quite ready for. Her female friends thought David was dreamy, him with his smirk and his pretty face and powerful body and big motorcycle. But her male friends were deeply suspicious of him, and she wondered if they knew something about him, if they could see something she and other women couldn't.

She moved to unbutton her blouse but David stopped her.

"Don't move. Don't do a thing. You're my slave now. You only do what I tell you to do."

His slave! She felt her stomach quiver and felt a heaviness in her loins.

He deftly unbuttoned her blouse and pulled it off, then quickly removed her skirt as well. He led her to the bed and pushed her down on it, then removed her shoes and socks before slipping her panties down her legs and off.

Lisa blushed a bit as he spread her legs wide. Her sex life, prior to David, had not been terribly exciting nor particularly stimulating. She'd had a few brief couplings with boys during high school, mostly in the backs of cars. They'd lasted minutes and brought her little pleasure. Then, in the two years since she'd had two sexual experiences, neither going much above her high school fumblings.

And then had come David, and his hours long lovemaking sessions that had brought her her first orgasms, had made her cry out with a lust she'd never imagined she could possess. He had been the first outside her doctor to actually spend any time 'down there', the first to show her how delicious a tongue could feel on her labia and clitoris.

He really opened an entirely new window in her life and she was determined to keep it open. And if that meant exploring bondage, which, while exciting was also worrying, then she'd have to have the courage for it.

He removed her bra, then had her spread out on her large bed. He winked at her, then left the bedroom for a few moments. When he returned he was holding four long black straps in one hand.

In a businesslike fashion he began to strap her wrists and ankles to the four corners of the bed. Even as she watched him do it Lisa felt a strange sense of being used, of him having coldly planned this ahead of time.

Yet that concern quickly evaporated as the leather closed tightly about her wrists and she felt the straps go taut against the top corners of the bed. She felt her arousal deepen, her breath quickening as he moved to the foot of the bed and fastened the straps to the bottom posts.

Then, when she was laid out helplessly he slowly unbuckled his belt, smirking at her as she lay there before him.

She strained against the straps, feeling her sense of help-lessness growing along with the heat between her thighs. At the same time she felt an odd delight at being so bold, at taking part in something that was, at least to her, so wicked, so far from the old boring, mousy Lisa.

When he was down to his underwear he paused and walked out of the room again, returning with something in his hand. His expression was, she thought, odd. He almost looked bored, and certainly far too casual for what was, to her, an incredibly exciting and novel experience.

He knelt on the edge of the bed and reached behind her head.

"Tilt your head back, slut," he said casually.

She felt indignation war with excitement at his crude words, but obeyed.

"Open your mouth wide. Wider. Wider!" he snapped.

She opened her mouth wide, startled, and he brought the thing he'd carried to her face, then jammed it against her mouth before she could protest. It was a thick rubber ball of sorts, and he shoved it into her mouth with brutal and painful strength, forcing her jaws wide apart and filling her mouth.

She rolled her eyes, trying to talk, trying to demand he take it out, but her tongue was jammed down by the thing, and he was pulling straps around her head and buckling the rubber thing in place.

He stepped back, letting her head fall, and again she tried to complain, tried to tell him she didn't like the thing, but she could barely make a sound as he casually stripped off his underwear and knelt between her legs.

He sneered at her, then his open hand lashed out and cracked across the side of her face, stunning her and bring-ing tears to her eyes.

"Stupid whore," he said in disgust.

He gripped himself, pumping his fist up and down his

erection as he watched her writhe helplessly, then he pushed the head of his cock against her and thrust into her.

She cried out in pain, staring up at him in shock and fear. Again she cried out as he dropped his heavy weight atop her and drove the last inch of his manhood into her opening.

He began to thrust into her wildly then, grunting as he pounded himself up into her belly. This was not the gentle lovemaking she'd become used to. This was not the considerate lover who's hands did marvellous things to her body.

He was not making love, he was fucking her, she thought, for the first time really understanding the distinction between the terms. His hips ground against her as he slammed himself into her again and again, making no effort to give her pleasure, using her like the cheap whore he had just called her.

He finished quickly, as he must at the pace he'd set, and heaved a sigh of relief as he pulled back onto his knees.

"What? Too rough for you?" he said with a smirk. "Come on, baby. You know a slut like you loves cock any way she can get it."

Why was he talking to her like that? Was this all a game? Well, of course it must be, she thought. It was a rough kind of game, a role playing game, and she wasn't at all sure she liked it.

He ran his hands over her body, fingering her nipples and pinching them, then moved a hand between her legs, slipping two fingers up inside her.

"Think I can make you come on my fingers, baby?" he taunted.

And he could. She knew he could, for even as her anger grew at his treatment she felt her heat reawakening as his expert fingers probed within her and his thumb worked away at her clitoris.

It was just a game, after all, and she could talk with him later about making it more gentle. But in the meantime, she

12

felt the sexual heat rising within her, and gave herself over to a fantasy of being the helpless prisoner of an evil madman who was intent on molesting her for his own evil purposes.

The fantasy added to her pleasure, and she strained against the straps holding her, gasping and moaning as he continued to finger her in a careless, almost contemptuous manner.

"Maybe I should bring in a ruddy football team to use you," he said. "I bet you'd like that, wouldn't you, you tramp! You'd love to get yourself done by a dozen men at once, to get yourself gang banged!"

Lisa whimpered into the gag, her head jerking back in tight little movements as she sought to drive herself up against his fingers. A sexual haze was surrounding her, growing more dense with each second, catching her up in a world where nothing mattered but her own pleasure, her own lust.

Her movements became more and more energetic as she ground herself up at him, groaning and gasping as she pulled at the straps binding her. Her body throbbed with sexual need and the intensity continued to grow.

He pulled his hand away and stood up, then moved out of the bedroom again. She moaned and rolled her eyes towards the door, mentally begging him to return, to give her the relief she so desperately needed.

She heard his voice, and strained to hear what he was saying, but in a moment she felt a dagger of shock hit her as she realized he was not talking to her. He returned and with him were two more men, neither of whom she knew.

"Very nice," one of them said as he moved to the bed and limbed into it.

"Aye, nice piece of meat that," the second said, nodding his head. "Good body, nice face, nice hair."

She stared at them both in shock, unable to understand this betrayal, feeling her face go scarlet as they eyed her exposed body.

She jerked her eyes to the men who'd climbed into the bed and her eyes widened as he dropped his pants and produced a large erection.

He shuffled forward, and she watched with a mixture of embarrassment, astonishment and, much to her bewilderment, excitement as he pushed himself against her moist, reddened labia, then thrust himself into her.

He chuckled as he met her wide eyes, his fingers sinking into the softness of her breasts, squeezing them together as he humped into her with a deep, steady stroke.

She turned her head towards David, but he was talking with the other man, ignoring her as this man raped her.

She felt a deep indignation, and furiously tried to push down her growing sense of delight as the man using her stroked his cock back and forth against her buzzing, burning clitoris.

Bastards, she thought. Rotten dirty bastards!

Yet her groin was alive with heat, and it surged upwards into her belly and up through her chest as he drove himself into her again and again. She became desperate in her attempt to resist it, but as it caught hold of her mind she resigned herself to it, no longer having the will to fight against the bliss engulfing her.

She laid her head back, grunting in time to his hard thrusts, moaning as his hands crudely mauled her breasts and moved with outrageous familiarity over her nude body.

She felt herself rising towards an orgasm, her mind fluttering wildly in the stormy winds of intense sexual pleasure.

Her head jerked back once, twice, then she cried out, the sound barely audible through the gag, arching her back, her body stiffening then shaking violently as the climax rippled up and down her spine.

And as the howling sexual maelstrom collapsed the last vestiges of her resistance she felt nothing but the hard, steady pounding of his tool into her seeping cleft, and the crackling sexual electricity that was setting her muscles to spasm in helpless delight.

She went limp, groaning, eyes closed even as he continued to pump into her. She felt him stop, but didn't even open her eyes to acknowledge it as he moved away from her and got off the bed. She opened them only when she felt the bed shake again, opened them to see the second man leering at her as he moved into position.

Gripped by a deep, languorous afterglow she could only watch with dull eyes as he entered her and began a high-speed rutting that set her and the bed shaking.

She noted David and the other man placing her open suitcases on the nearby dresser, and saw them taking items from her closet and dressers.

Then she gasped, her attention diverted by the man atop her as he gripped her long blonde hair, yanked her head up and back and began to chew painfully on her exposed throat.

Fortunately he spent himself quickly. Then he joined the other two, ignoring her there on the bed as they loaded up several suitcases with her clothes and toiletries and removed them from the room.

She pulled again at the straps, but they were immoveable, and despite a growing fury she could do nothing but lay there.

Finally David moved to the bed and unstrapped her ankles. She glared at him balefully, just waiting for him to remove the gag. Then he was out! She'd toss him and his filthy friends out of her flat and out of her life!

One of the men joined him as they unstrapped her wrists from the bedpost, but her sudden furious attempt to pull away was met by a slap across the face that sent her head whipping backwards.

They took her by the arms and dragged her out of the bed, pulling over to the table and sitting her roughly in the chair next to it. David slapped a piece of paper down in front of her and then placed her hand on it, sticking a pen into her fingers.

"You're going to write a letter to your girlfriend Susan," he said. "I'll dictate. You write."

She rolled her eyes at him and struggled but the other man forced her left arm up behind her back painfully and she screamed, tears filling her eyes.

"Just do as you're told or else," David snarled, gripping her hair and twisting it violently.

"Start the letter. 'Dear Susan'," he said.

She moaned and turned her eyes away, then screamed as his open handed blow sent her head flying back.

"I gave you an order, you slut! Now do it!" he snarled.

He gave her the pen again and she wrote as he dictated, telling Susan she was going on a sudden holiday to Africa with David and wasn't sure when she'd be back. After she signed it David and the man behind her stood her up, then quickly strapped her wrists together behind her back.

The two men moved ahead of them, and she and David followed behind, David keeping a firm grip on her arm as he led her to the front door. She tried to draw back as she realized his intent but a slap to the head dissuaded her as he led her outside into the cool night.

She had a basement flat in the back of the building. Its entrance was at the side, and no windows faced into the small parking lot as he led her across it to a small gray van parked nearby. Her mind was filled with terror as she tried to understand what was happening, and why.

He thrust her into the van, then he waved at her and winked. "See you again sometime, baby," he said with a grin.

The door slid shut and the van started forward.

"Cheer up, love," the man in the back with her said as he slipped his hand between her legs. "You won't have to worry about paying the rent where you're going."

He laughed in delight at his own wit.

3

Amanda Graham fought hard to keep her eyes open as Professor Jennings droned on and on about the merit's of charting a decade long corporate history of any intended investment, filling the board with a veritable blizzard of graphs and scrawled formulas.

It was a quarter to ten in the morning. The class had begun at eight thirty, and though she'd been up until four (her boyfriend Neil having been particularly enthusiastic in his lovemaking the previous night) she had faithfully dragged herself out of his warm bed to make the early morning jaunt here for this class.

And now she could hardly wait for it to end.

Finally he assigned homework and she shoved her things into her bag and stood up, rubbing her eyes tiredly. She trotted down the hall and took the stairs two at a time, knowing that if she was quick she'd get home before Neil was even out of bed, and wouldn't that be fun.

She had to be quick with several young men of her acquaintance who tried to discuss this or that with her, for she knew that anything but brusqueness would only encourage them.

Male attention, mostly unwanted, though not always, had been both a pleasure and a cross to bear since her twelfth birthday. She'd always been extraordinarily attractive, a girl adults loved to hug and pat and fawn over, but at twelve she'd developed into something else again.

She retained the adorable face, though it slowly took on less that of the wide-eyed innocent child then of the sleek, sophisticated young woman. Her long, lush, chestnut coloured hair flowed about her like a lion's main, and tumbled past her shoulders like a silken waterfall. It framed a softly rounded face with a small nose, piercing green eyes, full, sensuous lips and perfect glistening teeth.

She was six feet tall, and had always been quite athletic. Her long, exquisite legs were perfectly sculpted, her buttocks tight and round, her waist narrow.

Her breasts were high and on a smaller woman would have seemed overly large, yet on her frame seemed in perfect symmetry with the rest of her. She had grown yet another bra size just before starting university, and now wore a size thirty-eight D cup, which she hoped would be her last for quite some time.

Despite their generous size her breasts were astonishingly firm, the small, neat nipples tilted slightly upwards when she stood straight.

All in all, she presented the absolute height of feminine beauty and desirability, and had been pursued rabidly by boys, and then men, from before she'd even begun her teenage years. Now, as she faced the end of them, her twentieth birthday a few months off, she often found herself the subject of lust and flattery from hungry males of all ages and descriptions.

She had a whip-sharp intellect, and refused to be condescended to or patronized by men seeking to ingratiate themselves to her by flattery. She knew what they were after and would have none of it. Dignified and proud, she had cut a swath through high school and was doing so in university as well, leaving legions of male admirers in her wake.

"Damn," she said softly as she rounded a tree-lined curb and saw a long van parked across the road.

She braked sharply, bringing the Jag to a halt. She glowered at the two men ahead of her even as he noticed another car coming up behind her and stopping with its nose against her bumper.

One of the men with the van walked over and bent over next to her window.

"Is there a problem?" she asked.

"Just a slight one, miss. Step out of the car, would you?"

She frowned at him in surprise. She looked behind her and saw a tall woman in a leather jacket climb out of the Fiat behind her so shrugged and opened the door.

"I don't understand," she said. "What is it you want?"

The man was large and rough looking, with long brown hair. His chest bulged against a dirty T-shirt. She looked around warily and was reassured to see the other woman sit back against the front side of her own car, folding her arms across her chest as she looked on.

The second man came over then and looked her over, folding his arms across his chest.

"Aren't you something!" he said.

"Look. What is this about?" she demanded firmly, keeping the tremor from her voice only with the greatest of effort.

"Get your clothes off," the first man ordered.

"I beg your pardon?"

His open hand lashed out and cracked against the side of her face, flinging her back against her car. She gasped as she saw stars, clutching the side of the car to keep from falling.

"I said get your clothes off. We haven't got all day."

Amanda staggered to her feet only to meet the other man's open hand. Again her head whipped back and she cried out as she fell across the front of the Jag.

"Clothes off," the first man said, sounding almost bored.

"P-please," she gasped. "I - I have money and -"

A fist slammed into her stomach with enough force to double her over and knock the wind from her lungs. She collapsed to her knees, gasping and choking as she clutched her aching stomach and fought nausea.

"Do as you're told," the man said.

He gripped her hair, winding it around his fist and yanking her to her feet. She screamed and clawed madly at him only to get another slap, then another, then another. She staggered back and fell on her back at the side of the road, gasping dazedly.

"Strip," he ordered, his feet stepping into the dirt next to her head.

The other man came and stood on her other side, reached down and yanked her up to her feet. Her face was hot and aching from the slaps and her mind was fluttering like a butterfly. She had no experience with violence and it had deeply shocked her.

The man raised his hand again and she cowered back with a cry, her hands going to her blazer.

He halted as she jerked her blazer off and dropped it into the dirt at the side of the road. Her trembling fingers went to her blouse and she undid them slowly then pulled it open and off.

"Please," she whimpered.

Another blow sent her head snapping back and again she hit the ground, sobbing now, whimpering. She rolled onto her stomach, covering her face with her hands but screamed as her hair was again used to force her back to her feet.

The other woman was looking on, obviously a part of things. She was older than Amanda, close to thirty. Cooly sophisticated, her make-up perfect, her pants and top tight but stylish, she calmly smoked a cigarette as she watched.

There was no boredom in her eyes, but neither was there the hint of help or sympathy. Instead she smiled and looked excited as Amanda removed her shoes then shakily undid her trousers and slipped them down.

Tears trickled from Amanda's cheeks as she moved her hands behind her and undid her bra.

"M-my father has money... NO!"

She cowered back as the man raised his arm again, sobbing.

"Strip."

She was behind embarrassment now as she slipped her silky bra over her shoulders and let it fall. The men eyed her breasts with smirks and she cringed mentally as she undid her panties and cowered there naked.

"Stand up straight!" the man said sharply.

She gasped, standing straight, chest heaving.

"Hands behind your head! Push those fat tits out!"

She obeyed, whimpering as he kicked her feet apart in the dirt, and jerked her arms back harder, forcing her back to arch. The two men ran their eyes over her but didn't touch her.

Then the woman came forward slowly. She wore stiletto heels and carried herself with confidence and authority. She was taller than Amanda, and much broader at the shoulder, muscular and powerful looking though obviously in excellent shape.

She looked Amanda up and down, moving slowly around her, and Amanda gasped as she felt the woman's finger slide down her spine and between her buttocks.

She jerked aside, her hands coming down only to be cuffed across the face and flung back into the dirt.

"Please! Please!" she sobbed.

"Come here, girl," the woman ordered, pointing at the dirt next to her feet.

Amanda moaned and pushed herself up.

"No! Crawl here! Now! On your belly!"

One of the men moved beside her and she cried out as his boot pressed down against her back between her shoulder blades, forcing her breasts into the dirt.

"Now! We haven't all day. Sooner or later someone is going to wonder why this road is closed."

She crawled forward on her belly, panting for breath, eyes blinking back tears as she pulled her nude body through the dirt and weeds and stones until she was at the woman's feet.

"Look at what you've done," the woman said angrily.

"You've made my shoes dirty. Clean them off. Now, girl. Before I lose my temper with you."

Amanda raised her head, gulping in air, confused and flustered.

"With your tongue, you dog!" the woman snarled.

Amanda looked at the woman's shoes, then cried out as one of the men stomped his foot down on her back.

"Do I need to take a belt to you?"

They were mad! They were all mad! Why were they doing this to her?

The woman growled and Amanda hurriedly lowered her lips to the gleaming shoes. She hesitated briefly, then pushed her small pink tongue out and licked tentatively at the side of one shoe.

"Hurry!"

She licked harder, her tongue darting out, lapping across the
side of the shoe as the two men watched and sniggered.

"Yes, you learn quickly," the woman purred.

A knee slammed into the small of her back and Amanda grunted as her arms were yanked up and back behind her. She continued to lick as she felt her hands placed together and a thick strap slipped around her wrists snap tight. Another strap went around her arms just below her elbows and she let out a cry of pain as her arms were forced painfully back until her elbows touched.

The woman gripped her hair then and yanked her to her feet. She smiled and then crushed her lips against Amanda's mouth, her tongue plunging deep as her hand came up and cupped one of her dusty breasts, squeezing hard.

Then she shoved her back into the arms of the two men and Amanda screamed as her hair was pulled back savagely. With her mouth wide a spongy rubber ball was jammed into it, keeping her jaws wide. The ball was attached to a strap which went around her head and buckled behind her.

Moments later the woman marched her to the van and flung her inside, smiling as she stood back and let one of the men get in.

"I'm sure we'll meet again, my dear," she said with a cool smile.

The door closed and she was in darkness for a few moments. A light was turned on and the man leered down at her, his eyes moving over her body.

"Now you just hold still, love," he said, removing a syringe from his pocket.

He rolled her onto her side, then plunged the needle into her upper arm. Almost at once she began to feel light-headed, then the world faded slowly around her.

4

No matter what awaited her, Lisa moaned in pathetic gratitude at the sudden touch of a hand on her bare breast. She had been held utterly immobile, blinded and deaf, for what seemed ages. Her throat and mouth ached with dryness and her limbs were cramped from lack of movement. Anything, even rape, was better than that!

She felt the straps unbuckled, then hands lifted her up from whatever box she'd been in and set her down on a hard surface. Her arms were numb, but her legs groaned in pleasure at the sensuous delight of being able to bend just a little, even if for a moment.

She felt the sheath unrolled, pulled down her legs and off, and spread her legs slowly, utterly heedless of who might be there, who might be looking down at her nude body.

It felt glorious, and the pleasure rolled up and down her body. She slowly bent her legs up, keeping them well apart, and even when a hand slipped between her sweating thighs and began to squeeze her pussy it did not detract from the sensations.

In fact, as the fingers began to rub against her clitoris she felt a rapid buildup of sexual heat. she drew her knees up even further, back even more, groaning into the gag as she spread them and opened them, bent them and opened them. And as the finger rubbed insistently at her clitoris a small orgasm rolled over her dazed mind.

Her legs dropped back, her back arching, her head turning from side to side. She cared nothing for pride, only for the pleasure that was rippling through her body. Her heels drummed against the surface below as she shook violently.

Then she lay still, gasping desperately for breath.

It had taken much less than a minute for her orgasm.

Hands rolled her onto her stomach and the sheathe was unstrapped and rolled down her arms and off, then her hands were unstrapped, and finally, the hood was unbuckled and slid free over her head.

She squinted and blinked as bright lights assaulted her eyes, tears starting to fill them as her ball-gag was removed.

She was in a long, low stone room sitting on a high, wide work table of sorts. The walls were lined with cabinets closets, and strange looking devices whose purpose she couldn't even guess at. Two men were in the room, both clad in dark coveralls, both grinning at her even while treating her with a casualness that was both reassuring and frightening.

She tried to speak but her throat was too dry and she coughed instead. One of the men pulled her head back and held the plastic tube of a drinking cup against her lips. She sucked greedily, swallowing the cool liquid with a relish she never thought she would accord mere water.

She tried to reach for the cup herself but her arms would hardly function. They had been pinned back for so long - how long she didn't know, that they were only now beginning to throb painfully with reawakened feeling.

And even as she sat there drinking one of the men was placing a thick padded leather restraint around each wrist, locking them in place calmly and efficiently.

There was a rail running along the ceiling just overhead, long meat hooks hanging from it on rollers. As the drinking cup was pulled away her wrists were fastened together in front of her by means of a small round metal link, then she was lifted up by the two men and the link slipped over one of the hooks overhead.

She gasped and groaned as her full weight dropped on her wrists and aching arms and shoulders, but the men seemed unconcerned with her discomfort. One gave a hard shove to her back and the hook glided briskly along the rail, carrying her towards an opening in the far wall.

She saw the box she had obviously been inside of pushed aside and another come forward, rolling through a small opening in the other wall on a treadmill. The two men lifted the box off and onto the table, opened it, then took another woman from the box, laying her out on the table as Lisa herself had been.

That girl was also hooded and bound, and Lisa had no opportunity to see the face as one of the men came over and gave her another casual shove, sending her gliding through the narrow opening in the wall and into the next room.

Another man waited her there, wearing a heavy leather apron and gloves. He gripped her hip and slid her further into the room then picked up a hose and pointed it at her. Water poured over her as she gasped and sputtered and twisted on the end of the hook.

Still, in a way she was grateful for it. The tight leather had made her sweat, as had her desperate predicament, and she felt filthy and bedraggled.

She had barely had enough time to get over her pathetic gratitude at being freed of her bondage. Yet she wondered at her lack of embarrassment around these men. Perhaps it was her confusion and weariness, perhaps the strange kind of hospital mentality which people got after repeated exposures to indifferent strangers.

Still it felt odd, like she were a piece of meat, or some kind of product. The men paid little attention to her displayed body, moving around her as he soaked her with the warm water from the hose, eyes calm and indifferent.

He set down the hose and picked up a large sponge then began to scrub her down, starting at her chest. The sponge was soapy, and he quickly raised a lather across her body, moving quickly and efficiently from top to bottom.

He put the soap down and moved behind her, then pulled her head back and poured something liquid into her hair. His rubbery fingers scrubbed and another layer of soap rose as he shampooed her hair. A radio was playing in a distant room, the music soft and dreamy.

He moved around in front of her and lifted her left leg up and apart, slipping a strap around it to hold it in position. Her right leg was likewise lifted up and apart, baring her loins and buttocks in a quite lewd manner.

He hummed to himself as he picked up a narrow tube and slowly pushed it up into her cleft. Lisa grunted and felt a new embarrassment, yet again, the man was so casual that it was obvious he was merely doing his job.

The cone pushed deep and she felt warm soapy water pumping out and then spilling out between her pussy lips. The cone moved around inside her a little, then pulled back. He pushed another narrow cylinder into her body, this one made of a soft spongy substance. Like the cone it slipped up high into her pussy, and he began to pump it slowly in and out, twisting it from side to side as he cleaned her out.

She never spoke, did not try to ask any questions. Her mind was still trying to come to terms with what had happened to her, what was happening to her, and she knew that demanding she be freed was utterly pointless.

The cone was re-inserted and more water washed her out, pouring down onto the floor below to disappear into a drain obviously made for this purpose.

He picked up another tube and she gasped as he pushed it against her rectum, then thrust it slowly inside and drove it deep. More water pumped into her, yet this time it didn't dribble out, for the pump had a rounded plug which had been slipped into her as well, blocking her neatly.

She whimpered softly as she felt the water filling her, felt her bowels getting heavy with it and her stomach starting to ache. She imagined she saw her lower belly actually begin to swell outward as the water continued to pump into her gut.

"P-please" she whimpered.

The man ignored her. It was as if she hadn't spoken. He looked at the machine attached to the hose, then to her rectum, then to the machine again. Finally, when she thought she would absolutely explode, he turned a switch on the machine and it stopped.

He moved away as another girl, the one she'd seen unloaded, came sliding through the opening on the end of another hook. Like Lisa she was a brunette, her hair a tangled, sweating mess, her face red, body flushed and sweaty. She blinked her eyes in confusion and groaned, her chin falling to her chest as the hook came to rest.

The man ignored her, moving to a table and making notes on a clipboard there.

Lisa felt her insides throbbing and aching, the water stretching her bowels to the utmost. The man went to the phone and talked briefly in a low voice. She could not make out the words. Then he came back to her and flipped a switch on the machine. The hose began to suck the water out of her and she felt the ache receding as she was emptied out.

After all the water was gone she could feel the vacuuming pressure of tip of the hose inside her as he moved it around. She gasped and yelped several times as it sucked at the sensitive flesh deep inside her. Then it was withdrawn and water poured over her once again, rising off her hair and body.

Her legs were unstrapped and allowed to fall back into place below her, then he gripped her arm and slid her along on the rail, through his small room and into through another narrow opening that led into the next.

Another man was there, and another naked girl hanging from a hook. This one was a blonde, and the two got only a few second to exchange frightened glances before the man gave the blonde a push and sent her sliding out of the room into whatever awaited her next.

Then he pulled Lisa further into the room. As in the previous room her legs were lifted up and well apart to expose her groin, then strapped into that position. The man picked up an electrical barbers razor and ran it carefully down her abdomen and between her legs, sheering off her pubic hair in seconds. Then he pulled a machine over and sat down with his face directly between her legs. He turned on the machine and picked up a narrow instrument with a sharp little edge and stabbed it into the soft flesh between her legs.

She yelped, then yelped again, then again, as sharp little pains made her jerk and shake. She quickly realized that what she was undergoing was electrolyses, that the man was ensuring her pubic hair would never regrow!

"Please," she whimpered. "Why am I here? Where am I? Why are you doing this?"

He sighed and put down the hose, then walked to a nearby shelf and lifted up one of several ball-gags sitting there, bringing it back to her.

"No! Please! I'll be quiet!" she promised.

He jammed it into her mouth regardless, and buckled it behind her head, then sat to continue his work.

The second brunette slid through the wall behind her and

was allowed to hang there watching and waiting her turn as the man worked quickly but carefully over her soft flesh, then did the same to her underarms.

When that was done he sprayed her down again then sent her sliding on to the next room. There, mercifully, she was lifted down. The gag was pulled free, and tossed away, and she was put into a barber's chair, her arms strapped down as another man in an apron did her hair with considerable care. He cut it, combed and brushed it and styled it in a way she'd never imagined.

When he was done her previously plainly hanging hair glowed with life and appeared to have the texture of feathery silk. It was parted in the middle, with thick, shimmering waves spilling down just to the sides of her narrow face, half covering her cheeks.

He nodded his satisfaction, then unstrapped her and locked her arms behind her back before walking her to the next room.

This room was an odd one indeed. There were a number of men there, some in flowing Arabic robes, some in business suits, some in shorts and polo shirts. There were also about a dozen other girls, all, like Lisa herself, nude.

A series of thick metal poles protruded from the ground at regular intervals along the walls, and she was led to one and placed over it. Then she was held in place as a man pushed down repeatedly on a pedal set into the floor. The metal pole rose and pushed against her bare pubic lips, then forced them aside and slipped up inside her, going higher and higher, until she gasped and rose onto her toes.

Then the man slipped a chain over her head and dropped it so that a narrow brass tag hung just below her neck, a tag with a number on it.

All the other girl were similarly tagged, and all standing atop poles as the men moved around, chatting casually and inspecting them. There were several men in dark black uniforms of some sort who appeared to be in charge of the girls.

When one of the girls, a petite blonde, cursed a man who pinched her nipple one of the men moved forward and sternly spoke to the girl, then his hand went to a small black device at his hip and a moment later the girl began to tremble and shake frenziedly.

Lisa was at a loss to understand what was being done to her. It was only some minutes later when she tried to ask one of the black clad men what was happening that she learned.

"You do not speak unless spoken to," he snapped. "Not ever!"

With that something in her belly burned like fire and Lisa felt the hair stand up on her head as pain tore into her in waves. It stopped a few seconds later but left her gasping and shaking with its memory.

Then she knew - the poles were electrified!

She whimpered softly but made no further attempts at speaking as men moved around and before her, speaking, often in foreign languages, reaching out and caressing her skin or hair, squeezing her breasts and running fingers along her straining pubic lips.

Lisa stood among a row of a half dozen other women, all nude, all staring in fear. They were the women she had seen in what she thought of as the exhibition room, and like her, they seemed new to whatever place this was.

All seemed to be in their late teens or very early twenties. All were beautiful, with lush, firm, curvaceous bodies and large, firm breasts. All had their wrists locked behind their backs by leather restraints. And all had varying looks of fear on their beautiful faces. None seemed embarrassed, however, even though several strange men stood across from them.

There was little modesty left about nudity, not after having been leered at and fondled for almost a full day.

They'd been given little time to sleep, and all were exhausted, both mentally and physically as the men walked up and down their rank, slapping riding crops against booted legs.

An older man came into the room, dressed, as the others were, in a blue shirt and pants, a kind of uniform she supposed. He looked them over, then gazed at a clipboard he held for a long moment.

"Very well," he said, looking up at them. "I'll say this once, and only once. You are slaves. I realize this might be an astonishing concept to some of you, but there you have it. You are on an island protected from intrusion both by us and by a very nicely paid foreign government. No one is searching for you, for all of you are thought dead or gone willingly. Even if anyone were to search for you they'd certainly have no reason to be looking in this empty little corner of the third world. So you can leave off fantasies about being rescued because it won't happen.

"Now then, you all know what a slave is. You are property, to be disposed of as your masters choose. If you don't behave satisfactorily you will be punished. Severely punished. You are here for sexual purposes, as you may have already suspected. You will do your level best to please the members of this organization. You will never, under any circumstances refuse any order of any kind, and will always comply with a happy, delighted look on your face, eager to please your master."

"This can't be happening," she heard a quavering voice say from the side.

The man smiled. "It is indeed happening. I should add that speaking without being spoken to is one of the things which bring punishment, and now that I have shut up or else. Also, any time you are addressed you will respond with yes master or no master. Am I understood?"

He glared at the woman a moment.

"Am I understood?" he snarled.

A ragged chorus of women said yes, or yes master and he slapped his crop against his boot. "Am I understood?" he demanded again, even louder.

School memories kicked in and Lisa, along with the other young women shouted "Yes, master!"

He nodded and began walking back and forth along their line again.

"Don't like the thought of fucking anyone who wants you? Tough. That's what you're here for. That's the only reason you now exist. So get used to it. Abandon any thought you have that your body has any worth, or that you should be choosy about who does anything to it. Your body belongs to us now. Some of you, of course, are not yet fit to entertain our members, so you will all be trained. The faster you learn, the less painful that training will be."

Another of the men moved forward at his gesture, his face stern, his voice loud and harsh.

"Stand up straight, you whores!" he shouted.

The women all straightened their shoulders fearfully.

"I am one of your masters," he said. "You will treat me like a God! My wish is your command! You will leap eagerly to obey my slightest desire!"

He walked forward to one end of the line, glaring down at a trembling red-headed girl.

"We expect our sluts to stand straight and push their breasts out. At any time if you are seen to be slouching or not standing straight you will be rebuked for it!"

He moved behind the redhead, and his riding crop suddenly slashed out, cutting through the air and then slashing across her round buttocks. The girl screamed in pain, leaping forward, twisting and trying to cup her wounded buttocks.

"Get back in line!" he screamed at her.

Sobbing, she hurriedly got back in line and tried to

straighten her shoulders, arching her back so her breasts would push out.

He moved along the back of the line, then around in front, right in front of Lisa.

"Good morning, Lisa," he said calmly.

"Good morning, master!" she said, trying to sound eager.

He passed on and she felt a deep thanks.

"Good morning, Susan," he said to the blonde girl next to her.

"G-good m-m-m-orning, master!" the girl whimpered.

His arm snapped out, the riding crop lashing her breast. Susan screamed, and Lisa almost did to, staring in horror at the bright red line of pain that appeared across the girl's round breast as she staggered back, twisted, and fell to her knees, sobbing.

"Get back in line!"

Another of the men gripped her by the hair, yanking her up brutally, savagely forcing her head so far back it was upside down, ignoring her scream of pain as he forced her back into position. Only then did he ease up on his grip and let the sobbing, whimpering girl stand in place.

"I did not find your greeting enthusiastic enough," the first master said. "Now you will apologise, greet me properly, and thank me for the corrective action I have taken."

She continued to sob and whimper.

"Good morning, Susan," he said.

"Good morning, master!" she exclaimed desperately.

He waited, then his eyes narrowed.

"I'm s-sorry, master!" she cried.

"What else, you filthy, vile little whore?"

"Th-thank you for correcting me, master!" she gasped.

"Better. Good morning, Susan," he said.

"Good morning, master!" she cried again.

He passed on to the next girl and greeted her by name.

Her reply was quite enthusiastic.

After going down the line he returned to the first girl, Lisa.

"Step forward, Lisa," he ordered.

She quickly moved forward but he halted her, gripping her hair and yanked it back hard. She cried out in pain as her scalp burned.

"You will answer when a master gives you an order!" he shouted into her ear.

"Yes, master!" she cried.

He let go and pushed her forward so she was in the middle, in front of the other girls.

"On your knees, slut," he ordered.

"Yes, master," she gasped, thinking, as the other woman had said, that this surely could not be happening.

She watched him unzip his trousers and bring out his flaccid cock and felt a wave of horror and fear.

"You will perform oral sex on me in front of these other women. We will see how good you are at it and how much you have yet to be taught," he said.

"Y-yes, master!" she gasped, trying to appear eager.

"Begin."

As three men and five women watched, Lisa leaned in, fighting the humiliation she felt, and after only a brief hesitation, slipped her lips over his cock and began to lick and suck. She took it deep into her mouth as everyone watched, licking and sucking awkwardly as he stared down, arms folded across his chest.

"Lick my balls, you stupid dog!" he snapped. "Take them into your mouth and work on them! Don't you know anything!?"

Lisa let his soft cock slip free of her lips, desperately licking up along his balls, sucking them into her mouth one by one until he forced her head back by the hair, then flung her back across the floor. She landed awkwardly, gasping in fear.

"Useless sow!" he snarled. "We ought to just kill you and not waste our time!"

He looked at another of the women. "You, Karen, come here and take over!" he ordered.

"Y-yes, master!" she squeaked, hurrying forward and dropping onto her knees in front of him.

Lisa started to rise but a hand on her shoulder kept her on her knees. She watched as Karen licked his balls eagerly, pushing her face in against his crotch, her tongue whipping out again and again until his cock started to harden. Then she began to bob up and down on it, sucking as his hand stroked the hair back from her forehead.

Suddenly, though, he seized her head in both hands.

"Of course all of you must learn how to take a man into your throat," he said. "Every true whore learns it, and every one of you is a true whore!"

With that he thrust his thick, glistening cock forward, and Lisa and the others stared in horror as the woman struggled weakly, watched as her throat bulged and her eyes got wide.

The man's cock disappeared between her lips and he held her head in a tight grip, her face crushed against his groin as he stared at the rest of them with a cruel smile.

"All of you will learn to take any size cock down your pretty throats without hesitation," he said as the girl wriggled and twisted beneath him.

Finally he eased his cock back, sliding it out of her throat and mouth, and as it popped free she gasped and coughed, gulping in air as he held her hair in one hand and used the other to rub his spit-wet cock all over her red face.

He flung her back then, as he had Lisa, and pointed at her.

"You. Whore! Come here."

"Yes, master!" Lisa gasped.

"No! Crawl here! On your belly, you miserable slut!"

She bent over, grunting as she fell to the floor, wriggling forward awkwardly, her breasts grinding and rolling beneath her as she made her way up in front of him.

"Keep your face on the floor where it belongs, but raise your behind high and spread your legs," he ordered.

"Yes, master," she gasped, drawing her knees in under her and raising her backside high.

Another of the masters walked over beside him and the two watched her as she made her way up to them.

"Now I want you to clean this master's boots," he ordered, "With your tongue. You will continue to clean them until I tell you to stop. If you stop for any reason you will be severely punished, instead of being given only a gentle rebuke!"

"Yes, master," she gulped, staring at the other master's gleaming boots for a moment.

In one sense she was appalled, for licking the man's boots was an intensely degrading act. Yet, oddly, in another way she was delighted, for it was a simple task.

She began to lick at it, her pink tongue sliding over his gleaming boot. The first man then moved behind her and she sensed him dropping to his knees.

"All of your holes will be used, of course," he said, "Including this one."

She felt his cock, wet with pre-cum and Karen's spit, pressing against her nether hole and her mind blanked momentarily, then she sagged weakly, almost forgetting to lick as the master forced his cock slowly down into her rectum.

How long had it been, that she had been lying on the sofa watching the television? And now she knelt bound on a floor, licking a man's boots as another sodomized her, all while others watched.

His cock pushed deep, and she moaned weakly, her tongue still licking out, sliding over the man's ankle, then around

36

against his heel, moving from one boot to the other as the master behind her began to pump, all the others watching her being sodomized there on the floor.

He pumped for long minutes, often talking, telling them what whores they were, and how every one of them should be delighted any man would deign to pay them the slightest attention. Every one of them was a worthless slut, a piece of woman flesh made for men to enjoy, and their bodies were the only excuse for their existence.

After he had finished she was dragged to her feet and pushed back in line.

Then they were put through their paces, running around the room, then unbound so they could crawl around in a line, following one another, then crawling to the masters, bunched up around their feet like packs of dogs to lick at their shoes. Any girl unable to push in close enough quickly felt the bite of the crop against her back or buttocks.

Leashes were attached to their collars then and, crawling, they were led out of the room and down a narrow hall to what the masters called the feeding room. Their plates and bowls were on the floor, and they crawled to them and began to eat their morning breakfast. It was nourishing and tasty, for the masters wanted them to be healthy looking.

After breakfast came classes in obedience. Each of these classes was generally spent impaled on a shorter version of the metal pole she'd first been introduced to. The poles generated a soft, low level hum, a buzzing which was disturbingly comforting and made Lisa's pussy hum with helpless pleasure. But a wrong answer or incorrect response would quickly shoot a hot blast of agony into her.

In addition to the electrical shock, each wrong answer brought a demerit. Ten demerits would require punishment, and none of the girls wanted to know what the men considered punishment since they obviously did not mean the frequent blows with riding crops, slaps, kicks, or the shocks from the electrical probes.

As luck would have it Lisa was the first to feel real punishment. She was led into a small cold room, and two of the masters pressed her forward against a kind of table. The table seemed to have the middle part missing at first, and her breasts were allowed to dangle down as she was strapped in place.

Then the narrow empty spot began to get narrower, and she felt the two sides of the table pulling together, sliding in against her breasts. She gasped, trying to pull up, but couldn't.

The hole narrowed, and then she began to scream in earnest as her breasts were crushed, only an inch separating the two leaves of the table when its movement was halted.

That was only the beginning, however. One of the masters pulled her legs far apart and strapped them down, while another moved beneath the table.

A metal rod had been behind her, but now one of the men gave it a touch and it angled sideways, pointing directly at her gaping sex. The top foot was a studded rubber dildo, and then just below this was a heavy metal plate with a thin leather coating.

The thing hissed and eased up slowly, until the dildo lined up perfectly with her opening, then it slid up into her, slowly, so she hardly noticed. The pain in her nipples and breasts obscuring any other sensations.

It was thick, and her soft pussy walls were spread wide as it drove higher and deeper. When it was almost fully inside her she felt the ache inside her as it hit the bottom of her sheath, yet still it pushed, and the ache grew.

It drew back, then pushed forward, drew back, then pushed forward. Again she began to ignore it, even though she knew all the other women were watching. She was trying to catch her breath, trying desperately to apologise and beg their forgiveness.

The thing moved faster, and faster, then deeper still. Finally it was so deep each time the nose thrust into her it jammed painfully against her cervix. That was when the master moved to it and adjusted the plate, sliding it slightly up.

Again it thrust in hard and she felt a terrible blow, for as the thick rubber penis buried itself within her body the plate, slightly curved to match her anatomy, slapped brutally hard into her groin, crushing her pubic mound.

Her eyes bulged and she felt a deep nausea and dizziness along with a horrible pain. She screamed, in shock and agony, but moments later it thrust back in and again she felt the twin agonies as the rubber penis slammed into her cervix and the plate slapped brutally up into her soft, bare mound.

"We will leave her here for a time," she heard one of the master's say "Perhaps she'll learn faster after this little demonstration."

Lisa wanted to beg him not to, wanted to say anything, but all she could do was scream and howl as each new blow landed. Pain burned through every fibre of her being as the plate slapped up into her sex and the dildo pounded into her cervix.

Again and again the blows came, threatening to drive her insane as the other girls filed out and the door was shut behind.

She sobbed hopelessly, wanting to die, screaming now and then, howling at the top of her lungs. The pain was maddening, and that she could do not the slightest thing to hinder it was infuriating.

She screamed in rage, then broke, sobbing, whimpering, gasping with each new blast of pain, knowing she would surely go insane if it continued.

And perhaps, after a time, she did. Somehow her body adjusted to the brutal raping dildo that was thrusting up into it, and it no longer seemed to strike her cervix with quite so much energy.

Or perhaps, she thought dazedly, it had simply driven right through into her womb.

Still, there seemed less pain from there. The nausea had faded, even though the plate continued slap quite hard up into her sex, jamming her forward each time. Every blow felt almost like a kick between the legs, and yet she had to take them again and again and again.

Her mons felt afire, and terribly sensitive. Yet through the pain, somehow she felt a strange stirring there, a strange little thread of sexual heat running through the fabric of pain hammering against her. It grew, and she seized on it, encouraging it, hoping desperately it could help hold back the blasts of pain assaulting her.

She pretended it was a handsome man behind her, a well-endowed, handsome man rutting into her, his hips slapping against her.

The sexual heat grew, small embers igniting something within her, growing hotter with each passing second. And slowly, ever so slowly, the burning pain was absorbed into the heat of pleasure, and without even being aware of it at first the gasps and grunts of pain became those of sexual arousal.

As her sex moistened her breasts burned and the pleasure spread throughout her body. Coated with sweat, gasping, near senseless, she felt a wall of pleasure rise up around her, then collapse inwards.

She shook to the tune of a powerful orgasm, the repeated blows from the pad merely flinging her higher and higher as the orgasm burned through her mind and body. For long seconds nothing mattered but the pleasure, then she tumbled free of the climax and back to reality, groaning as the plate continued to pound her, the tube continued to skewer her.

Yet the pleasure rose again, greater than before, and another orgasm shook her body, then another, then another, her mind swamped by contrary sensations of wildfire pleasure and terrible agony.

Battered and tormented, her thinking processes began to shut down, and she became little more than an animal, a slab of living meat there on the table, grunting in tune to whatever sensations moved through her system.

She slept...

She wakened in her cell, lying on the cold stone floor, arms and legs chained wide. Her sex felt raw and swollen and hot, and every movement made her ache.

After a time one of the masters came in and looked down at her. He gazed at her sex, then took his crop and pressed it against her. She whimpered in pain, but as he began to rub the narrow leather up and down against her clitoris she felt the sudden explosion of sexual heat within her, and within seconds she climaxed.

She resumed her training, desperately eager to please the masters, to ingratiate herself with them any way possible.

Often she found herself left alone, though, stranding upright usually, arms overhead, impaled on a pole with wires clamped to her breasts and clitoris, blindfolded and unmoving, long hours would pass in a strange but oddly enticing rhythm.

First would come pain, usually a cane or crop applied to her back or buttocks. Several blows would strike her, and almost immediately thereafter the soft hum would begin, the pole and wires sending electricity into her body in such a way that she vibrated in response.

Her clitoris would began to twitch, her pussy to lubricate and her breasts to swell.

Modesty had disappeared after the first day, misery after the second, hate after the third. By the fourth day all she wanted was to please the masters in order to avoid pain.

Real pain, that was, the kind that made her howl and

shriek her voice ragged, the kind she had got on the table, the kind she could get at any time were she to displease the masters.

By comparison the blows from crops and canes were like soft stings and hardly important.

Besides, they were always followed by the most delicious waves of pleasure, pleasure that grew and grew until she squirmed and moaned and tried to slide her aching, sopping sex up and down on the metal pole she was impaled upon.

5

Edward gazed at the girl in delight. She was a luscious morsel indeed. Her naked body gleamed with health, her silky brown hair soft and shining. She had an hourglass body, with heavy, but firm breasts and an adorable behind.

He reached out and squeezed it, and she whimpered, but arched her back, pushing her buttocks back against his hand. She turned her head, staring at him anxiously as he slipped his fingers down under her buttocks and palmed her shaven mound.

He licked his lips and sighed, then moved back, inspecting the rack on the wall then taking down a particularly nasty crop.

He swung it several times and it hissed as it cut through the air. He shuddered briefly, then turned and looked at the girl again. She stood straight, arms up and apart, manacled to chains hanging from the ceiling. Her legs were tightly closed, her back arched, her buttocks pushed out for him.

He moved around in front of her and touched the tip of the crop to her bare little cleft, stroking it back and forth before letting it slide slowly up her body. He nudged her right breast, lifting it then letting it fall again. He saw her staring anxiously at the tip of the crop as it rasped against her nipple.

"What is your name, slut?" he asked, forcing her chin up with the crop.

"Lisa," she stuttered.

"L-L-Lisa?" he said mockingly. "You've been a very bad little girl, haven't you, Lisa."

She stared at him beseechingly, and opened her mouth as if to deny it, then lowered her eyes submissively. "Yes, master," she whispered.

"And how have you been a bad girl?"

"By - by being a filthy slut, master," she moaned.

He reached out and cupped one of her deliciously full breasts, squeezing it, spreading his fingers so the malleable flesh would ooze out between them.

"A filthy, cock-hungry little trollop, aren't you?"

"Yes, master," she gulped. "I'm sorry, master! I'm so sorry! Please, master I -"

"Silence!" he snapped, his hand tightening in the flesh of her breast, squeezing and twisting painfully so she cried out, then shook with suppressed tears.

He slid his hand up into her hair, then wound it around his fist and forced her head back.

"You've been a filthy, vile little slut," he said. "And I hear you've been well-raped for your temerity. Now you'll start being punished."

"Please," she gasped. "I - I'll do anything!"

"You certainly will," he said.

He released her and moved into position behind her. He slid the crop between her trembling thighs, sawing it edgewise along her tight cleft, against her pouty lips, then pulled back, drew back his arm, then lashed out and down. The crop struck directly across her buttocks with a crack! that echoed off the mahogany walls and was absorbed by the thick, plush carpeting.

The girl screamed in pain, but after the initial shock she pushed her behind back, arching even further. He saw her rise onto the balls of her feet, thrusting her behind out even more vulnerably as a red line of pain appeared across her buttocks. He paused a moment to admire whomever had trained her.

He slashed the crop down again, harder this time, and she jerked violently, giving a choked cry of pain. Another blow landed, and then another, as the Crack! Crack! Crack! of the crop filled the air with its enticing melody.

The more he struck the more aroused the girl seemed to become. As for Edward himself, his erection was almost painful as it thrust out against his trousers. He landed a dozen blows on her lusciously soft behind, then tossed the crop aside and hurried back to the rack. He took down a cat-o-nine-tails and returned, drawing back his arm and then lashing the whip down across the young woman's back. Her scream was one of shocked agony as she lost her balance, thrown forward and off her feet briefly by the impact of the thongs against her soft skin.

Streaks of red marred the perfection of her back, then more, then more again as the cat clawed at her skin again and again.

He stopped, panting, then bent and raised the cat again, moving around in front of her. She was perspiring heavily now, her skin glistening hotly, her hair matted against her forehead.

Her soft, lovely face was flushed, her eyes filled with pain, but also a strange need. Tears trickled down her cheeks as he looked her up and down, then she gasped, swallowed, and arched her back again, thrusting out her breasts.

Lisa's mind lay in twisted turmoil, the pain blinding in its horror, clawing away at her ability to think, burning her alive even as she trembled in the grip of a pleasure more consuming than any she had ever felt before in her life.

It had been hard, those first days and weeks here, but her thinking processes had been radically altered, her concept of self blurred, her desires, appetites and emotions violently rearranged.

She had spent long days of torment as the 'masters' had shown her her place in life as a slave, then many long hours, days even, though she had no way of knowing how much time had passed, tightly bound, blindfolded, voices washing over her as pain and pleasure were forced upon her again and again. And somehow they had become intertwined, somehow she had become addicted to the pain, dreading it even as she craved it. For the pain led to a pleasure so great she would sacrifice her soul for it.

And as she stood there and saw him through tear-filled, slitted eyes, she hated him, she loathed and despised him with every fibre of her being, and she knew without being told what he wanted. She whimpered within herself, filled with terror of the pain she knew was yet to come.

Yet she needed it. She tried to catch her breath against the agony, then closed her eyes and slowly, weakly, arched her back, thrusting her proud young breasts up and out at him.

Edward reached out and ran his hand over one of her breasts, squeezing it, letting his fingers crush the malleable flesh. Then he drew back and raised the crop, lashing it directly over one of her breasts.

Her head whipped back and she shuddered and gurgled as the intensity of the pain took the breath from her. Another blow landed, this time on her other breast, then a third, setting it jiggling and shaking.

She gave a choked sob of pain, then her thighs ground together furiously as an obvious orgasm took hold of her.

Cursing her, Edward lashed the crop down again and again

across her proud breasts, his arm a blur as her head jerked feebly back, spasms racking her body.

He continued whipping her breasts until her shudders eased and she sagged against the chains holding her, then he cracked the crop down against her lower chest, then her belly, then her abdomen, watching her jerk and shake and moan under the blows as stripes appeared all over her pale white flesh.

He licked his lips and stepped back, then reached down for her right ankle. He jerked it up, lifting her leg high, then taking one of the loose chains hanging from above and fitting the hook into the ring set into the manacle around her ankle. He then lifted her other ankle just as high and again fitted the manacle to a hook.

He stepped back briefly and worked the controls on the wall, controls that worked how high and far apart each chain was from the other. With a simple motion he lowered her slightly, then had the two chains holding her ankles high move further apart and back behind the ones holding her wrists.

This tilted her body up and back, lifting her buttocks and crotch for his enjoyment.

He moved forward and opened the front of his pants, drawing forth his blood-engorged organ and staring at her gaping cleft, the pink flesh inside so lewdly revealed. In a single motion he pushed himself against her, then thrust in powerfully, drawing a grunt of pain from the girl as he buried his tool deep in her warmth.

His hands reached out and crushed her breasts, twisting them painfully from side to side as he ground his pelvis into her wounded buttocks. Then with a sneer of contempt he began to pump himself inside her, building up speed rapidly, using his tool as a weapon, stabbing it into her again and again with cruel lunging strokes.

He could not hold out long, for he was simply too aroused.

Nevertheless, the girl climaxed again, her head thrashing wildly as she sobbed and whined through the powerful climax. Edward felt her insides clasping and spasming around him even as he rutted down into her, and cursed her furiously, both proud and angry at her pleasure.

He felt himself explode, what felt like a massive wave of juices spewing down his shaft as he emptied himself into her womb.

He staggered back, glaring at her furiously, then picked up the crop and raised his arm. It hissed through the air and struck the dazed girl directly across her bare mound, the blow shocking her and tearing a scream from her throat.

She shook violently, her mouth opening and closing like a fish out of water. "Ooohh... ooohh God," she said with a choked sob.

His teeth gleamed in satisfaction, and the crop landed again, directly along her still moist partially open cleft, striking her pink flesh with a wet sound that was instantly eclipsed by her shriek of agony.

His arm rose and fell, rose and fell, rose and fell, the crop beating down on her exposed pubic mound as she howled and jerked in her chains. Then the tenor of her screams changed, and again Edward felt that curious mixture of pride and anger as she tumbled into another powerful orgasm.

He threw down the whip and stormed from the room, grabbing a towel from a nearby rack and wiping at his face as he did up his trousers. He made his way down the hall, then took the elevator upstairs to his suite.

"Welcome home, master!" his personal slave Bambi said with a delighted smile.

She was kneeling before the door, head up, chest thrust out, legs spread wide to reveal her bare, shaved mound.

"Get me a drink. I want a shower," he growled.

"Yes, Master!"

Bambi had once been Elizabeth, a law student at Harvard

University in America. For two years now, however, she had been Bambi, a slave-slut, used as a personal servant and slave to whichever master had the desire for one.

She scurried to obey as he tossed the towel on the floor then went down the hall to the luxurious bathroom. He stripped quickly, tossing his things on the floor, then reconsidered and turned on the bath instead.

Water gushed into the huge marble tube from four separate jets, the temperature preset, and he climbed in with a sigh of relief as Bambi hurried into the room, squatted next to him and handed him a glass.

He took it, sipping lightly. He looked up at her beaming face, then reached out and fingered her lewdly bared slit.

Her eyes closed and she moaned in pleasure, her crotch grinding against his fingers as it began to almost instantly moisten.

It was a wonder to him how they'd made these sluts the way they were, but he only wished they'd expand and make all the world's whores behave in the same fashion, especially those snotty bitches he'd gone to school with.

"Get me another drink," he ordered, drawing his hand back.

"Yes, master!" the girl cried, rising and rushing out of the room.

He watched and snorted, then sank deeper into the water, sipping again from his glass.

This was undoubtedly the most expensive club he'd ever heard of, but it was more than worth it. The food was excellent, the service unequalled, and the women, the women behaved as women ought, and every damned one of them was available for whatever he desired.

Bambi hurried back and squatted next to him, holding his glass.

"Set it there, then get in, slut."

"Yes, master!" she squealed.

She slipped into the water across from him and he raised his foot, pressing it against the centre of her chest. She took it in small hands, for she was a little thing, and pressed her breasts around it. Then she reached out and bottle of creamy soap from next to the tub, spraying it over her breasts and his foot.

She used her breasts on his foot, squeezing and rubbing them back and forth, then lifting his leg higher still, sliding her heavy round breasts around his ankle, scrubbing from either side as she bent over and worked her breasts up to his knee.

The rest of him was under water and he didn't feel like moving just yet, so he shoved her back with his foot, then lifted the other. She repeated her cleaning actions, the smile of delight never leaving her face.

He wondered how many times she'd been beaten before she remembered to keep smiling.

He pulled his leg away and reached out for her, seizing her arm and yanking her forward so she fell across him. He brought his hands back behind his head as he spread his legs apart.

"Blow me," he ordered.

"Yes, master!" he said with a wide smile.

She plunged her head below the water and he smiled. "Stupid slut," he muttered.

Her lips slipped around his cock and she sucked it into her mouth, her hands massaging his testicles as she slurped expertly on his shaft, her tongue whipping up and down in exceedingly clever and effective ways.

She raised her head above the water and gulped in air, then plunged down again, taking him into her mouth and sucking heavily, bobbing her lips up and down.

The way women should, he thought.

For a moment his mind turned back a few months. He was at Kevin Darnel's party. He hadn't been invited, but he'd come anyway. He'd had more than a few, annoyed at the way some of the young ladies were showing less than delight at his propositioning them.

Then he'd seen her, an absolutely delectable brunette standing at the stereo and inspecting some disks. She was young, like he liked them, possibly not even out of high school. He hurried over, wanting to reach her before she straightened.

She was wearing a mini, short and tight, and her long legs drew his eyes like magnets.

As if she knew he were coming her legs shifted apart slightly. Oh she knew, all right. The slut. His hand slipped in under her skirt, up between her warm thighs, and he felt the crotch of her panties against his palm as he squeezed softly.

He had a phrase in mind, one he'd been practising in his mind, one he thought sounded particularly suave and sophisticated. He never had a chance to utter it, however. The girl in question turned instantly and her elbow slammed into his belly with such force it knocked the wind out of him.

He grunted in stunned agony, clutching his stomach just as she whirled fully and slammed her knee up into his crotch.

He'd been hurled backwards, then fallen against a table, clutching at a large bowl of punch which, as he collapsed, fell over him. Laughter had erupted throughout the room as he'd curled up on the floor, soaked, with bits of fruit punch over his face.

For long minutes he hadn't been able to move until the nausea went away and he'd got his wind back. By then she was gone, but her image lived on his mind, and her name. She'd humiliated him in public out of pure spite, out of vicious female treachery.

He scowled angrily across the room, then at the top of the blonde girl's bobbing head. He reached down and grabbed her by the hair, forcing her down and holding her in place. After a short time he felt her begin to struggle. Her small hands slapped at his face and reached up for his wrist.

He laid back with a cruel smile, holding her easily. Her struggles grew more desperate, then faded and she went limp.

He held her for a second longer, then pulled her up by the hair. She hung limply in front of him as he held her by her soaking, tangled hair. Then he flung her backwards and she splashed back on her back, floating there for a moment before he got up and lifted her out of the water, throwing her roughly onto the floor.

He pressed a button and sat back in the water. Seconds later another woman appeared, this one a redhead.

"Yes, master?" she asked with a wide smile.

"Have someone remove that offal," he said, "And get in here."

"Of course, master!" she said, beaming in delight.

She bent and pressed the button twice, then slipped into the water, pressing her full breasts against his chest. Seconds later two more women appeared, picked up the limp body of the blonde, and carried it out of the room, out of his sight.

He laid his head back, then frowned as he heard the blonde coughing. They should have taken her further before working on her, he thought. He would have to complain.

He gripped the redhead by the hair and forced her head under water. Her lips slipped around his cock and he sighed, reaching for his drink.

6

Amanda's eyelids fluttered slowly, and light hit her eyes, hazy as yet, but clearing rapidly.

She groaned weakly, fighting back a feeling of nausea as she lay still. After several minutes both her eyes and her head were clear enough for her to look around her.

She was in a small room with mirrored walls. The only furnishing was a low, narrow white table on which she lay. The room was very bright, and she blinked her eyes as she slowly sat up.

There didn't appear to be any door, though there must be, she thought. She remembered the men, and the woman, and her mind filled with terror as she sat up and looked around.

She was dressed again. That was reassuring. She wondered... but then her mind shied away from the thought of what they might have done to her while she was unconscious.

She swung her legs over the side of the table she had lain on and looked around, anxiously studying the mirrored walls.

An odd place to keep a captive, she thought in confusion. She'd expected a small dank basement or something of that sort. Why this place? What was it for, and why was it so brightly lit?

She stood up slowly, clutching the table as her weakness overcame her. She stood there on rubbery legs for a long moment, then went to the nearest wall. Well, it was all one wall, really, since the room was circular. It was barely eight feet around, and she couldn't fathom why she was placed in it, or where the doorway was.

She returned to the table and sat down, wondering why she had been taken. Her parents were well-off, but hardly as wealthy as many others. And why had they gone through that brutal, humiliating stripping by the road if they were going to dress her once again?

The only reason she could think of was they wanted to humiliate her. But why? What kind of people were they? Were they terrorists? She'd heard of some cases were wealthy young women were sexually abused by those who kidnapped them. Her heart fluttered at the thought of what might await her.

Then a section of the wall pushed inward, revealing a door. She whipped her head around, then stared, eyes widening as two enormous black men stepped inside.

The door closed behind them...

Each of them was well over six feet in height, and wearing nothing but a loincloth. Their heads were shaved bald, and their bodies bulged with enormous muscles. They smiled at her and she felt a stab of fear, slipping off the table and placing it between them.

"What do you want!?" she demanded, fear crawling up her spine.

Neither spoke. They split apart, each going around one side of the table until they hemmed her in against the mirrored wall, smiling, doing nothing but smiling down at her as she jerked her gaze from one to the other and back again.

"What do you want!?" she demanded. "Where am I? What am I doing here? Who are you!?"

Edward took his seat next to the glass. There were three tiers of seats surrounding the small glassed in chamber, and though not all were full, there was a nice turnout as the men watched the small play unfolding within the room. Here and there naked young women knelt beside their masters, massaging their crotches or gazing up adoringly.

He watched the girl cowering back. A fierce grin of triumph appeared on his face as the two big blacks gripped her arms and dragged her away from the wall. He rubbed his hands in anticipation, reaching down and turning up the sound slightly.

Amanda knew fighting was useless. These men were the largest she'd ever seen. Their arms were easily larger than her thighs, and they were each more than twice her weight, possibly three times.

One gripped her wrists, then lifted her arms high, so high

her feet left the ground and dangled uselessly as he held her up and stared at her.

Then the other moved behind her, taking her arms and holding her like that as the first released his hold. He moved his hands down and cupped her breasts through her blouse, then gripped the material and with effortless motion, tore the blouse open, shredding it like it was tissue paper and flinging the front part of it behind him.

His hands undid the belt around her waist, then opened the clasp of her pants and tugged, pulling them down to her ankles and then off over her shoes.

Amanda quivered in terror, her mind reeling with anger, humiliation and fear. Doing anything to resist seemed pointless against this massive men, intellectually she knew that, yet she couldn't help trying to pull her leg back as one gripped her ankle.

It was like pulling against steel. He removed her sock and her shoe, then released her foot.

The one behind her set her down, then his grip shifted to her blazer and blouse, jerking them back over her shoulders and down her arms with a swift, practised motion.

Clad only in small black string bikini panties and matching bra she darted away from between them, her chest heaving as she backed against the wall and stared at them with wide eyes.

"Please!" she gasped. "I... my father has money! He'll pay you if you don't hurt me!"

They approached her from either side, then one gripped her arms and jerked them back behind her, holding them in tight fists. The other smiled as he gripped her bra, then tore it apart, baring her proud young breasts.

Her face scarlet, she fought back tears as the man smiled thinly, his eyes enjoying her nudity. Furiously she kicked out, but he seemed to expect it and caught her ankle easily. Then his hand cracked across her face very lightly.

Still, it was like getting hit by a cricket bat and her head whipped to one side as she tasted blood. His other hand cracked against her opposite cheek and her head was thrown to the other side. He slapped her again with his first hand, then again with his second, then again, then again.

Amanda's mind was dazed as he halted. She tasted blood in her mouth as the world swam around her. The hulking man slipped a hand behind her back and pulled, forcing her chest out, then ran his other hand over her breasts, squeezing them and pinching her nipples into erectness. He bent and fixed his lips over her nipple, suckling and chewing as she regained her breath and senses.

He eased down onto his knees and gazed into her crotch, then tore her panties off.

Amanda sobbed as her last protection was removed and the man stared at her with obvious lust. She tried to cross her legs but he simply yanked them apart. His strength was frightening.

He pushed his face into her sex, his tongue lapping up and down her cleft as he held her thighs in a vice-like grip and tongued her up and down. It was all a dream, she thought. It was all mad. This was the product of some dark, bizarre fantasy. She would waken and it would all be over. But as much as she willed herself to wake nothing changed.

The man in front pinched her pussy lips, pulling them apart, even painfully so, his tongue slithering in and out of her, driving impossibly far inside her and wriggling around like a snake.

He pulled back after what seemed an eternity, and rose. He nodded to the one behind her and she was marched forward to the table, then lifted onto it. They turned her onto her back and spread her legs far, the tendons in her thighs aching at the strain as the first one moved into position.

"P-please," she whimpered. "Please..."

His hand cracked across her face and she cried out as

pain hit her. Then she felt his heavy fingers at her sex, felt herself pulled open, then, as she lifted her head dazedly, she saw him draw back his loin cloth.

He was impossibly large and thick. She'd never seen one that big in her life, not even in the adult movies she'd watched. Her jaw dropped and she gazed at it in horror as he pushed it in against her opening.

"No!" she cried, but her hands were caught by the second man, pulled up above her and held easily. She strained and pulled, her back arching repeatedly as her buttocks ground against the table, but the two men held her without effort as the first pushed his thick head against her, jabbing with more and more pressure.

She felt the strain against her pubic lips, felt them slowly forced in and apart. She sobbed in fury and frustration, unable to do anything to hinder the man as her opening was forced wider and wider. It stung, then ached as she was stretched wider than she'd ever been in her life.

She cried out in pain as the blunt head of his penis pierced her. He chuckled, the first sound he'd made, then put his weight behind his monstrous tool, forcing it deeper.

Amanda felt every ridge and vein on him as it scraped slowly through the taut, straining lips of her sex and forced its way upwards through the soft, elastic layers of her pink pussy sheath.

Amanda strained and writhed, sobbing in pain as his immensely thick organ bored its way into her inch after agonizing inch, straining her sheath out like an overinflated balloon.

"Oh God!" she cried, her head thrashing as he lurched forward again.

Inch after inch drove remorselessly through her aching, straining pubic lips until he was so high inside her she thought he meant to force his way into her stomach. Still he pushed forward, and she desperately jerked her head up, staring down between her splayed thighs, her eyes widening in horror and disbelief as she saw how much more of him remained.

"No! I can't! It won't go!" she screamed, her voice breaking. "Please!"

He halted his forward pressure, and remained still inside her for a long moment. Her head fell back onto the table as she gasped in relief. She felt him easing slowly back, then suddenly he slammed his hips forward. She felt the blunt nose of his tool slice upwards and slam against her cervix. Her eyes bulged as she screamed in agony, her body thrashing and wriggling, muscles standing out beneath her glistening, sweat-covered skin as she strained again and again.

He was impossibly deep inside her, and she thought he must have burst right through the back of her womb. She screamed as he ground his pelvis against her, his long, thick steel-hard organ twisting around inside her abdomen.

She felt her insides being torn and twisted, and screamed as cramps ripped through her belly.

"Stop it! Please God!" she screamed, sobbing helplessly as he leered down at her.

He drew back slowly, and she sobbed anew at the blessed relief as the pressure relented against her cervix. He pulled back slowly, then pushed back into her again, taking his time, enjoying himself as he used her for his pleasure.

But his slow, steady stroke did not last long, and was more for effect, more so the watchers could see the immense side of his tool each time it moved into her, each time the full long length of it slid past her entrance and disappeared up into her body.

Once he thought they had had their fill of watching that he picked up the pace, his tool, pre-oiled to prevent damage to the female glistened as it pumped in and out of her.

Edward gasped in delight, his cock pushing up eagerly against his pants as he watched the slut being raped. It was just the first of the punishments that awaited her, he thought with vindictive lust, and not nearly the worst either.

His slave moved forward and reached for his crotch but he slapped her away, sending her sprawling. He wanted nothing to touch him, not until he spewed himself over that bitch's face!

Amanda could hardly breath as the powerful man slammed his hips forward against her again and again. She'd never been so brutally ridden before, and never by such a monstrously long and thick organ. It was pounding up and down inside her, tearing her vitals apart, churning her guts to a heaving pulp as the man hammered his hips into her belly with unrelenting fury.

Small choked sobs escaped her lips as she moaned and gasped and grunted in an agony of pain and fear, the brutal raping seeming to go on forever.

Then with a groan he released his hold and she felt...for the first time in her life actually felt a man's semen gushing down into her body. He continued to pump, though more slowly, and she felt his juices spurting out around him each time he sheathed himself in her body.

His member slowly softened and he pulled it free. Amanda felt hollow inside, and groaned as the taut pressure on her pussy lips eased finally.

Then he reached forward and gripped her by the throat. The second man releasing her as he yanked her up into a sitting position, then off the table. He raised his arm high into the air, extending it fully as the weakened, dazed woman struggled feebly, then he dropped her down and forced her onto the ground on her knees, then onto all fours.

She collapsed, but a quick grip on her hair, yanked her upper body back off the floor, and held her there until she steadied herself.

The second man moved in behind her, lowering himself

to his knees, his hands moving slowly over her back and buttocks, then underneath, thick fingers probing her sex, feeling the slickness there, the juices of her previous rapist oozing out.

Amanda felt tears slip through her tightly clenched eyelids,
tears of misery and anguish as his cock pushed at her, tearing her lips open again, then sank down into her raw, aching belly.

His big hands went almost completely around her waist as he jammed himself in to the hilt, and she sobbed in pain as he mashed the nose of his tool against her cervix.

Then he began to ride her, to use her like a bitch dog, his hips working up to speed quickly until they were slamming into her with bruising force.

He shifted his hands upwards to her shoulders, yanking her back to meet each thrust, increasing the force of his deep, vicious thrusts so the pain screamed along her nerve endings. Her entire body shook, jerked back and forth by his rutting strokes. Her head bounced up and down and her vision swam dizzily.

Suddenly he slowed, and she tried to catch her breath, groaning as her insides throbbed and burned.

"Are we enjoying ourselves?"

It was a new voice, but at first she hardly noticed. Only slowly did Amanda raise her tear-stained face, looking up higher and higher until she saw the smiling face high above her. It was not one of them, one of the monsters as she thought of them, yet he seemed oddly familiar...

"Well, Amanda," he said. "It's been some months now, has it not? You were quite rude to me last time we met. I trust you regret that behaviour now."

Who was he? The face was a little familiar, but she didn't think it was anyone she'd met before.

His smile turned to a cold, angry glare at the confusion on her face.

"Don't try to pretend you don't remember, you little slut!" he snarled in an oddly high-pitched, petulant voice.

Memory dawned and she stared up at him, not understanding at first. He was... Sir Edward something or other, an old lech who had groped her at a party.

"That's right, you whore," he spat. "I had you brought here to punish you for your insolence! I hope you begin to understand what a mistake you made!" He gestured to the man behind her, who immediately picked up the pace, battering her insides with his giant cock, bruising her buttocks with his muscular hips.

"This is perhaps more of what you wanted, slut? Hmmm? This is the reason you would have none of me? Because you wanted to be ridden like the she slut you are! Well here you are, ridden by an animal barely out of the trees! I hope you like it!"

She gasped and gurgled as the man pounded himself into her, her insides burning like fire as he plunged down her aching hole again and again and again.

She gasped as the man above gripped her hair and yanked her head up to face him, staring at him through desperate, pain-filled eyes as he smirked down at her.

Then the man behind spewed into her body, pouring what felt like gallons of hot cream into her wounded cavity before withdrawing.

She felt her arms pinned behind her, then shackled there as the man in front, the white man, lifted her to her knees by the hair and undid his pants. He pushed his red penis against her face, rubbing it there, then forcing it into her mouth.

"You could have saved yourself a good deal of difficulty if you'd only done what I wanted back then," he said. "Now suck this like a good little whore."

His cock lunged into her, and she choked and tried to

twist away, but he gripped her hair tightly, sneering down with a cruel, shark's smile as he forced himself into her mouth and almost into her throat.

Desperately, gagging repeatedly, she bit down on the intruding member. He squealed like a pig in response, batting at her head and dancing backwards, then stumbling against the table and falling.

She stared at him as she gulped in air, then got to her shaky legs and tried to run to the door. One of the tall black men easily grabbed her, however, turning her to face him and holding her in place by a fistful of hair.

"You... You... You'll pay for this!" he gasped, cupping himself.

7

It was going to be a day to remember.

Lord Andrew of Scotland Yard could hardly contain his enthusiasm when he woke Ms McDermitt of the Home Office up in the middle of the night to invite her to a raid he had planned on the 'secret headquarters' of the white slavery ring she had accused him of doing nothing about.

He picked her up shortly afterwards, annoyed somehow that she appeared perfectly awake and dressed, wearing an expensive and obviously tailor-made blue suit with a high collared silk blouse beneath.

"This better be good," she grunted as she slipped into the back of the Rolls.

"Oh I promise you it will be memorable," he said, barely containing his glee.

Behind them, as the Rolls moved out, two shadowy figures entered her flat, but Victoria McDermitt didn't notice as she demanded information from him.

"It seems these cads had an insider within Scotland Yard," he said. "They also have several highly placed members of the government helping to keep any investigation of them from getting too close."

"I knew it!"

"You informed no one that I had called?"

"I said I wouldn't," she said crossly.

"Good. There's no telling who's involved."

"Bloody macho men so proud of their ability to over-power helpless women," she said. "This bloody thing should have been crushed in its infancy."

"Well, don't worry, thanks to good solid police work we've ferreted out their headquarters."

"Thanks to a young that policewoman Meghan Sims, you mean," McDermitt retorted.

Sir Andrew smiled, inwardly snarling. He should have known that little blonde slut would go over his head. Probably another lesbian! He allowed himself to imagine the two attractive young women in each others arms, naked, kissing, and felt his manhood stir. He turned his mind away from such thoughts as the Rolls raced through the night. There would be plenty of time to enjoy his fantasies soon.

They were soon near the docks and driving amongst warehouses.

The car turned into one particular warehouse and stopped. The overhead door rose and they drove through. It closed behind them.

There were several men gathered around a desk set against the wall. Two were apparently unpacking a crate. Two others were drinking coffee at the table, while another was leafing through a clipboard. The only woman aside from Victoria herself was a tall broad-shouldered Mediterranean beauty leaning against the wall, a look of aloof contempt on her lushly attractive face.

They got out of the car and Lord Andrew took Victoria's

arm, leading her towards the desk. She shook it off brusquely.

"Gentlemen," he said. "I have here Miss Victoria McDermitt."

"Fancy that," one man said. "Looks nice. Like to see what her legs look like, though."

Victoria's eyes widened and then storm clouds appeared in them as she jerked her head around to glare at Lord Andrew.

"Well?" he said.

"Well what?" she snapped.

"Well show him."

"If this is your idea of a joke you old -"

"Oh I'm not joking at all," he said, calmly removing his own blazer.

"Lord Andrew if you don't explain..."

The back of his hand caught her in mid sentence, smashing into her mouth and knocking her backwards. She fell against some boxes then stumbled to the floor with a cry of shock.

Lord Andrew cracked his knuckles as he walked over to her, a smug smile on his face.

"You... you..."

"Indeed," he said.

He dropped to his knees, straddling her, another backhand sending her reeling back to the floor as she tried to sit. He gripped the front of her blouse and tore it open, exposing a frilly little half bra containing her full breasts. He tore the bra open and let his pudgy fingers sink into them, groping and mashing them together.

"B-bastard!" she half sobbed, sitting up, clawing at him.

Another backhand sent her flying back, then he straddled her body, his knees pinning her arms at her sides as he began to methodically slap her face. Again and again and again his heavy blows sent her head jerking from side to side, until her face was beet red and her mind spinning dazedly.

63

Then he moved down her body, bending and sliding his lips and tongue over her breasts. He bit freely and deeply, ignoring her sobs of pain and feebly flailing hands, chewing and digging his teeth into her sensitive nipples.

He lifted his head with a crow of laughter, then opened her trousers, unzipped them, then simply tore them open wider, ripping the thin fabric at the crotch to completely expose her inner thighs and the soft white panties she wore. He gripped her panties, tearing them off and then snickered at her tight cleft.

"Here's one that's long overdue to get plugged," he called to the watching men.

Victoria groaned weakly, wriggling and trying to pull away. Lord Andrew spread her legs wide and knelt on her thighs, then began to slap at her breasts with both hands, slowly, enjoying every second and every cry of pain.

"Slut! Filthy, despicable pervert!"

He undid his pants and pulled free his engorged cock, then thrust it into her with every bit of force he held. She was no virgin, but she was quite tight, and entirely dry as he pounded himself into her, and she screamed in pain and shocked humiliation as he laughed and dropped heavily atop her body.

She gasped in horror, humiliation and terror as he thrust into her, his heavy body pinning her to the floor as his man-hood tore in and out of her despoiled sex. All around her she could see the others watching, smirking, laughing at her rape. She cast her eyes in mute appeal to the single woman but that beauty looked back in amusement and even excitement.

Lord Andrew rutted fiercely, thrusting into her again and again, his lips crushing down on hers as he gripped her hair and forced her head back. She whimpered helplessly, feebly trying to push him away as he continued to drive himself into her with brutal and relentless energy.

Then he was done, pouring his semen into her. He lay

atop her for a few moments, then rose to his feet, putting his cock back into his pants as he looked down with contempt and satisfaction.

"Well that's about done for you, you slut," he said.

Victoria lay there spread-eagled, gasping, whimpering, her blazer and blouse wide open, her pants torn open at the crotch. She made no effort to close her legs for she hurt terribly there and her mind was still dazed from the sudden violence which had been inflicted upon her.

Lord Andrew knelt, gripped her hair, and lifted her head, jamming the muzzle of a gun into her open mouth.

"In the morning, a warrant will be issued for your arrest," he said with glee. "Your flat will be found to be stuffed full of kiddy porn, and we'll have produced at least one pathetic young girl who'll tell the world how the nasty old bull dyke raped her at an early age. You, of course, will have fled, and despite our best efforts it's most unlikely your body will ever be found."

The woman stepped away from the wall and came over to them. "Don't kill her. Let me have her."

"I've decided to kill her, Lisette," Lord Andrew snapped.

"That would be a waste. I can make considerable use of her. Besides, you don't really want her misery to end so quickly, do you?"

Lord Andrew snorted and glared down at the terrified woman below her. "Very well. Have your fun with her, Lisette."

He pulled the gun out of her mouth and stood up as the woman moved forward with a slow smile on her face. "Get up, you," she ordered.

Victoria stared up at her dazedly, trying to come to terms with the fact that she had almost been murdered, that Lord Andrew was actually been going to kill her.

Lisette leaned over and gripped her hair, yanking her up off the floor. Victoria screamed in pain, clawing weakly at the woman's powerful arm even as her pants slipped down around her ankles.

Lisette dragged her forward but she stumbled over the pants around her ankles and dropped to the floor again. Lisette sneered, dropping onto her back. In seconds she had yanked her blazer back over her shoulders, then pulled the torn remnants of her blouse and bra back over her shoulders and bound them in tight knots behind her, pinning her arms behind her back.

She snatched off the pants along with Victoria's shoes, then dragged her to her feet by her hair again.

"Owww! Oh please!" she cried as the big woman laughed. "Come with me, sweet girl," Lisette said with a smile, leading the mostly naked woman along the floor and into a small room set into one of the walls.

There she flung her against one of the walls, eyes gleaming, then forced her to her knees. She pulled a heavy belt from around her slim waist, then slipped it around Victoria's throat, yanking it up tight. "You do as I say, understand?" she said calmly.

Victoria gasped and choked, then nodded desperately.

Lisette smiled and let go of the belt, though it remained looped around Victoria's throat. She stood back, her tongue flicking out teasingly as she reached down and pulled open her leather jacket and slipped it off. She ran her hands tauntingly over her own body, then lifted her short skirt and moved forward.

"You know what I want, my dear," she said with a leer.

"Please don't," Victoria gasped. "D-don't make me do this!"

Lisette gripped the belt and yanked up hard, choking off her words. She lifted higher and higher, forcing Victoria to her feet, then her toes, watching with a smile as her face turned red.

"You do as I say. Yes?"

She loosened her hold and Victoria swayed, then fell to her knees, gulping in air desperately.

Lisette was barely twenty-one, but deep in depravity. She loved the power she held over others, be they men or women, and had a wide and varied knowledge of perversity, a knowledge she loved to share.

She gripped Victoria's head and jammed her face up into her sex, grinding her moist pussy up and down against her gasping lips.

"Lick me," she growled. "Now! Now!"

She tugged and pulled and twisted at Victoria's hair until the sobbing woman complied and began to push her tongue out and up into her sex. An hour later she was still lapping and sucking as Lisette sat back in a chair, slumped down, legs spread wide and sighing in pleasure.

"P-please... please I can hardly move my jaw any more," she whimpered.

"Please mistress," Lisette said with a smug smile.

"Please m-mistress," Victoria gasped.

Lisette giggled, then stood up slowly. She gripped the belt and with a yawn, pulled Victoria after her as she left the small room. Victoria cringed as she came under the eyes of the men in the warehouse. Lord Andrew was gone, but half a dozen men remained.

"This is my little pet, Fifi," Lisette said with a giggle. "She's lonely and so wants your company."

"Glad to give it," one of the men said.

Victoria moaned as the men crowded around her, their hands fighting for possession of her body. They dragged her back to the desk and across it, gathering around as her legs were spread wide. Then, one after the other they raped her, cruelly, savagely, pouring verbal abuse down on her as they used her body for their pleasure.

And through it all Lisette looked on coolly.

Victoria, like other women, had imagined what rape

would be like, but her worst nightmares could not begin to match the terror and humiliation she felt as the men used her again and again, slapping and groping her as they poured insults over her.

And all the while Lisette smirked, glorying in her degradation. When the men were done Lisette had led her by the belt around her throat, forcing her to crawl along after her on the floor as the men looked on.

She was taken back into the back room and her hands and arms strapped together behind her back. Then a leather arm sheath was forced up high, making her elbows press together and nearly dislocating her arms at the shoulders.

The bottom of the sheath had a long leather belt which held two large dildos attached to one side. Lisette giggled as she pulled the belt down between her buttocks, forcing the dildos up into her anus and vagina, and not incidentally forcing her arms down and back even more painfully.

The strap separated into two just past her mound, with the twin straps going up and over her hips to fasten to the side of the strap behind her. Lisette jerked the belt up high, hooked it to a heavy nail set into the wall, and left Victoria like that, on her toes, gasping for breath.

An hour or so later she returned, smiling as she ran her hands over Victoria's full breasts.

"You enjoy yourself, English lady?" she smirked. She pinched her fingers together against one of Victoria's nipples, jamming the sharp nails in against the sensitive pink flesh. Victoria screamed in pain, tears filling her eyes as the younger woman smiled.

"You forget who your mistress is, yes?"

"I-I'm sorry, mistress! I'm sorry, mistress!" Victoria screamed.

"Now that you've had so much rest I'm sure your tongue is feeling ready to pleasure me again."

She took the belt from the wall and pushed Victoria down

to her knees, lifting her skirt, and once again Victoria was forced to lap at the younger woman's sex until her tongue ached.

A ball-gag was forced into her mouth then and she was led out to a car and pushed into the back with Lisa. They drove through the industrial part of the city until getting onto the highway and driving to the airport, to a secluded private hangar.

Lisette got out and pulled on her leash. This was no longer the belt, but a chain which was attached to the centre of a second chain. The second chain had a rounded loop at either end and those loops had been closed tightly and painfully around Victoria's now aching nipples.

She hurried along behind Lisette, burning with humiliation as the woman led her over the concrete pad and up to a small private plane. Two large men lifted her up the stairs and she then followed Lisette to the small private cabin in the back.

The plane took off and Lisette smiled as she removed all her clothing for the first time.

"You like?" she purred, running her hands over her nude body.

She removed Victoria's gag, then pulled the dildos free of her and slipped off the sheath. Then she took her hand and led the shaken woman into a large bed, slipping under the covers and drawing Victoria in after her.

There was absolutely nothing she could do, Victoria knew. the woman was not alone, and even if she could somehow overcome her, which seemed most unlikely, she could hardly take over the plane.

Lisette drew her lips back with a pout, then pinched one of Victoria's nipples hard enough to make her gasp.

"Kiss back better," she demanded.

Their bodies rolled together as their lips joined again, and this time Victoria pushed her tongue out to meet the younger woman, moaning in despair as Lisette's hands roamed her body and the woman's sex ground against her own.

All through the flight, hour after hour, Lisette forced Victoria to make love. The girl was insatiable, and whenever Victoria showed a lack of eagerness she had quickly found painful ways of bringing it back.

It was dizzying and humiliating, for not only was Lisette ten years younger than her, but obviously uneducated, if shrewd. And Victoria was a sophisticated woman who had worked many years to make others aware of her status, taking great care to always retain her dignity. To be forced to grovel before this French bitch had been almost more than she could bear. Lisette sensed that, she thought, and delighted in it.

Lisette called her Fifi, and forced her to crawl the length of the plane, then down the stairs to the airport Tarmac. Even there, with the sun beating down, Victoria had to crawl along beside the woman while men walked back and forth, many of them Asian, smiling, grinning and pointing.

They were at a small, private airport, and despite her desperate search she found no sign of any kind of authorities. Mortified, she crawled beside Lisette, gasping in pain as the weights hanging from her nipples and clitoris swung and bounced below her.

A Rolls arrived and they got into it, Victoria laying on the floor in back, for, as Lisette told her "Bitch dogs don't get on the seats, Fifi."

She had tried a small rebellion in the car. Lisette had ordered her to lick her feet while she was down there and she had refused. Almost instantly, moving so quickly Victoria was astonished, the woman had her hand buried in Victoria's hair, and had yanked her head so far back her spine was burning before she was even able to scream.

Then she felt one of the chains attached to her nipple yanked hard, then again, then again, as Lisette shook her like a rag doll.

"You do what you're told, English bitch!" she hissed. "Or your death will be so painful you will welcome it!"

The rest of the trip had been spent with Victoria licking Lisette's feet and whimpering, cupping her aching nipple and trying to forget how much her scalp had hurt.

She crawled from the Rolls, again on the leash, and into a small bare looking building. Inside was all luxury, with Persian rugs and marble floors. Lisette handed her leash to a stout, older woman, obviously a servant.

The woman looked down at Victoria in disgust, and she dropped her eyes, humiliated anew. The two spoke in a language she didn't know, then the older woman led her away, with Lisette calling after her, warning her to obey. She went to the sink, and when she returned she had a straight razor and a small bottle of shaving cream. She roughly forced Victoria over onto her back on the floor, then spread her legs and lathered up her mound. She said something in a warning tone, glaring at her, then began to shave her.

Victoria didn't dare move as she stared at the straight razor and felt it sliding along the most tender, sensitive parts of her anatomy. The woman was careful, but the chances for a terrible cut were ever present.

She felt the woman work thick, stubby fingers into her sex, using them to keep her flesh taut as she sliced along next to her cleft. She burned with the indignity of it all but dared not move as the woman shaved her as bare as a child, then positioned her on all fours again and began to scrub her with rough hands and an even rougher brush.

Again water was poured over her, this time very hot, steaming as it hit the floor around her. She gasped and felt her flesh throb with the heat of it as the woman emptied several buckets over her body.

She leaned over her then, with a towel, and began to wring the worst of the water from her hair, then patted down her body with the now damp towel.

A man came in then, watching with a sneer on his lips, adding to her humiliations. He spoke to the woman for a moment, and the woman rose, muttering, and walked out. The man came over to her then, looking down. He reached down, gripping one of her arms, and pulled her to her feet, then looked her up and down.

Tired, exhausted, and still damp and hot, she did not react, merely looked at the floor until he forced her chin up. He turned her then, roughly, shoving her against the stone wall, pushing her hard against it so her breasts pillowed out.

His hand moved up and down her back, along her spine, down over her buttocks, then between her legs to cup her now bare mons. She clenched her teeth, fighting back tears of rage and misery as his fingers probed at her opening.

Then she heard his zipper, and a moment later his erection was pressed against her. She thought at first he meant to turn her around, but his heavy body pressed into her, crushing her into the wall as his male organ pushed against her rectum.

Her eyes widened in horror, and she struggled, but she had little strength of either will or body then, and gave up after a slap to the side of the head, sobbing lightly as she felt the sharp pain of his penetration, felt his cock forcing its way up into her anus.

His hands ran over her damp, overheated flesh, pinching and squeezing as he burrowed deeper. Cramps rippled through her belly and she felt sharp twinges and burning from her rectum as he jammed it ever higher. She rose to her toes, gasping, yet still he forced more in.

"God! Please!" she sobbed.

He ignored her, thrusting in again, and now she could feel his pubic hair against her buttocks, could feel his flesh against her damp cheeks. He laughed, bending and biting down on her shoulder, then the side of her throat. His hands came around and cupped her breasts, mauling them, crushing and squeezing them as he ground his loins into her backside.

"Bastard," she sobbed. "Bastard."

He drew back, then thrust forward again, rapidly building up speed so she thought her insides were being torn apart, grunting with pleasure at his crude sodomy.

Then he gave a sudden gasp and pumped desperately, his hips slapping into her behind, grinding her against the wall as he came inside her. The realization that his male semen was pumping into her bowels made her sick, and she almost threw up.

She turned her head to one side, gasping, eyes closed, and when she opened them Lisette was there.

8

The pain was intense, and Amanda had never imagined her feet could hurt so much just from standing on them.

Of course, she had never tried to put all her weight on the balls of her feet for so long either.

She was standing in a small brick-lined room, on a small round platform surrounded by deep plush carpeting. She was nude, her lush young body glistening with sweat, her breasts thrust out and up. A heavy leather strap bound her arms behind her back, pinning her elbows together. A second bound her wrists.

She was wired to a thick glistening steel pole and her toes were locked into two narrow metal braces so she could not move them even an inch. Under her heels were two pedals which, were they depressed, would cause an electrical contact to be made, thus sending powerful jolts of electricity up the metal pole and into her body.

Her back was arched strongly, painfully, aching only slightly less than her feet. Her long lustrous hair had been wound into a tight, thick tail, and pulled back crudely, forcing her head back, her eyes facing the ceiling. Standing in front of her was another metal pole, thinner than the one she was straddling. The top of this pole was flat, unlike the rounded one up inside her pussy, and dangling perhaps a half inch above it was a small but heavy metal contact held aloft by a narrow wire.

That wire ran upwards to approximately the height of her shoulders, then over a small wheel, splitting in half and extending to two strong metal alligator clips with sharp teeth. These clips were firmly biting into her nipples, which throbbed and burned with pain.

She had already had the experience of allowing that metal contact to touch the pad below, and her breasts still tingled with shocked pain even several minutes after the event. So now she was doing her very utmost to prevent a recurrence.

But it was hard, so hard. Her breasts and back and nipples hurt so, and her feet... she didn't know how much longer she could keep her heels off those pedals. Her feet trembled and shook every few seconds, and she whimpered in misery and fear, her mind frantic and bewildered by how her life had changed over the previous twenty four hours.

In a corner of the room was a luxurious recliner, deeply padded and comfortable, made of the finest leather. Edward sat in the chair, sipping brandy and smiling as he looked on at her torment.

He was nude, and a lushly endowed young redhead knelt between his legs softly mouthing his flaccid penis, not with the aim of either arousing or sating his excitement, but for comfort, to soothe his aching member.

In truth the doctors had found nothing but a little bruising and a bit of scraped flesh, but the psychic wounds ran much deeper. Edward found himself feeling fear whenever one of the whores started to mouth him, and, enraged, had beaten several since his second humiliation at the hands of the vile Graham woman.

Allowing the redhead to lick and suckle softly was his way of showing his bravery, both to himself, and to anyone else who thought the slut had frightened him.

Of course, the redhead, barely five feet tall and weighing under a hundred pounds, was tightly bound. Her arms were encased in leather sleeves and pulled not only behind her back, but painfully high behind her back, her hands up behind her neck, where they were bound to the collar around her throat.

Her arms were strapped tightly together as well, as were her ankles, knees, and thighs. Next to him on the table sat a heavy whip, and the girl well knew what would happen if he even imagined he felt her teeth on him.

He raised his eyes and looked at Amanda again, hating her, despising her, and imagining cruder and fouler punishments with each passing minute.

She screamed and he looked up to see her shaking violently, swaying slightly as she yanked the contact point off its pad by arching her back even more. His lips curled into a slow, evil smile and he felt his loins stir anew.

Amanda could barely breath as her chest burned. She felt her mind growing faint and fought to keep from collapsing. She sobbed piteously, not caring any longer about pride or dignity, unable to stand the horrible and perverse punishments she was subjected to.

"Please!" she sobbed. "I beg of you! Please!"

"Please?" he said lazily. "Please what, slut?"

"P-please no more! I'll do anything you want! Anything!"

"Will you suck my erection?"

"Yes! Yes!"

"And kneel on all fours like a bitch in heat while I ride you?"

"Yes! Please!"

"And of course you'll let me sodomize you?"

"Anything!"

"Well now. Why don't we see just how much you want to suck my wonderful penis, hmm? Let me hear you beg me. Beg me like the filthy, miserable whore you are. Beg me to let you get your ugly lips around my beautiful cock. Go on, slut! Beg!"

She swayed and her feet trembled, her right heel touching the pedal beneath her. She whimpered again, trying to raise it, but it lowered and she felt a tingling between her legs, a tingling that moved upwards into her sheath, setting her abdomen quivering.

"Please, please, please let me suck you cock! Please let me wrap my miserable slutty filthy lips around your beautiful, wonderful cock! Please! I'll give you a wonderful blow job! I will, truly! Please, oh please!"

She raised her heel slightly, at terrible pain, and the tingling eased, but then her left dipped and she felt the tingling again, stronger now. She tried to rise and in doing so leaned forward just slightly, fire shot into her nipples and she screamed, lurching back.

This time her heel pushed down harder, and the tingling became a crackling charge of electricity. It surged up the metal pole and blasted deep into her belly with terrible results. She shrieked in agony, vibrating like a plucked guitar string, her body bathed in fire as she lurched up desperately.

Too much, and the fire caught at her breasts, consuming them. Again she screamed, pulling back, just enough, holding her heels aloft.

She sobbed in misery and pain, her body still tingling in the aftermath of the voltage which had coursed through it, her mind still stunned in the aftermath of the pain.

"Would you, er, repeat that please? I don't think I quite got it," Sir Edward said.

"Oh God, please help me!" she whispered.

"I'm God here, slut. I'm your god. And I am most displeased with you. Now let me hear your beg to be sodomized, you miserable, wretched, diseased little trollop. And don't forget to call me master this time."

"Master," she croaked. "Please, master. Please sodomize me. Please rape me in the ass. Please use me. I... I'm a filthy, worthless slut. I'm sorry, master. Please let me show you how sorry I am."

He stroked the hair of the girl fellating him and tilted his head back, appearing to consider it.

"Uhmm, no," he said.

Amanda moaned, fresh tears spilling from her open eyes. Long minutes passed. She swayed forward and another blast of pain hit her chest, then she slipped backward, her heels depressing the pedals.

She screamed, the sound echoing against walls long familiar with screams, as the power threatening to rocket her upwards off the pole as it crackled up into her body.

Again she managed to drag herself up high enough for the pedals to rise, and held there trembling for long minutes.

"Perhaps I should get this on video," Edward said. "You really do look quite erotic like that, you know. I'm almost tempted to take you down and ram myself up your tight little rectum. But I'll restrain myself. I know how you hate forward men touching your pure little body."

Amanda barely heard him. She had never felt such pain, had never imagined there could be such pain. She had thought she was in pain during her terrible rape, but now she longed to be back in the room with those monsters. For things had only become worse since then.

Her heels sank, and try as she might overworked muscles would not respond. Her heels touched the pedals and the tingling began between her legs, getting more and more powerful as her heels lowered, crackling up the pipe and into her guts like a rising scream.

And then she realized the scream was hers...

There was a knock at the door, and Edward motioned the slave girl sitting by it to turn and open it. A man came in, smiling to Edward, and, with barely a glance at where the girl was writhing in the grip of an electrical storm, came forward and shook his hand.

"How do you do, Sir Edward," he said. "My name is Prince Achmed Abdullah."

"Uhmm, well, hello there, er, Your Highness," Edward said, standing awkwardly as he stuffed himself back into his trousers.

"I am glad to meet you as your companies and mine have numerous dealings which perhaps we might use to our advantage," Achmed said in heavily accented English.

"Well, er, I'm always glad to do business, but, well, uhm..." He nodded at the girl on the pole.

"Quite right, of course. Business before pleasure," Achmed said, looking dispassionately at Amanda. "Your intend her death?" he asked.

"I suppose. Well, er..."

"She is, I hear, quite new here, yes? You western men do not understand that revenge is best if it lasts longest. If she dies after so little time..." He held up his hands regretfully.

"Well, er, yes, now that you mention it. She would be getting off easily. There are so many other, uhm, things I had in mind for her."

"Exactly."

Edward moved to the machine and shut off the power, but the girl kept shivering and trembling for a full minute even as he turned back to Achmed.

"I'm er, new, as you might know," he said.

"Oh course. I am fairly new myself. Perhaps I could show you around, and we could devise more interesting punishments for this impertinent female. I myself brought just such a female here two weeks ago, you know."

"Oh, really? Well, er, uhm, what did you do to her?"

"Come and I will show you," Achmed said, smiling broadly.

He led Edward down the hall, then around a corner. There were many sections of the club Edward had not yet fully explored, so he was glad of someone to show him around, even if it was a damned wog. Still, he thought, surely the wogs knew quite a deal about punishing and torturing people. They were all damned barbarians anyway. It would be interesting to see what Achmed had in mind for the slut back there.

He was glad he'd stopped before killing Amanda. What had ever possessed him anyway? That would have ruined his fun with her. He wanted her crawling to him on all fours, not dead. He wanted her begging for his attentions. He wanted her as degraded and demeaned as possible.

He really did have to mind his temper, he thought. It was because he was so strong-willed. Strong-willed men always had tempers, he told himself.

9

Achmed led him into a wide room lit by crystal chandeliers, a kind of grand hall of the tormented, where delectable young women were placed out for the amusement of jaded guests.

As they entered, the first thing the came to were a row of low marble pedestals. The first pedestal had a young blonde lying back, arms stretched straight down along the far corners of the pedestal, legs stretched straight up and apart. Her head hung down over the far side of the pedestal, her hair bound and pulled down to keep her from rising.

A man stood in front of her, using her mouth casually, and Edward felt his lusts stirring as he saw the bulge in her throat and watched the man's cock slide right into her to the balls. He'd heard of this sort of thing, vaguely, but never experienced it himself. To push himself right down her throat like that!

He simply had to do it to Amanda!

The next pedestal had a girl bent over on her belly, legs straight and bent, head pulled up and back, and bound back by her hair, which was pulled back in two tails and chained to the near corners of the pedestal.

Achmed led him around to the far side, where her face was, and stroked her cheeks before pulling his cock out and placing it in her open mouth. She closed her lips - though not without some difficulty - and he began to thrust into her.

Edward licked his lips hungrily as he watched Achmed's tool slide right into her to the hilt, and watched the Arab grind his pelvis into her face as he sighed in pleasure.

He moved to the next pedestal, where another girl, this one a redhead, was bound on her back, head hanging free. His fingers fumbled at his trousers, then opened them and drew out his semi-hard cock, pushing it into her mouth.

She started tonguing it immediately, sucking and lapping as he drove it in deep. He felt a tremendous wave of pleasure and satisfaction as he entered her throat and slid right down it. His hands gripped her neck, squeezing as he pumped up and down, trying to feel himself moving inside her.

That she was breathing with difficulty was apparent, but not terribly relevant to him as he pumped harder and squeezed harder. He came quickly and softened, then pulled out, fumbling himself back into his clothing even as Achmed pulled his still hard prong from the other girl's mouth and put it back into his robe.

"I hate to waste myself on one when there are so many deserving of Allah's seed," he said piously.

"Uhm er, yes, of course," Edward replied, somewhat bemused.

"Observe," Achmed said, lifting a foot long metal baton of some sort off a nearby shelf.

He turned to one of the women on her back and thrust it deep into her bare little pussy opening, then pushed a red button the end.

She started shuddering and shaking, her body bouncing wildly on the pedestal as she warbled and moaned in pain.

"There are many uses for electricity," he said.

"I see." Edward nodded.

He took one of the batons as well, then picked up a short, heavy riding crop as well.

The two moved along the row, zapping this or that girl in whatever hole presented itself, and Edward tried out the crop on a very round little behind.

In the main part of the room women hung from the ceiling in various positions. Achmed motioned towards one girl hanging upside down, legs spread wide, and smiled at Edward. Edward showed his teeth and lashed her several times as she shivered and shook and sobbed in pain.

They went on to the next girl, who hung from joined wrists, whipping and shocking her for a few minutes.

The next hung by both wrists and ankles. She was older than most of the others, perhaps by ten years. Still, she was lovely and full-bodied, with an intelligent, aristocratic face and soft brown hair.

She eyed them anxiously as Achmed produced another curious device. It appeared to be a foot long tube made of interlocking plastic mesh. It was open at one end, and at the other had a small oddly shaped hole.

"What is your name, bitch?" he demanded.

"V-V-Victoria, Master," she gulped.

"Another English girl," he said to Edward.

He slid the device deep into her opening, then slipped a thin handle into the end and began to twist it slowly. At first Edward didn't see what effect this had, but then he realized the tube was noticeably thickening. The wire mesh was unwinding inside her, uncoiling and expanding.

Victoria groaned and her head fell back as she began to strain at the chains holding her. The tube widened and the plastic mesh pushed out tightly against her pussy and vaginal opening.

She cried out, sobbing, her body trembling and shaking.

"Can you make it any wider?" Sir Edward asked.

"Not without doing a great deal of damage."

"Go ahead."

"Regrettably, to damage the club's general property requires permission first. It is in case someone has reserved her use, you see, who might be inconvenienced."

"Oh, I understand. Of course. But I could use this on one of my personal slaves, right?"

"Yes, of course."

So she was not to die yet. She groaned as the thing inside her grew smaller and smaller, then pulled free. Her vaginal opening remained open for some time, her muscles strained beyond instant recovery.

Achmed led Edward further into the room and they found a big busted blonde hanging by her breasts. They were tightly encased in leather straps, and her arms were tightly bound behind her back. She swayed slowly in place, whimpering and moaning as men passing by pushed to set her swinging.

Edward pushed his baton into her rectum and shot a burst of electricity into her, giggling in delight as she screamed and danced wildly.

Next were traditional rowing machines with a little extra. Achmed sat in the seat and gripped the oars, smiling up at him, then turning and beginning to stroke.

The difference, of course, was that the oars were attached to a long rounded wooden pole directly in front of where the rower sat. A dildo sat poised on the end of that pole, directly before the bared cleft of a delicate looking Japanese girl. Each time he jerked the oars back the pole rammed forward a full foot, burying the dildo into the girl.

There was nothing she could do about this, of course, since her knees were tied apart and back and her arms were bound behind her. Nor was there anything she seemed to want to do, as her head began bobbing back with each hard thrust and she began whispering and moaning in Japanese, her grunts obviously that of pleasure rather than pain.

"Slut loves it," Edward sneered.

"Ah, but think of the effort it required to teach her to love it," Achmed responded. "It's so easy to give pain, but to force their minds to accept pleasure is something of considerably more satisfaction."

He got up and moved to a weightlifting machine, turning and sitting on the bench, then grasping the handles and lifting slowly. A willowy blonde was lifted into the air by her wrists, then lowered again.

Achmed got up and Edward saw her ankles were locked to a metal bar. Achmed strapped several weights onto the bar, then sat back and pumped the handles again. He could see the strain in the girl's face now as her arms were lifted up against the weight trying to hold her down.

"How much weight is on her ankles?" he asked.

"One hundred pounds."

"How can you lift that much and her?"

"I am stronger than I appear," Achmed said with a smile. "Also, the weight of the girl is offset by pulleys, see? So all I lift is the weights."

"Ah, so you could strap a couple of hundred pounds to

her ankles and lift her up and down?"

"Certainly."

"Just like the old English rack, huh?" Edward said with a smile.

"Same basic affect." agreed Achmed. He got up and then suddenly took Edward's arm and led him towards a staircase. Edward chuckled when he saw it, for each stair was a naked girl lying on her back. He mounted slowly, to the sound of gasps, grunts, and groans from each of the girls he trod upon.

Soft music played in a lounge upstairs. Comfortable chairs were dotted about the room, as were small stylish pedestals.

On one pedestal two lovely women, one black, the other white, stood together, arms about each other, hands and lips moving softly and seductively over each others bodies.

On others women were dancing, masturbating, or simply posed for artistic effect. Achmed sat him down in the seat next to this one, sitting back comfortably.

"So tell me, Sir Edward," Achmed said. "How did you come to join the Viceroy Club?"

"Well, er uhm, they contacted me, you see."

"Oh really? How did they know to do that? A member recommend you?"

"Er uhm, not quite, though yes, I suppose you could say that. You see, I'd er, well, I'd been sort of, uhm, amusing myself, enjoying myself, as you can imagine, and well, the local authorities were starting to take notice of it."

"I don't understand."

"Well, er, you see, it was like this. About a month or so, I was walking along, well, er, driving along, and there was this young lady, you see, quite lovely, wearing revealing clothing and well, obviously just asking for it. You see?"

"Of course."

"Well, I had this American gadget, this electrical stun gun thingy, you see. And, er, well, I stopped and, you see, tested it on her. Worked delightfully well, actually, at least that first time, and I er, well, pulled her into the car you see and headed home."

"For a bit of sport, as you English say."

"Precisely," Edward beamed. "But unfortunately, she woke up before I got home and, well, started becoming rather violent. I quickly subdued her, of course."

He dropped his voice and glanced round before continuing...

10

I remember it so well, Edward told Achmed...

The girl had struggled frantically, and it was all he could do to keep his gloved hand across her face, preventing her screams, and drag her down the stairs to the basement. His heart was pounding madly and he was sweating as she clawed at him, her legs kicking out, her entire body writhing and thrashing furiously.

He was appalled at the fight she was putting up. He had chosen her as much for her small size and meek appearance as her lush young body, yet he could barely restrain her.

"Little bitch!" he gasped, twisting her arm as he dragged her the final few steps. He lifted her, swinging her around, then marched her to the small hidden door to what had once been a bomb shelter. Again she struggled and he cursed as her heel slammed into his shin. He flung her into the wall, using his body to hold her there as he clawed at the release. The hidden opening slid aside and he caught the girl by the short hair and flung her down the stairs.

He hurried after, hitting the release so the door closed after him. The girl bounced a few times, then scrambled to her feet and screamed so loudly his ears almost popped. She turned and raced down the narrow corridor, passing the open blast door with Edward following.

He heaved a sigh of relief, closing and locking the door behind him. There was no way the girl could escape now, nor would anyone hear her, however loudly she whined.

He rushed forward after her and almost ran into her. She was wide-eyed, having run right into his torture chamber, stared around in horror, then fled right back at the man who'd hit her with one of those electric shock devices then dragged her into his car.

"No!" she screamed, turning and trying to flee once more.

His hand shot out and gripped her hair, yanking her head back, bowing her body, then twisting her, gripping her arm and slamming her into the stone wall. She yelled in pain, but he pinned her arm up behind her back now and marched her back into the small room he'd fitted out to exorcise his personal demons.

A fist to her gut halted her wild and desperate struggle, and as she sagged to her knees he hurriedly fetched a rope from the cupboard and squatted before her. He wound it tightly around one slim wrist, then pulled the other out from where it was clutching her stomach, wrapping the rope around it, then binding them tightly together.

It was a slapdash affair, but no less tight and effective for that. He heaved a sigh of relief, then looked upwards to the several hooks he'd hung on chains from the ceiling. He dragged the girl to her feet by the hair and led her under one, then lifted her arms high above her and, with a deal of effort as she began to struggle again, slipped her wrists over the hook.

He stepped back, panting for breath, then stumbled to the cupboard and poured himself a stiff brandy, shaking his head as he turned to regard the girl.

About twenty, and not much over five feet tall, the young

woman he'd captured with that difficult to obtain (and faulty) stun gun was stretched tightly before him. Her toes barely touched the floor and her wrists were tightly held high above her. She had a small rounded face with large brown eyes and a pouty little mouth. Her chestnut hair was cut short, and she was wearing a tight black mini and a now-torn white blouse.

"Bastard!" she groaned, half sobbing.

"You'll soon find out what I am," he gasped, recovering his breath even as she recovered hers.

He moved over to her, then undid her skirt. She tried half-heartedly to kick out at him but the fight seemed to have gone out of her. The skirt dropped to the floor and he licked his lips as he beheld her bare thighs, his erection well under way now.

She wore a pair of small, silky, high cut pink panties, and with a single strong pull he tore them away, baring her small, neatly trimmed bush and the darker line of her sex hidden between her thighs.

Tears filled her eyes and she struggled weakly, wriggling like a fish on the end of a hook as Edward tore at her blouse. It was harder to remove, but in less than a minute only shreds remained, and then not even shreds. Her bra he had to cut off, but then he stood back to admire his handiwork, trembling with excitement and lust, his cock hard against his tight trousers.

The girl groaned, her face filled with terror and humiliation. Her toes twitched above the floor, and her belly was indented below her shapely full breasts.

Edward moved around her slowly, admiring her firm round buttocks. He reached out and squeezed them, making her cry out in alarm and kick out with her feet.

"That's not on, girl," he said roughly. "If you do anything more to get on my nerves I'll teach you just what I do to nasty little girls around here."

87

His voice was icy and she halted her struggles, gasping for breath as he moved around in front of her. He reached out, his angry eyes boring into hers, and cupped her right breast. He smiled thinly as his fingers sank into the soft flesh and she made no resistance.

"Slut," he spat, pinching her nipple cruelly.

She gasped and whimpered but did not attempt to kick out as he bent and folded his lips around her nipple. He chewed hungrily at her flesh, his tongue whipping across the sensitive surface of her nipple, his lips sucking furiously as his fingers mauled both her prized orbs.

He stepped back, gulping in air, his face alive with excitement and passion.

"Slut!" he repeated.

His hand drew back and then lashed out, his open hand cracking against the side of her face and sending her head spinning to the side.

She cried out, then cried out again as his other hand caught her on the opposite cheek and flung her head back. Again he slapped her, then again, then again, each time cursing her.

Dazed, moaning, she let her head hang down as he moved behind her, this horrible man who hated her for no reason she could imagine.

He stood behind her, his eyes fixed on her beautiful form, on the smoothness of her back and the spine running down to her rounded buttocks. She was so helpless, so utterly helpless, and he could do anything he wanted to her.

Anything.

He picked up his strap, the one he'd taught the others to fear, and twisted it through his fingers again and again as he ran his eyes up and down her soft ivory skin.

Then he stepped forward and raised his arm, pulling it back. His eyes were fixed on the centre of the young woman's back. With a shudder, he drew his arm back and then swung it forward. The strap flew through the air and whipped down across her lower back with a crack! that echoed around the small room.

The girl's back arched as her lower body tried to instinctively pull away from the pain that bit into it, and after an instant's hesitation she cried out in pain, her voice high-pitched and filled with terror.

Again he lashed out, another crack! testifying to the strength of the blow. This time she screamed, her legs kicking out wildly, her body twisting and spinning.

He waited for her movements to ease, breathing hard, knowing from the feel that if he reached down and squeezed himself even once he would explode.

"Please! Please, sir!" the girl cried, tears trickling down her cheeks. "Please don't hurt me! I'll do anything you want!"

"Of course you will," he murmured, moving behind her.

Crack! Crack! Crack!

The girl howled as the strap whipped across her back, jerking and dancing wildly on the end of the hook. She tried to keep him from her back, twisting to face him, or trying to, even as tears poured from her eyes.

Impatiently he swung his arm cruelly and the long leather strap cracked down across one of her breasts.

Her scream made him wince even as his cock pulsed with delight. He watched the soft round orb redden even as tears fell from her face onto the softly rounded surface and trickled down over the small pink nipple.

"Slut!" he said with a cruel smile.

He moved behind her and the strap began to fall again, raising angry red lines of pain across her shoulders, her lower back, then her buttocks and upper thighs. After dozens of blows her screams faded, became soft cries and grunts.

He halted, panting for breath, then moved in behind her. His hands shook as he undid his trousers and pulled his erection free. He jammed it in between her red buttocks, rubbing it there for only seconds before he exploded, his come spewing out across her wounded flesh.

He staggered back and fell into a padded chair, gasping for breath.

He was neither surprised nor annoyed at his quick climax. He had always been like that - the first time. This had made relations with women under normal circumstances embarrassing. But he would hold out longer the second time, and still longer the third. Edward's required little time between climax and erection provided he had the proper stimulus. And hanging there in front of him, groaning weakly, helpless, aching with pain, was more than enough stimulus.

No doubt she would be easier to handle now. They always were.

He did up his trousers, then stood and moved forward. He gripped her arms and raised her, lifting her wrists over the hook, then letting her sag to her knees on the floor before him.

He looked down at her teary-eyed face, feeling tremendous power. He smiled at her, revelling in her helplessness, then slowly undid his zipper and opened his trousers. He let them fall and smiled again as she tried to turn her head away.

He gripped her hair and she cried out in pain, fresh tears filling her eyes.

"You know what I want, slut," he growled.

He pulled her face in against his crotch, rubbing her face against his groin.

"Do it," he ordered. "Take it into your mouth."

With a brief sob she obeyed, and he sighed as her lips slipped around his tool and she took him all inside her warm oral cavity. She sucked and licked at it tentatively and he quickly began to harden.

Soon he was fully erect again and she was bobbing her lips up and down his length, or as much of it as she could take into her mouth without choking.

He pulled out at the last instant, squeezing himself as his

juices spurted forth, splattering across her upturned face.

She whimpered, but was held tightly by the hair. He rubbed his organ against her face, smearing his juices into her pores, then flung her back roughly so she fell on her back on the floor.

He removed his trousers and strode back to the chair, sitting comfortably, facing across the room where the girl still lay as she'd landed.

"Come here," he ordered.

The girl began to rise but his voice beat her back down. "Crawl!" he yelled. "Crawl on your belly!"

She trembled, then sank back to the floor. She took two deep breaths, then slowly began to wriggle forward, her breasts cold against the stone, grinding below her as she moved slowly forward.

When she reached him he placed his foot down against the back of her head, pinning her face to the cold concrete.

"I want you to remove my shoes," he ordered, "then clean my feet with your mouth."

She looked up at him in misery.

"Now, slut!"

"Please," she said in a small voice. "Please, sir, I -"

His hand cracked down across her face, hurling her back onto the stone floor.

"Now!" he ordered.

Helpless, she crawled back to him and obeyed, whimpering and cringing, then her small pink tongue licked out almost delicately across the heel of his foot. He smiled down at her as her tongue lapped reluctantly along the top of his foot, then downwards over his toes.

At his orders she took each of them between her lips, sucking at it as she licked, then worked her way across the bottom of his foot.

When he felt himself hardening again he reached down and gripped her hair, dragging her up and into his lap and pushing his cock at her again.

She took it into her mouth, bobbing her lips up and down it as he watched, hands folded across his chest, a smirk on his face.

"That's enough," he said. "I want you on all fours like the sow you are. Go on. Now!"

She moaned as she obeyed, and he rose, walking slowly around her as she knelt submissively. He prodded at her heavy, hanging breasts with one foot, then at her pussy with the other.

"This is what you were made for, slut," he said. "This is the natural position for a slut like you, on all fours like a bitch in heat, ready to be mounted by her master."

He moved behind her and dropped to his knees, rubbing his spit-wet erection back and forth over her sweating cleft. He reached down with his hand, prying her tight lips apart and baring her pink inner flesh, then pushed himself forward into it, jabbing at her hole, forcing himself into her inch after inch as she trembled and shook and tears dropped to the floor.

He used his erection like a sword, jamming it into her, forcing it higher and higher into the young woman's sheath, griping her hips tightly to yank her back as he stabbed deep and buried himself inside her hot young depths.

Giving her little chance to get used to it he began to rut into her, his hips pounding into her round buttocks with bruising force, his hard cock pistoning up and down her tight pink tube.

For long minutes the only sound in the small enclosed space was her ragged breathing, grunts and whimpers and the soft slap slap slap of his hips striking her buttocks.

"So you had your own little impromptu version of the Viceroy?" Achmed said with an indulgent smile.

"Well, rather," Sir Edward chuckled. "But then the very

next morning, with the little tramp still downstairs, I had this visit, you see, from a gentleman representing the club. It seems some information had drawn the attention of a high ranking member of Scotland Yard, a Lord no less, regarding my little, uhm, adventures, and he had some connection with the club. So he was good enough to, well, to destroy what evidence there was and issue me an invite."

"It's good to have friends in high places," Achmed said. "And the club has a good number of them."

"Yes. Delightful people. A real gentleman's club."

"Quite a few people from all over the world here."

"Yes. Quite so. A goodly number of English gentlemen too, and, of course, quite a number of your people."

"We know how to treat women in my land," Achmed said seriously. He leaned forward and slid his hand between the girl's thighs, fingering her cleft. He stroked gently alongside her clitoris, then tugged lightly on the chain hooked to her labia. She whined softly and trembled.

He eased a finger up inside her, gently caressing her soft pink flesh, pumping it in and out as his thumb moved across her clitoris in a circular motion.

She moaned, then gasped as her small motions tugged against the chains holding her so tightly in position.

Achmed smiled and continued to stroke her clitty, causing her to quiver and shake, her juices to flow down his fingers.

He halted and drew his hand back, turning to Edward.

"Now you see what true torment is? I shall leave her like this, wanting more, needing relief, but unable to obtain it."

"You're a cruel man, Achmed, to treat a slut like that," Edward said with a sneer of contempt for the girl.

11

Agent Sarah Bergstrom stared after them as they left, fighting to control her breathing as she considered ways to get back at 'Achmed'.

Achmed was Agent Paul Stern, like Sarah, from the Mossad, Israel's intelligence service. It had taken them a long time and a lot of effort to infiltrate the Viceroy, and many times they had risked their lives so that they could get as far as they had.

It wasn't because of the way the men of the Viceroy Club treated women that Mossad had become involved. At least, not women in particular. It had been ordered to find three young Israeli army junior officers who had gone missing over the past three years. Each of them was young and beautiful, and had disappeared without a trace.

The immediate suspicion was a kidnapping by Arabs. The fact that they were all so young and beautiful pointed to a motivation, and the Mossad began to search for powerful Arabs who were known to have a reputation for abusing young women. Since that was a fairly common perversion among a number of powerful men in the middle-east the search had taken some time.

A number of powerful and wealthy Arabs belonged to the Viceroy Club, and it was through them that Achmed had managed to gain an invitation. His cover was solidified by his desire for them to kidnap an Israeli tourist he'd run into in Cairo.

Sarah was the tourist, masquerading as a college student. She had been well-briefed in advance as to what her role would require of her, and chosen for two reasons in particular. First, she was extremely beautiful, with a slim, athletic, but curvaceous body. And second, though she had tried to hide it from her superiors, careful checks into her background had shown her to be deeply involved in bondage and sadomasochistic sexual practices.

Sarah had been a masochistic person for many years. Since it only aroused her in a sexual context and she was able to separate her sexual life from her working life, nobody bothered her about it.

Until they needed a woman to do something they could not ask any normal woman to do.

Normal, she thought. She had been 'normal', once, years ago, before... David.

She'd been a teenager still, eager to explore strange realms of sensuality. The sex she'd experimented with had seemed tame, and lacked the kind of excitement and pleasure she had heard and read of. David was far older, and seemed - dangerous, somehow.

Yet the moment they had been alone she had begun to suspect she had only the merest hint of what lay beneath his handsome exterior.

He'd ordered her to strip, and she had, feeling excited, but quite self conscious. After all, just stripping, alone, was not something she had any experience with. All the boys she had had sex with had groped and kissed her as they were both undressing.

Once naked she had stood there, trembling slightly, and he had ordered her to turn her back to him. Then he had pulled her wrists up behind her back and tied them there.

The instant she realized his intent she felt a surge of excitement that almost made her faint. She'd never really thought about bondage, nor really heard much about it, but as her wrists were bound tightly together she knew something deep inside her had finally been satisfied.

He had treated her cruelly, demeaning and degrading her, using her roughly, contemptuously. Yet she had revelled in it, and come back for more. The next time he had slapped her repeatedly, her face, her breasts, her buttocks, making her squeal each time. Yet her climaxes had been so powerful she again came back, like an addict, knowing what she was doing wasn't good for her but unable to resist.

The third time other men were there. They had raped her under his eyes, and she had cursed him in her mind, yet climaxed powerfully. He hung her by her wrists for the first time that day, and whipped her back until she had been sure it was bleeding.

Each visit grew worse, until she had finally broken off with him, a mass of bruises, cuts and welts.

Yet he had opened a new doorway in her mind, and always afterwards she had needed bondage and pain to arouse her. She had hidden this from everyone, of course, or thought she had, until the Mossad had told her they knew it all.

Though embarrassed initially, Sarah had agreed to help. She had thought she had some idea, as did her superiors, of what she faced, of what they were up against. However, all her experiments and sexual games of bondage paled in comparison to the perversions of the Viceroy Club, and that posed a danger she could not admit to Paul.

It wasn't that the pain or humiliation were more than she could take, though they often came close, it was that she was finding herself being sucked in to the role of obedient slave, to that of sexual playtoy and victim.

She had been kidnapped just as expected, and, unharmed but with a tracking device planted inside her body, delivered to an island, which, she had since discovered, was in the middle of the South Pacific.

She woke in the strange mirrored room, wearing, not the civilian clothes she had worn on being kidnapped, but an Israeli army uniform. This had puzzled her greatly, and at first she had feared that their cover had been seen through.

She had suspected immediately that the mirrored walls were one way mirrors, had been certain she was under observation, but had still almost given the game away when a section of it opened and Paul had come through.

His behaviour had alerted her, of course. He was leering at her threateningly, and he called her a filthy Jewess and Israeli pig. She had glared at him, called him vile names, and then he had raped her.

He had whispered an apology in her ear as he had torn her clothes off, and she knew he had no alternative, yet it was still a bizarre experience. It had been a rough, violent rape, and the only thing that had saved her from real pain was that he was playacting, at least in a sense, and because it had aroused her.

That shocked her, for knowing she was under observation during it was embarrassing, and though she had played many bondage and rape games she had not thought of herself as an exhibitionist. But as she had slowly let Paul tear her uniform off her, and as he had slapped at her face and torn at her hair she had gradually lost some awareness that what they were doing was in a sense, an act, and had begun to fall into her old role playing, as she had with former lovers.

She had fought hard, but he had stripped her. Then a fist in the belly collapsed her resistance long enough for him to bend her over the table there and enter her from behind.

She was wet, very wet, and her body charged with sexual desire. Fortunately her gasp of pleasure was interpreted by the watchers as pain, and her subsequent cries, moans and whimpers were likewise thought of as the pain she was receiving from the brutal rape by Achmed the evil Arab.

But inside her pleasure had soared, and her mind and body had rolled up and over successive waves of scorching sex-heat that threatened to drown her. She had barely had enough presence of mind to disguise her orgasm when it came, for it had been intensely powerful.

She was still caught up in the sexuality of her degrading rape when her wrists had been bound behind her back and she had been led out into a much larger room. There she had seen the crowd which had gathered around the circular glass room. She had felt humiliation and anger, yet something deep inside her was touched as she was led, bound and naked amongst the sneering, spitting crowd of men, led down a narrow hallway and then thrown into a cell.

They had imagined something like captive sex toys, like a bordello for rich men to amuse themselves with pretty young girls, possibly a little bondage, spanking, that sort of thing.

They had expected her to be bound and used by other men too, that Paul, to maintain his cover, would have to offer her 'services' to other members.

They had quickly come to realize how wrong they were.

Immediately after her rape, when Paul/Achmed showed no further desire to abuse her, two other Arabs, two of the ones they had targeted, as a matter of fact, joined him and persuaded him to loan her to them. He really had no choice, especially as ingratiating himself with them was part of his cover.

She was subsequently dragged downstairs and hung naked by her wrists. Paul was nowhere in sight as the two Arabs leered and groped her, making bloodthirsty threats and cursing Jews and Israel.

She had been frightened, of course, but she had found her sexual juices flowing freely and her body quivering with excitement. Even as she feared them she found herself wishing for their abuse, wanting them to do unspeakable things to her.

And they had.

Sneering at her, slapping and pinching and kicking her, they had quickly bent her across a low bench, her legs strapped straight to one side of the table's legs at ankle, knee, and thigh, her arms strapped to the second set of legs at wrist, elbow and biceps. A final heavy strap was pulled across her back and cinched so tightly she could hardly breath.

They took turns raping her then, rutting as hard and furiously as they could, pounding their erections into the softness of her silken tunnel as she gasped and moaned helplessly.

Then had come the caning as bad as any she'd ever had, if not worse, the thin cane cracking down across her upturned buttocks at a slow, measured pace that she thought might drive her insane. Blast after blast of incredibly sharp pain bit into her exposed behind as the men laughed and jeered.

One of them had lifted her head at the end, lifted it by the simple expedient of yanking up on her hair. And as she screamed in pain his once more stiffened penis had thrust into her mouth and, without hesitation, plunged straight down her throat.

It had certainly halted her scream, and her eyes bugged out as she felt he unfamiliar thickness of the object invading her throat. She gagged repeatedly, choking helplessly, her face going scarlet as she tried to get control of her reflexes.

He giggled cruelly, his smelly groin mashing into her face, grinding down against her nose as he tugged at her hair. She felt her breath going, felt herself becoming light-headed from lack of oxygen as her head threatened to explode.

He pulled back slowly, and she fought another battle to control her gagging reflex as his cock slipped up her throat and the head popped out into her mouth.

He pulled it free, wiping the spit-wet thing all over her face as she gulped in air.

And all the while the man behind continued to cane her fiercely burning cheeks.

He pushed himself into her again, thrusting himself deep into her throat, and she gurgled for a moment before his cock slipped into her and drove down to the hilt. It felt like her throat was going to tear, felt like his cock was right down inside her very chest cavity.

Then he started pumping, using her throat as he had her pussy, his steel hard prong sliding up and down her throat, the glistening shaft appearing from between her lips only to disappear into them again as he held her there and used her.

Yet it was not as bad as the first time, for she knew she could take it now. The gagging reflex was less, and she controlled herself and her fears as his tool pumped inside her throat. He pulled out once again and she gulped in air before he could sheath himself again.

The man behind finished beating her, and after some discussion in Arabic, which she wasn't supposed to know but did, they unstrapped her and pulled her upright.

She had been caned many times before, of course, and strapped, and spanked and paddled, but as she they hung her by her wrists there in the small room she had tasted the bite of the whip for the first time, and across her back.

The pain had driven the breath from her, and she had screamed helplessly. But almost at once she had felt a hot gut churning surge of high-pressured sexual desire and heat flooding her body.

To be hung by the wrists and whipped! Actually whipped across the back! It was the fulfilment of more fantasies than she could possibly remember. She had never dared actually go through with it, though eventually she would have worked up the courage.

But now she had no choice. For the first time in her life she was truly helpless. There were no safe words here, no coded words that would cause her partner to halt and release her. These men were not acting, not playing, and she truly was their prisoner.

The next blow had drawn another scream, the pain terrible, yet her nipples hardened into hot little pebbles and her loins quivered hungrily as her legs kicked spastically.

Again and again the whip lashed across her back, each

time drawing a scream of pain and a flashing blast of raw carnal lust that had gripped her body and mind and shielded it from the full effect of the pain.

And when one of the Arabs slipped his hand between her legs and squeezed her mound she had been unable to suppress a soft moan of pleasure. Cursing her, sneering at her in contempt, he had roughly thrust his fingers up into her, pumping them savagely as her legs writhed and her body shook with helpless pleasure.

The whip had continued to lash her back but she had ignored it. Or rather, each blast of pain served to rocket her bliss higher and higher. The orgasm almost consumed her mind. It was more powerful than any in her previous experience, and she had screamed in wanton bliss even as the two Arabs cursed and spat on her and whipped her furiously.

The Arab in front had even begun to slap angrily at her face and breasts as he plunged his fingers up into her, yet still her climax rode on, screaming higher and higher until it finally spent itself and she hung dazed and limp.

God, how she had hated them, despised them. They were evil, despicable men, her enemies, and the enemies of her people.

Yet how she had loved it, how she had revelled in her torture!

And that had been just the beginning. She had rapidly discovered just how much delight the Arabs of the club took in degrading and tormenting Jewish and Israeli girls.

They lowered her to the floor, then led her to a small corner of the room. There she saw four red shackles bolted to the floor. Her ankles were shackled to one set, then she was bent back, back, back, and her wrists buckled to the other set only a couple of feet behind her feet.

As encouragement for her to keep her body violently arched up they rolled over a small wheeled cart which they placed beneath her. The top of the cart was lined with needle sharp metal spikes.

And then the two had picked up riding crops and stood on either side of her. One began to methodically whip her breasts while the other rained blows across her inner thighs and mound.

They took their time, obviously enjoying their work immensely. The one at her head alternated between breasts, though sometimes, perhaps to throw her off, he would strike one twice, or even three times running. The other slashed the whip against one thigh, then the other, then down on her mound, though, like his companion, he altered his rhythm so she couldn't brace herself.

She screamed until her voice was a raspy croak, her body seemingly aflame with agony as the men jeered and cursed her. Yet quickly the heat seemed to shred the intensity of each new blast of pain. The throbbing pain itself became a kind of fog over her mind, absorbing and diffusing the jagged-edged agony as the crops struck anew, toning it down and absorbing it into itself.

She felt the sexual songs singing within her body and mind, felt her outrage melded with the shock and fear and turned into something stunningly wicked and wanton. Her legs were splayed wide, yet she opened them more, gasping, crying out, screaming with each new blast that struck her pussy.

Yet she wallowed in it, her body revelling in the blows to her mound and breasts especially. She rose higher and higher towards the peak of pleasure, her mind swimming, drowning in sensory overload.

Then she came again, her voice unable to bare the howls of pleasure, becoming little more than a hoarse gurgle and grunting as she raced up from the peak rather than down, upwards towards a previously unattainable plateau of ecstasy, her mind stunned by the power of the orgasm as it went on and on, carrying her ever upwards.

Every muscle in her body was spasming and twitching, her nervous system in melt-down as convulsions tore through her in an endless procession.

Her mind was shattered, flung back from the cataclysmic ferocity of the orgasm that was rippling back and forth along her spine. She was on the verge of passing out, and knew only a small dart of fear at what would happen when she did.

But the men halted their beating. One of them, the one between her legs, cursed her and slammed his boot into her open and vulnerable sex. Then they pulled the cart out of the way and moved to unshackle her.

She collapsed soon afterwards, lost to blackness.

12

Amanda had been given precious little time to understand what had happened, to cope with it and adjust. They had given her all night to 'rest' after her shattering electrical torture.

She was taken to a stone cell and placed down on the floor, her aching, shocked pink pussy slipped over and down a ten inch long metal tube protruding from the stone. Her legs were spread so wide apart she was doing the splits. Her thighs ached as each leg was forced straight out to either side and shackled there.

Her arms were pulled straight up above her, shackled together and locked in place to a low hanging chain.

And there she was left to contemplate her sins for several hours.

Then they came for her, to rearrange her position, they said, so she would be more comfortable.

They unstrapped her, then strapped her ankles together

tightly before pulling them up behind her buttocks and encircling them and her thighs with a heavy strap to pin them together.

Her wrists were strapped back against her upper arms and she was forced to kneel there on elbows and knees. Her hair was wound into a single tail again, this time from the very top of her head, and lifted up high, forcing her head and upper body high, then an alligator clip was slipped around her clitoris, drawing a scream from the half unconscious woman as the tight, sharp little teeth bit into her ultra-sensitive button.

A wire pulled up above her and was attached to a hook high above. Then two more clips were attached to her nipples, and weights hung from them. As a final measure for her comfort, they pulled her tongue out with tongs, attached another clip to it, and pulled a wire taut to force her to keep her tongue sticking out painfully far.

Then they shut off the lights to let her sleep and relax.

When Edward casually opened the door of her cell the next morning, accompanied by two of his slave girls, Amanda looked somewhat the worse for wear. The straps were gone, and a coarse, heavy rope had taken their place. A belt around her hips had been made of it, with a length then descending down her abdomen and up between her whip-marked buttocks, pulled very, very tight so it was forced up between her pubic lips.

Her breasts were thrust out like two overfilled balloons, for rope encircled each at the ribs, squashing them painfully. The rope then went behind her under her arms to be tied so tightly she could hardly expand her chest wall enough to breath. Her arms were tightly bound together behind her, above and below the elbows, and again at the wrists, the elbows touching firmly.

Her ankles were bound together and then bound to her thighs so her feet were pushed up against her buttocks. Her feet were also bound together, though with cord rather than heavy rope. The cord wound neatly around her feet mid-way between toes and ankles. Her two big toes were bound tightly together, apart from the rest, and the cord pulled them up and back painfully hard.

Likewise her hands were bound together just below the thumbs, in a praying position. Her little fingers and thumbs were bound together separately, her thumbs forced up and back and her little fingers forced down and in.

Amanda was on her knees on the cold stone floor, but no other part of her body touched the floor. She was balanced perfectly on her knees with only the help of her hair, which was bound still and held high to a hook. A heavy leather blindfold covered her eyes and a thick ball-gag filled her mouth, keeping her jaws wide.

Seeing her like that made Edward smile in delight, and had he not already used both slaves within the past half hour he would have raised his erection to full attention.

But he was content to merely observe her, then go to his breakfast, the two giggling slave girls following to feed him.

Sarah recognized the newcomer to breakfast as the one Achmed had been speaking to the other day and her lip curled upward in disgust before she caught herself. Then she hurried down to greet him, as was her job in the dining room that morning.

Sarah was dressed in thigh high black leather boots with stiletto heels, shoulder length leather gloves, and a leather harness that was something like a corset, though not nearly as comfortable or concealing.

The harness had two rounded, hard-leather cups which encircled, squeezed, and slightly raised her breasts but certainly did nothing to cover them. Lower down it consisted of strips of hard leather which encircled her lower chest and waist. The strips had been pulled tighter and tighter and tighter as she had knelt before one of the attendants, until she had felt like the life was being squeezed out of her.

She had felt her internal organs being pushed downwards, pressing down on her lower organs. The result was not only could she barely breath she could barely move, and the downward pressure made her feel her labia and sex organs distended, pushing out with the pressure coming from above.

But lest she fear they would tear open and let her insides spill out a tight, two inch wide leather strap was cinched tight against her pubic mound, yanked up hard, with painful pressure, then fastened to the harness.

The strap, though unseen, had two long, thick dildos attached to the inside, both of which were now deep inside her lower belly.

To complete the ensemble a heavy leather collar was around her neck, hard and thick, forcing her to keep her head up firmly.

"Welcome to the dining hall, master," she said gaily. "We're so happy you could come! Where would you like to be seated?"

"I don't care," he said.

"Would you like to come this way then, please, master?" she asked.

He motioned her ahead and she led him to an available table, then bowed - with great effort - and presented him with a menu as the two slaves, clad only in chains and G-strings, knelt at his feet.

"It is our pleasure to serve you in every way, master! What may I bring you?"

"Shut the fuck up until I decide."

"Yes, master! Sorry, master!"

Sarah stood there in discomfort, considering the hundred different ways she could end his life, and which would be more painful and take the longest amount of time. It wasn't that this Englishman was particularly more brutal than any of the other men around. It was more, she thought, that he was so much less of a man than he seemed to think.

Word had quickly got around that he had had two of the attendants conduct the rape of that girl he had brought in rather than do it himself as almost all the members did with personal prisoners. And then she'd bitten his cock and sent him squealing like a pig! Since then he'd made sure she was tightly bound whenever he was in her presence, and had hadn't yet even dared to use her sexually, contenting himself with torturing her.

Not that being used by such a dog wouldn't be torture in its own way, she thought wryly.

"Bring me a couple of poached eggs and a coffee, black," he said, dismissing her.

"Yes, master! Right away, master!" she sang, turning and hurrying - as much as she could - away.

Among those who showed up for breakfast - many members had breakfast delivered to their rooms - was Paul/Achmed.

He came to her section of the dining room, and pulled her across his lap so they could talk without arousing suspicions.

"Ow. God!" she whispered.

"What's the matter?"

"What's the matter is I have two large dildos up inside me," she gasped, still trying to smile in case any others were watching.

"Really? Well, that must make you happy," he said, reaching out and cupping her breast.

Sarah restrained a glare, keeping her face smiling as he tweaked her nipple.

"I have some news," he said. "I've found one of the girls. Gabrielle. She's a privately owned slut that belongs to a man named Omar. He doesn't let any other men touch her except to beat her."

"Was he one of the men who beat me when..."

"No, those were other admirers. By the way they want to do it again tomorrow."

She shuddered and he smiled and pinched her nipple.

"Don't worry. I said you were busy."

"Thank you," she said, both relieved and oddly disappointed.

"I've offered you to Omar instead."

She blinked her eyes and opened her mouth.

"I told him you could do a lesbian show with Gabrielle. He hasn't subjected her to anything like that yet, and as you know she was quite religious. So she won't be happy. But with the two of you close together I'm hoping you can say something to her, letting her know to hold on, that help will be here soon."

"If I do then she might tell them the next time he beats her."

"I don't think so. I think given what she's already been through it will allow her to take his new torments without going insane. She must be halfway mad by now. Unlike you she isn't a crazed slut."

"I'm not a slut," she said resentfully.

He pulled back on her hair and she gasped in pain.

"You're as much of a slut as it's possible to be," he said coldly. "You think I don't see you coming whenever any man sticks his cock into you!? Now do what you're told, or it won't be the Arabs taking a whip to your back, but a Jew!"

He loosened his grip and she looked at him strangely, then swallowed whatever she had intended.

He felt a little uneasy, for he was finding himself much more relaxed about giving pain and abuse to the sluts here - and he had to continuously remind himself they weren't sluts, but prisoners.

For that matter, Sarah was a fellow agent playing a role, yet he kept seeing her as a nympho slave and feeling the urge to treat her as such.

He started to apologise, then abruptly halted and changed his tone.

"Tell me, slut," he said, noting the arrival of one of the Arabs he was seeking to ingratiate himself with, "does that strap push up very hard against your little bare pussy?"

"Yes, master," she said.

"Hello Achmed," the man said.

"Omar. How good to see you," he said, rising and shaking his hand.

"The strap not only pulls up tight but it has other advantages, doesn't it, slave," Omar snorted.

"Yes, master!" she said gaily.

"What other advantages?" he Paul curiously.

Omar sniffed in amusement, then reached behind her and unbuckled the strap, letting it fall away, at least as far as it would. Then he gripped the bottom and pulled until the two thick leather dildos began to slide out from her rectum and pussy.

"Ah, keeping them happy," he said.

Omar pulled the two long dildos almost completely out, then thrust them back up sharply, making her gasp and shudder and rise onto her toes briefly.

"Who has shaved her mound?" he asked, scowling. "I did not give permission for that."

He found himself both aroused and worried as he looked at Sarah's soft white mound.

"It's standard procedure for them all, Achmed," Omar explained. "Keeps them cleaner."

He tugged the dildos completely free and lifted the belt, displaying her barren sex.

"It is attractive, in a way," Paul said, licking his lips.

"It shows what they are, anyway," Omar said. "Just walking cracks waiting to be used."

Omar moved to shove the dildos back in but Paul halted him, reaching up and running his hand back and forth over

109

her mound, rubbing it softly as she squirmed inwardly.

"You can see she likes that," Omar said.

"Yes. I like it myself," Paul agreed, grinning at Sarah.

He pulled her over his lap, his fingers probing her swollen labia, stroking against her throbbing sex as she as she gasped and moaned, and ground her helplessly behind back at his fingers.

He knew he would get in trouble for this if his superiors ever found out. On the other hand it wasn't likely Sarah would tell anyone, and his erection was getting painful.

"Hot little slut, isn't she?" he said.

"Some of them take to it like a fish to water," Omar said. "Though others have to be broken."

"Uh... Uh... Uh... Uh... Uh..." Sarah groaned, her behind bucking and grinding as sex-heat flooded her body.

Then she was pulled off and stood upright on shaky legs.

"Go and get my breakfast, slut," Paul/Achmed said.

She almost glared at him, but that would have required a beating with Omar as a witness, and she caught herself in time, stumbling off to the kitchen to get the food he'd already ordered.

She could not touch herself between there and the table, for to do so was to bring on the most severe of punishments, and as a result she was hot and frustrated when she brought the plate back to Paul's table.

He promptly fingered her again, to the point where she was dancing from one leg to the other, her body undulating helplessly.

And again he stopped, turning to his meal and his conversation with Omar as she stood there panting and gasping.

"You're being very cruel to the little Jew slut, Achmed," Omar said in amusement.

"It's a rough life," he said with a shrug.

"I think she needs a little relief. Come here, Jew," he ordered. He turned to Achmed. "With your permission, of

110

course."

Achmed shrugged and nodded and Omar yanked her down across his lap, let his fingers trail up and down her sopping cleft, then began to spank her, not on her behind, but on her bare mound.

At first the blows sent shock waves of pain and nausea through her body, but even as she squealed and kicked help-lessly the sexual heat overcame the pain, and soon she was gasping and bucking back, thrusting herself up to meet each new blow until the orgasm howled through her system and she began to shake and tremble violently.

A portion of her felt humiliation at this public display of her weakness, especially in front of Paul, but she could do nothing to repress the massive release of sexual energy as it flared around her. Each new slap against her exposed pussy made her squeal in new pleasure, until she finally collapsed limply across Omar's lap, groaning exhaustedly.

She then dazedly licked Omar's hand clean, before hav-ing the dildos stuffed back into her belly and the strap buck-led behind her. Then she went back to serving the new arriv-als.

A couple of hours later, after a shower, her hair made up and make-up on, wearing the same leather boots and gloves, but with a G-string now and a soft glistening leather bustier, she accompanied Achmed to see Salaam, the Arab in per-sonal possession of one of the Israeli girls.

Sarah was not enthusiastic about having sex with another woman. She'd done it on one previous occasion, an assign-ment involving a lesbian spy, but she didn't like it. Still, she was finding that she was so constantly and powerfully aroused these days that even the thought of going down on a woman was not nearly as unpleasant as it once had been.

Gabrielle Stein had once had long wavy hair. She had prized it so much that, despite how difficult it was to main-tain under military conditions, she had carefully washed and bound it up tightly each morning.

But that was gone now. When beatings and torture had failed to break her to the proper degree of respect Jubal felt was necessary for a Jewess her hair had been shaved off.

After the hours long gang rapes and then tortures she had been subjected to it was the final indignity, robbing her of last vestiges of humanity. Now she didn't seem to care what was done to her, and submitted meekly to whatever punishment or abuse was directed her way.

A deeply religious young woman, Gabrielle had been a virgin the night she had been kidnapped. Her brutal gang-rape, which had lasted through the night and on into the next morning, had seen so many gleeful participants she still had no idea how many men had taken part.

Then, naked, wrists bound tightly behind her back, she was thrown into the back of a trunk and driven into Beirut. Helpless and in both emotional and physical pain, she was dragged out of the trunk by the hair to find herself in a narrow alley just behind a dark street.

There her captor led her deeper into the alley and into one of the buildings through a small steel door opened by another man, a man who ogled her and groped her as she passed.

She was led down a narrow stone corridor to a small room at the end. There she was presented to a large, older man in expensive western style clothing. Money had changed hands and another man had taken her further along the corridor and into another room.

Her wrists were unbound, but she was too weak to take advantage of her temporary freedom. They were soon shackled together in front of her in any event, then she was hung from   hook as the man turned a fire hose on her, soaking her, freezing her, and not incidentally, having fun doing it, half drowning her as the powerful stream of water battered her body and set it swinging wildly on the end of the hook.

He had turned off the hose, then scrubbed her roughly, using strong soap and a rough cloth. He had even plunged a pipe cleaner of sorts up into her rectum and vagina, tearing them in and out as she had sobbed in humiliation and pain.

The firehose was used again to rinse her off, then the bedraggled girl was taken down and dried with rough towels. Her hair was brushed out and dried as much as it could be. Her wrists were handcuffed in front of her and she was led back down the corridor, up a flight of stairs, and out to a small truck.

She was driven to the airport, and then led out of the truck, across a few feet of Tarmac to a private, and luxuriously appointed helicopter, and then placed aboard, where she found the man who'd bought her, now wearing flowing Arab robes.

When she had been pushed to her knees in front of him her glare up into his face had met a brutal slap that sent her flying back across the carpeted floor.

Jubal tolerated no insolence, no rebellious looks, no hesitation of any kind from a woman, much less a Jewess, as he had been quick to make clear.

After raping and sodomizing her he had bound her ankles, then flung her out of the by then high flying helicopter, to be tossed and twirled and buffeted by furious winds as she hung a good hundred feet below at the end of a rope.

He had dragged her up, forced her to her knees, and demanded she curse Israel and Judaism and beg him to use her again. When she had refused, hoping he would kill her, she'd been thrown out again, the rope almost snapping her legs out when it had gone taut.

The helicopter slowed almost to a hover, then lowered her bit by bit. They were over water, and soon her face was crashing through the waves as the helicopter moved slowly forward. After a few minutes she was raised about ten feet, then dropped, this time splashing into the water up to her ankles.

She had kicked frenziedly, but the rope kept her tightly bound and she couldn't break the surface until it hauled her back up and she was dragged back about the helicopter. They threw her to her knees in front of him then and she had obeyed him, then kissed and licked at his feet until he gave her permission to take his cock into her mouth.

He ejaculated into her face, then flung her backwards and let her be for the remainder of the flight.

They'd got off at another airport. There, hands shackled behind her, ankles shackled, and gagged, she was led from the helicopter across the Tarmac to a private jet, then placed aboard for a long flight to she knew not where.

Several times Jubal had raped and sodomized her, but the real hell hadn't begun until they had arrived. Then the whippings and tortures had begun in earnest, sometimes lasting hours. At the end of each session she was flung onto a cold stone floor, then chained to the walls in awkward and painful positions.

Now she knelt respectfully, sitting on her heels, hands on her thighs, back straight. All she wore were the heavy iron shackles which had been permanently welded to her wrists and ankles and the heavy iron collar around her slim throat.

Master had a visitor, and she was to entertain.

13

Meghan was nervous, despite the fact that she believed that other constables had the place under tight surveillance and would be listening to her through the microphone she carried. Still, this was a major case. If she cracked it she would no doubt make detective constable far sooner than her classmates, despite the sexism of that old fart, Lord Andrew.

Besides, it outraged her that men would buy and sell women in this day and age, that they would take some helpless young woman and carry her off to the South Pacific to have their way with her. And there were dark hints that rape was the least of the things the poor victims of this group had to cope with. Whispered tales of whips and chains, of abject slavery and cruel tortures circulated amongst the wealthier members of London's sex club regulars.

Meghan could hardly wait to bring such men to justice and free the poor young women they held prisoners.

She looked around nervously, then knocked at the door. It had taken several more visits to the Carlyle to get the information that the group operated out of the small office and warehouse complex here on the edge of London. Nothing was nearby but scrub trees and the cold, eyeless walls of other factories.

A moment later the door opened and a tall, blonde haired man looked down at her.

"Yeah?"

"My name is Ann. I've come representing Lord Dodge."

He motioned her in, looked around, then closed the door behind her.

"Lord Dodge is interested in acquiring a companion," she said carefully.

"A slave, you mean."

"Well, yes."

"Why?"

She looked at him in confusion.

"He's got you, ain't he?"

She flushed angrily. "I am not a slave," she said.

"Why not? Got the looks for it. Got good looking teats. I could make ya a slave, girl."

"Lord Dodge wants me as I am," she said, feeling a tight dagger of fear.

He shrugged. "What's he looking for?"

This was too easy! Meghan felt herself become more excited as this fool showed so little caution.

"Well, someone young, of course."

"Come on down the hall and we'll discuss it in my office."

He led her down a narrow hallway and into a small, stone-walled office with no windows. A small ratty looking desk almost filled the room, with a ripped chair behind it and two small hard chairs sitting in front.

He beckoned her to one and she sat down, trying to appear casual.

"Yeah, yeah, they all are. We don't deal in old hags, you know. Does he want a blonde, brunette, or redhead? He want slim or buxom? Black, white, brown or yellow?"

"Well, uhm, white I suppose and er, a, uh, redhead."

"With big teats?"

"Well, uhm, yes, of course."

"Why don't he just dye your hair red and use you?" he asked with a sneer.

She flushed and looked haughtily down her nose at him.

"I am Lord Dodge's personal secretary," she said stiffly.

"You look like good girl flesh to me."

"We're not speaking of me. We're speaking of a girl you might procure for Lord Dodge," she said sternly.

The door opened behind her and two more men came into the room, halting behind her chair. She felt a quiver of alarm, even though provoking them with this obviously contrived story was the intention of her coming here.

"We've checked with Lord Dodge, darling," one of the men behind her said. "He never sent anyone down here to inquire about anything."

With that heavy hands came down on her shoulders and she was yanked roughly from her chair, arms quickly pinned to her sides as the man behind the desk eyed her dispassionately.

"Would you like to tell me what it is you're doing here now?"

"I... I'm looking for a girl that went missing," Meghan gasped.

"And what makes you think we'd know where she was?"

"I heard... that you're white slavers!"

"You heard quite right. We are."

She felt another surge of elation as the fool admitted it.

"Perhaps you might find that girl you're looking for after all. We're always looking for big titted blondes."

She glared at him then gasped as one of the men behind her gripped her hair and yanked her head up and back.

"Why don't we see what you've got that may be of worth," the man said with a grin.

She cried out in alarm as her blouse was shredded and torn from her body, then kicked out at one of the men holding her. He slid aside easily, grabbing her ankle and holding her leg up as his other hand went to the catch at the front of her jeans.

"Stop it!" she cried. "What do you think you're doing! Get your hands off me!"

She had no serious belief they would care what she said but wanted to communicate with the rest of the squad listening in on the microphone so they'd burst in before things went too badly for her.

Her jeans were yanked down and her face went scarlet with embarrassment as the men chuckled in lewd appreciation, then tore at her panties and bra. She thrashed wildly, furiously, knowing it would be the talk of the station when the men burst in and found her naked. They'd be telling tales in locker rooms all over London!

She grunted as she was lifted up then slammed belly-down across the desk and her wrists forced together behind her back. She felt a heavy rope slip around them, then cinch tightly together. It looped around her wrists again and again and again before it was tied off.

Then she was pulled upright by the hair, her head forced back to thrust her breasts out as the man smirked at her, his hands behind his head, his feet up on the desk.

"Very nice," he said. "Lovely breasts, nice body, delicious face. You'll make a lot of men very happy, my dear."

"Let me go!" she snarled, eyes filled with fire. "You have no idea of the trouble you're in!"

"You'd be surprised at the ideas I have," he said with a smile.

He gripped her hair and she cried out as she was forced backwards onto the desk. The men chuckled at her struggles, prying her thighs wide, their hands groping and fondling her in outrageous fashion.

"No!" she gasped. "You can't!"

"Shut her up."

She cried out in pain as one of them yanked her hair back, then a thick ball-gag was stuffed into her mouth and strapped behind her head. They held her legs wide as the man who seemed to lead them moved into place and undid his trousers.

"You'll like this, darling," he said with a smirk.

Meghan screamed into the gag, thrashing wildly, but she was helpless to resist as he pulled out his bulging erection and rubbed it lewdly along her cleft. He laughed to see her twisting and writhing, holding himself against her and slowly forcing his way through her tight pussy lips.

Meghan fought to keep from getting hysterical, for that would accomplish nothing. Every second she prayed her backup team would burst through the door and put a stop to this before it was too late.

And then it was.

She shuddered, her head falling back as he rammed himself into her. The pain burned through her as he thrust deeper and deeper, boring up into her abdomen, slamming his way through the soft aching flesh until he was buried within her.

She moaned helplessly as his hands moved up and down her lushly displayed body.

"Now this is what you were built for, darling," he said, grinding his pelvis into her crotch, twisting his cock around in her belly.

He began to thrust then, faster and faster, heedless of her pain and misery, grunting with delight as he used her for his own satisfaction. His heavy balls slapped against her buttocks as the other two men looked on and applauded.

Again and again he drove himself into her. It seemed to last forever. And after him came the second man, then the third. By the end she lay there dazedly, whimpering and trying to understand what had happened.

"Put her in the van."

She came back to life somewhat as she was dragged off the desk.

Where were they anyway, she wondered. What in the hell had kept her backup from bursting in?

She was yanked back out of the office, then further up the hall and around a corner to stop in front of a door. One of the men shoved it open and bright sunlight hit her eyes. She gasped and struggled to pull back, knowing the men watching would see her.

That was stupid, she knew, stupid self-consciousness about nudity. No doubt they were waiting for her to get outside so they could take the men without a hostage situation developing. Perhaps her microphone had failed and they'd had no idea what had happened inside.

A slap against one of her jiggling breasts made her squeal in pain and she rounded on the man who'd delivered it, trying to kick at him, but another hard yank on her hair forced her head way back. Then she was matched across the parking lot, the air chilly as it hardened her nipples.

She looked around wildly. What was keeping them!? What were they waiting for!?

Her bare feet stumbled on the cold wet pavement and the many small stones littering it, and she felt horribly exposed as she walked nakedly towards a gray van.

They halted by a van and opened the rear door, then forced her up inside.

She was lifted up onto a bench and shoved roughly against the side of the wall, then one of the men pulled a metal bar around on a swing arm. It was rounded and came around against her throat, pulling in firmly before snapping to the van's wall on the other side of her head. At the same time her ankles were strapped together, then a small chain bolted them to the floor.

The two men withdrew and slammed the door closed.

Now, she thought, they'll come. I'm alone and in no danger. They can take the men outside easily.

She wondered if they had held off just to taunt her, just to take their own sorry adolescent joke at her expense. She had no doubt she would be the victim of taunting for years now.

The men got in the front of the van, and she frowned as the engine started. The van lurched forward, and her mind spun as he tried to understand why her backup hadn't moved in. Was it possible they didn't know she was here? No! How could they not?

Perhaps the microphone really had failed. It must have. And maybe they hadn't been watching the parking lot. That seemed astoundingly stupid, yet she'd witnessed a number of ridiculous mishaps since becoming a policewoman.

Could that rotten bugger Lord Andrew have decided to let her stew for a while, to let them do with her as they would in order to lead to the others? Would the man dare to do that to her?

She felt terribly vulnerable in her nudity. Despite several

months playing a pretend prostitute she was inexperienced about sex and though not as shy about her body as she'd once been when younger was still terribly humiliated at these strange men, and probably a number of policemen watching, seeing her naked.

Bastards! All of them were bastards! When this was over she'd...

The van bounced, then made a sharp turn before picking up speed on what felt like a much better road. She tried to look around, but the tight metal pinning her head to the wall didn't allow much room for movement. She squirmed a little, pulling against the ropes binding her wrists, but that only made them bite in deeper.

The van halted and she heard conversation, then the back door was opened and another man she didn't know came inside, dragging a young woman behind him. Like Meghan, the woman was nude, her wrists bound behind her back.

She was gagged in the same way, and her eyes were wild as she was forced down onto the bench across from Meghan, her neck bound there and her ankles chained to the floor. The man cupped one of her breasts, then winked at Meghan before climbing down and slamming the door.

The van started off again and the two bound, gagged women stared at each other.

The girl was quite beautiful, Meghan saw, probably the same age as she, her breasts high and proud, her waist narrow, her legs exquisite. Meghan wanted to reassure her that the police would stop them before anything serious happened, but of course, couldn't make a sound.

And even if she could she was starting to have her doubts about that. Surely something desperate had gone wrong to have let the van take her away naked like that.

The van drove on, then stopped again. This time a young girl was lifted up into the back. A petite redhead who Meghan doubted was over sixteen, she had large breasts and a terrified look in her big blue eyes as she was strapped into position.

Half an hour later another woman was lifted in. This one was wearing a tight leather hood over her face. There was no eyeholes, no mouth, just two small holes where her nose would be.

Her arms were strapped tightly behind her back, and her legs were strapped together at thighs, knees, and ankles. Her chest rose and fell rapidly as she was placed on the bench, then the metal neck brace snapped around her throat.

The van drove on, and about half an hour later stopped once again. This time when the back opened no new girl was placed aboard. Instead half a dozen men came up and removed the four young women there.

When she was taken out Meghan saw they were at an airport. She looked around frantically but there was no sign of any police cars racing across the Tarmac to rescue her.

A private jet waited, its engines running, and though she struggled, she and the other three were quickly marched or dragged up its stairs and inside.

The four were placed in a small room, then the engines roared and the plane took off.

14

Amanda was not touched by anyone for two days. She was washed, then soothing balms were applied to her skin. For what seemed an eternity she hung upside down by the ankles, wrists shackled behind her, blindfolded, with soft music playing in the room and sweet voices telling her endlessly that she must obey, that she must serve, that she was made to serve the masters, that her only pleasure would come in serving the masters.

Then she was lowered, the blindfold removed, and forced onto her knees.

'He' was there, standing over her and smirking.

"Well, well," he said. "And how are you feeling today, my lady? You look much refreshed from your little er, ordeal."

He bent over her and ran a hand through her hair, then unbuckled the ball gag and pulled it free.

Amanda moaned in pain as her stiff jaws were finally able too close slightly.

"I trust you've learned some manners now," he said.

He sat down next to her and lifted a tall glass of ice water, sipping lightly from it.

Amanda raised her eyes to it desperately. She had no idea how long she'd been bound, but it seemed like forever since she'd had anything to drink, and having the ball gag stuffed in her mouth for so long had made it as dry as a desert. Right then and there she would have done anything for a drink of water.

"Like some water?" he asked.

"Y-yes," she croaked.

"Yes, what?"

"Yes please sir," she gasped.

"Sir isn't good enough. I am your master. If you want any water you shall have to learn to ask properly."

"Master," she whispered. "P-please may I h-have some water, master?"

He dipped his fingers in the glass and flicked them at her so droplets of water spattered over her face. She opened her mouth desperately and he chortled in amusement.

"You want some water, trollop?"

"Yes! Please! Please, M-master!"

He dipped his fingers in the water then pulled them out and placed them against her dry, cracked lips. She opened them at once, and unashamedly took his fingers into her mouth, suckling desperately at the moisture.

He smirked anew as he let his fingers slide around in her mouth. Then he pulled them out, dipped them into the water, and let her suck on them again, then again. Amused, he poured some water into the palm of his hand and held it out for her, giggling as she bent and pushed her mouth into it with an eagerness that made him feel all-powerful.

She sucked the water dry and licked at his palm.

Inspired, he removed his shoes and socks, then, as she watched desperately, dipped his toes into the water and held them out to him. With barely an instant's hesitation she leaned forward, her mouth slipping around his toes and licking at them.

He laughed gleefully.

"Not so high and mighty now, are you, slut? Starting to learn your place in things, eh?"

He let her lick at his toes again, then abruptly placed the bottom of his foot against her face and shoved. She flew backwards and landed heavily on her back, gasping in pain.

"Want the whole glass, slut? Let me hear you beg for my cock," he said. "Come along. Beg me to do you, you rotten little cow. Beg me to use you like the cheap slut you are. Show me how much you want me inside your filthy hole."

"Please," she moaned.

"Do it!"

"Please I... please, master... I need you inside me! Please, I want you to, to use me. I want to give you pleasure, master!"

She spread her legs, drawing her knees back, exposing herself lewdly to him.

"Please use me! Please! Please fuck me! Fuck me, master!"

"You're my little slut slave, are you?" he said in amusement.

"Yes! I'm your little slut slave, master! Do me good! Rape

me, master! Please rape me!"

He slipped off the chair and onto his knees, smirking again as he undid his trousers.

"You want it, slave girl? You want my cock inside your dirty hole?"

"Please," she whimpered. "Please, master! Please put your wonderful cock in my dirty hole!"

He ran his hands over her buttocks, then gripped her thighs and forced them wider apart. He pulled his erection out, slapping it against her bare little pussy cleft. Then he centred it against her and pushed it slowly down into her tightness.

"Yes! Yes! Yes!" she groaned as he filled her. "Do me, master! I want you innn meeeee!"

"It's what I want that matters, you filthy whore," he sneered, thrusting in sharply.

"Oh! Yes! Yes! I'm s-sorry! Ugggh! Master!"

He sank deep, his hands moving up onto her rounded breasts and luxuriating in their soft fullness. He kneaded them roughly as he began to work himself in and out of her belly, feeling a sense of tremendous conquest and power over her as his lower belly began to slap against her upturned buttocks.

He had her now! She was his slave!

He thrust in wildly, gasping and grunting as her insides squeezed and caressed his sensitive glans, then came with a wild flurry of strokes before collapsing atop her, panting for breath.

He pulled out quickly and sat back on his heels to catch his breath.

"Water? Master? Please?" she begged.

He glared at her. The stupid slut only wanted the water! He considered not giving her any, but then she mightn't believe him next time.

He lifted her roughly to her knees, then let her drink half the remaining water before taking the glass away.

"You weren't enthusiastic enough to suit me, slut slave. I think you need a little more time to think about things," he said.

He shoved the ball gag back into her mouth, then, ignoring her imploring eyes, blindfolded her and chained her upside down once again before leaving the room.

It was a long flight, and there was nothing for Meghan or the other girls to do but look at each other. The hooded girl didn't even have that luxury. Before very long they were all very thirsty, but nobody came to water them. They were left alone with their fears for the entire flight.

The plane finally landed, and men dragged them out of the small cabin then down the stairs of the plane. Meghan saw they were at another airport, a small one. It was very hot and moist out, and she realized with a shock that they were probably at the South Pacific location she'd heard discussed previously.

Where was her backup?

The four young women were led across the Tarmac to a helicopter, then placed aboard and again ignored as it warmed up and took off. This time the flight was not long. Again they were led across a small concrete Tarmac, to be placed in another van.

The van drove them along a bumpy road, then backed up to a building of some sort, where the four were helped down and led inside. Meghan had little chance to see anything around her as she was led quickly by impatient men intent on their business.

In a small stone room she was untied, and her hands were locked together in front of her with heavy, padded leather restraints, then raised high and placed over a hook which hung from a chain. All four young women were then roughly washed in a quick but casual fashion. The hood was removed from the previously disguised woman and Meghan saw she was a lovely, but delicate looking brunette in her mid-twenties.

After their washing their legs were spread wide and chained that way, then a man with an electric razor casually sheered their pubic hair off, leaving their clefts bare and excruciatingly naked.

Another man carefully spread a jell over their mounds. Meghan began to squirm as it burned, but the men left it in place for several minutes before wiping it off. When she looked down she saw that she had not even so much as a hair left on her body between her legs. She was as bare as a newborn.

A tall man came in then and stood before them, looking each of them up and down.

"You must all be wondering what has happened, and why you've been brought here," he said. "I will say this one time only. If you wish to avoid as much pain as possible you will listen very, very closely. You were taken here to become slaves. You are slaves. Do you understand that word? Do you know what it implies?"

He walked up and down in front of them, glaring at them.

"You have no freedom now. You belong to us to do with as we choose. Any resistance, any disobedience, any hesitation will be punished in a very severe fashion. You are here to give pleasure to our members. You will do that in any way which amuses them. You are on an island that is very heavily guarded. Nothing is nearby but miles of shark infested water. The government which owns this island and everything else within hundreds of miles is quite cooperative with us so you needn't look for rescue. Nobody on Earth has the faintest idea any of you are even prisoners."

He paused before Meghan, then reached out and pinched one of her nipples, rolling it between his thumb and forefinger before walking on.

"You will simply have to make the adjustment from

spoiled, pampered little trollops, to devoted slaves. And we will do our best to help. Won't we gentlemen?"

The men nearby chortled and laughed in agreement.

"First, we'll remove this ridiculous belief you have that your naked bodies... correction, our naked bodies since your bodies now belong to us... that naked bodies need to be covered in clothing. The female body looks best without any covering, and that is the way our members usually prefer it... Take them down to the lobby and place them where the members can see them.".

The men moved forward and the four young women were pulled down from their hooks, then, all except Meghan were dragged from the room. The man who seemed to be in charge, who had spoken, had her taken into a small side room first.

"Well, my dear," he said, stroking her damp hair from behind. "I must say you're the most lovely policewoman I've ever met."

Meghan's eyes widened.

He kissed the side of her throat as one of his hands slid down her back and cupped her buttocks.

"It was quite fortunate you brought your tale to Lord Andrew. He's a friend of ours, you see. That was a terrible breech of security on the part of those two gentlemen you told him about, and they have been warned never to speak about the club again in such a fashion."

His hand rubbed slowly up and down between her buttocks, then slipped down between her thighs to cup her now bare mound.

"Lord Andrew arranged this little trip for you in order to ensure you didn't say anything in the wrong ears. There never was any surveillance on that warehouse, nor anyone else involved. As far as your colleagues are concerned you are on a vacation in the south of Wales."

He kissed her shoulder as his finger pierced her and slid up inside her tight pussy.

"No doubt the police in Wales will search high and low for you when you don't return to work in a few weeks time, but I don't think they'll find you, do you?"

He drew his fingers out then abruptly gripped the back of her neck and slammed her down across the desk. She gasped in stunned pain as he kicked her thighs apart and squeezed her mound.

"And now, a small taste of what your new life will be like," he said.

She heard his zipper go down, and struggled wildly, twisting and thrashing in as she felt his erection against her newly shaved mound. But it was hopeless. With her arms bound in front of her she could do nothing as he thrust himself home in her tightness.

She sobbed in fury and terror, the full weight of her situation now coming down around her as she realized for a certainty that there would be no rescue, that nobody knew she was here besides traitorous Sir Andrew. She had hoped to arrest white slavers and instead had become a slave!

She whimpered as she felt his pubic hair against her bare mound, as he twisted himself around in her churning belly.

"Get used to it, constable," he grunted. "This is what you'll be doing now for the rest of your life! It's what you were made for anyway!"

He drew back, then thrust home again... then again... then again as Meghan sobbed and closed her eyes against the rough surface of the desk.

He used her casually and roughly, his hands slapping and squeezing her buttocks and moving up and down her back. When he was done he dragged her to her feet by the hair then gave her to another man, who took her out of the room and down a hallway.

She was led into a busy looking corridor, the rug soft under her bare feet. Men walked up and down the hall, eyeing her casually as they went about their business.

In the entrance hall she saw the other three girls kneeling on a small raised platform. A sign under the platform said 'New Arrivals'.

Like the other three she was forced to kneel on the platform, her knees far apart, shackled in place, then her arms were raised up and back behind her head, a studded collar buckled into place, and chained there.

The hall was a fairly busy one, and men passed back and forth in front of them for hours. Often a man or groups of men would pause to inspect them. Hands would slide between thighs to cup newly shaved mounds, or tug back on hair to force breasts to thrust out. They pinched the girls nipples and commented on their beauty and worth before passing by.

Meghan had never felt more mortified in her life. Yet, she was stunned to realize that even this terrible humiliation could become routine. For after hours she was no longer embarrassed when strange men looked at her or groped her, not even when they thrust their fingers up into her and told her how they were going to rape her as soon as she was made available.

She was gripped by a deep despair, however, and, like the other girls, could not quite believe that this was all happening, nor that this horrid experience was to be a permanent one.

15

When she was released again Amanda was half dragged, half carried down a hall and into a large darkened room. In the centre of the room was a large chair lit by a narrow beam of light. And 'he' was sitting on the chair, looking as arrogant as God himself.

She was unshackled and released, whereupon she sagged weakly to her knees in dazed mental exhaustion.

"That's the proper position, at least," he said with a sneer. "Are you willing to pay the proper respect a slave gives her master now, dog, or do you want more beatings?"

Amanda's thinking processes were too muddled to understand how to answer that one so she said nothing, staring at him blankly.

"Are you ready to obey?" he demanded.

That was easy. She knew what answer was expected of her.

"Yes," she whispered.

"Yes, master!" he thundered.

"Yes, master," she said bleakly.

"Prostrate yourself before your master, dog!"

Again she stared at him.

"On your belly, slut!"

She quickly lay down on her stomach, pressing her still sore breasts into the cold stone floor.

He lifted his bare foot out of a slipper and held it before her face. Again she stared at it, and he growled impatiently.

"Lick it, you bitch!"

She stared at it a moment in confusion, then obeyed, arching her slender neck and pushing out her small pink tongue, sliding it along his heel and the side of his foot.

"Keep at it, whore," he said with satisfaction and contempt. "Lick it all over. I'll tell you when to stop."

And so, on her belly, Amanda lapped steadily all over his foot. And when he ordered her she obediently took his toes into her mouth and suckled at them as she licked. Her mouth and throat were as dry as before, but she knew she had to obey.

"Would you like some water, slave?"

"Yes, master!"

He gripped her thick hair and yanked her up to her knees,

then let her drink repeatedly from his cupped hand before placing the glass to her lips. She drank deeply, never so delighted at the taste of clear, cold water.

When she had finished the glass he stroked her hair and smiled at her, and she felt an unreasonable delight and gratitude.

"Thank you, master," she exclaimed.

He smiled benignly as he looked down at her, then pushed his hand against her face and shoved her back, getting to his feet.

"Follow me, dog," he said. "On your belly. Crawl on your belly after your master!"

She felt a twinge of anger at that, but it was quickly suppressed by the desire to avoid the kind of horrendous beating and torture he'd inflicted on her before.

She crawled slowly across the floor after him, and she saw a small pool there, a sunken tub of sorts. At his order she slunk over the edge and into the water, crossed it, then climbed over the edge at the other side, still keeping her belly to the floor.

"Congratulations, slut. You are reborn as a slave," he said. "I want you to repeat the words when the uh, er, Bishop here says them. Understand?"

"Yes, Master," she said dazedly, more than a little out of sorts yet.

A man in impressive looking robes stood next to 'him', and next to him on a table with a silken cloth were several round metal objects.

"Do you wish to be this man's slave?" the robed man demanded imperiously.

She was tempted to say no, but could guess the results.

"Yes," she whispered.

"Speak louder," he snapped.

"Yes," she said.

"You will repeat these words after me: I give my life, my

body and my soul to you to do with as you choose."

"I give my life, my b-body and my soul to you do as you choose," she said dully.

"I willingly become a slave, the lowest creature in the universe."

She repeated it, and the rest that followed.

"I am a worthless, useless, filthy, evil creature who's only salvation lies in obedience and servitude. I will serve my master always, obey his orders with pleasure, strive at all times and in all ways to please my master. I abandon any pretence of humanity, becoming a mere thing, a possession, a tool of little use or worth in the hopes of redeeming my evil."

The robed man then handed her a large gleaming metal collar open at the middle.

"This collar has a lock with no key," he said. "Once it is placed around your throat you become a slave, and it can never be removed."

She stared at it, her eyes blinking rapidly.

"Place it around your throat and lock it," he ordered.

She hesitated, but at a glare from 'him' she raised her hands, slipped the thing around her throat and then, after another hesitation, pushed it together. It locked with an audible click and the man lifted another, smaller ring.

Soon she had placed the smaller metal bracelets around her wrists and ankles, and locked them in place forever, as the robed man intoned.

Each of them had a small round ring set into it, and her master quickly attached short lengths of chain binding her ankles together. Her wrist bracelets were snapped together, the two rings locking tightly, binding her wrists in front of her.

'He' smiled as he stood closer to her then. He opened his trousers and drew out his organ, gripping her hair tightly and pulling her head back as he rubbed himself over her face. He pushed it against her mouth and she opened her lips, sliding them down the length of his shaft as he sighed in pleasure and happiness.

She began to bob up and down, working her tongue against the underside of his tool as he loosened his grip on her hair and slid his fingers through the long tendrils.

He came quickly, filling her mouth with his semen, and she swallowed automatically, glad of the liquid, an image suddenly flickering into her mind of her boyfriend Neil and how he used to caress her as she fellated him.

Gabrielle took little notice of the woman who accompanied Jubal's visitor. There were many slaves around, and most men had one or two following him around. This one was partially dressed in thigh high leather boots, long black gloves, and a tight shining leather corset of sorts.

"Come here, Jew," Jubal ordered.

She moved forward quickly, her chains clanking, then stopped before them, head bowed.

She was wearing heavy shackles on wrists, ankles and throat, with thick chain linking them.

"What do you think of this ugly, Jewish slut, my friend?" Jubal said.

"She certainly is disgusting looking," the other man said. "What a sacrifice you make to make use of her."

"Yes, I almost vomit every time I am forced to bury my manhood in her, but she craves it so, and if I hesitate she whines and begs."

"You are a kind master."

"Am I not a kind master, Jew?"

"Yes, master," Gabrielle said softly.

"Do you think your Jew slut can make mine come?"

"She's a very talented little whore," the other man said.

"We shall see. If she fails we shall beat her severely."

"And if she succeeds?"

"Then we beat the other one, of course," Jubal said with a broad laugh.

The two women looked at each other doubtfully, and Gabrielle felt a sinking feeling in the pit of her stomach. Was there no perversion too disgusting for Jubal to subject her to? She felt a wave of despair swamp her as the other woman moved determinedly forward.

Gabrielle raised her arms instinctively to ward her off, then choked as Jubal yanked hard on the collar around her throat, flinging her back against the wall

"You dare oppose my wishes, Jew!?" he snarled.

"No, master! Forgive me, master!" she whimpered, dropping to her belly and grasping his ankle as she rained kisses on his feet.

"Get on the sofa, you stinking Jew," he said dismissively.

Gabrielle turned and crawled quickly to the sofa, then climbed onto it and lay down as the other woman moved towards her. Jubal unlocked the chains from her ankles, spreading them wide, then lifted her manacled wrists up above her head and locked them to the back of her collar.

Then he and the other Arab moved back a the girl climbed between her legs and laid her own body down atop hers.

Gabrielle looked up into her eyes, then closed her own as the woman leaned into her. She felt her lips touch her own, then press down with more intensity. She felt the other woman's bare breasts rubbing down gently on her own naked orbs as the woman settled her weight.

"Do not resist, Jew! Or your punishment will be doubled!" Jubal snarled.

Gabrielle moaned and opened her eyes, miserably accepting the other woman's kisses.

It was a novel experience for more than one reason. Not only had she never been kissed in this way by a woman, but it had been so long...or seemed so long since anyone had kissed her so gently.

The woman's hands moved very slowly and softly against her aching flesh, caressing her in intimate ways that should have mortified her, but no longer could.

Surely nothing could humiliate her any more, she thought sadly.

The woman's tongue dipped into her mouth, sliding across her own, then up along the inside of her cheeks before pulling back.

Gabrielle felt a strange attraction to this. She had been screamed at, snarled at, beaten and tortured for so long now that any tenderness of any sort was a wonderful change. And she would have not have been human had she not found herself revelling in that tenderness, however short it lasted and wherever the source.

The woman's fingers moved lightly across her flesh, stroking her nipples before moving down along her bruised ribs with the lightness of a feather. Her lips moved across Gabrielle's bruised cheeks and under her ear, her small tongue darting out and gently caressing her earlobe as her breasts moved back and forth against Gabrielle's.

Then her lips were back and Gabrielle was surprised at how much she welcomed them, even kissing back hesitantly. It didn't seem to matter that this was a woman. It seemed enough that someone did not hate her, was not trying to hurt her, and was kissing her with a tenderness she had all but forgotten.

Their tongues moved lightly together as the woman eased a hand up and stroked the underside of her breast. She groaned softly as she felt the other woman slip her thumb and finger against her nipple and rub them expertly.

"My name is Sarah," the woman whispered. "I won't hurt you."

Strange and conflicting thoughts drifted through Gabrielle's mind as Sarah eased her lips downwards along her throat and onto her breast.

It seemed strange for anyone to promise not to hurt her, and that only added to the confusion she was feeling as the woman's lips slipped around her nipple and sucked with infinite tenderness.

She closed her eyes, sighing as her sensitive nipple tightened, as Sarah's tongue stroked it teasingly. She felt one of the woman's hands ease down her belly and between her legs, felt her fingers stroke gently along her cleft.

New hesitation came to her, but she slowly relaxed as the woman continued to stroke slowly without entering her.

"Look at those filthy sluts," she heard Jubal say, but the words barely penetrated the fog rapidly growing around her mind.

Gabrielle lay back wearily, sighing in pleasure at this delightful tenderness, at this softness and gentleness, and the pleasure they waked within her. She felt an unfamiliar stirring in her loins and spread her legs, groaning softly as the woman's fingers at least eased between her newly moist lips and moved up and down between them.

Sarah shifted her lips from one nipple to the other, then eased downwards, her tongue trailing along the woman's belly and in between her legs. Her hands gently massaged her inner thighs as she pried her legs wide, then her tongue followed, circling Gabrielle's cleft teasingly.

Gabrielle felt herself grinding her body down into the sofa, and groaned in understanding, in realization that she was deeply aroused. She felt a new shame at that, a quivering uncertainty and misery, yet the pleasure, any pleasure, was too precious to withdraw from, so she embraced it hungrily.

Sarah slipped her tongue in between her pussy lips and drove it up into her body, and Gabrielle gasped and drove herself upwards, closing her eyes and rolling her head back in delight. It felt so good, and it had been so long since she had felt good.

She felt the soft little tongue squirming in and out of her, and lewdly ground her hips upwards, then it eased free and moved higher, and she cried out softly as it moved lightly across her clitoris.

Jubal spoke of removing it, so she could never feel pleasure again, and she felt a desperate wanting as the heat inside her grew and the buzzing warmth of her clitoris send rippling waves of wanton pleasure through her body. She trembled, panting for breath as Sarah licked again, this time harder.

She felt the fingers slipping inside her suddenly sopping wet entrance, felt them driving deep as her tongue lapped more quickly across her hot little button. She moaned and whined helplessly, glorying in the pleasure as she bucked upwards in ever more violent motion.

"Uhhhhh!" she groaned, arching her back.

Sarah licked even harder, and much faster, and Gabrielle's legs jerked and spasmed as the orgasm tore into her. It was her first orgasm - ever, for she'd strictly observed Jewish religious laws against sex and masturbation.

Her eyes rolled back a she humped up in mindless ecstasy, glorying in the wondrous pleasure engulfing her body and mind. Her right foot bounced on the floor while her left jammed against the back of the sofa. Her back arched repeatedly as she humped up against Sarah and her head shook from side to side.

"Look at that filthy Jewess!" Jubal snarled.

"Which one?"

"Both of them! They are both shameless!"

"Certainly true."

Jubal moved forward, gripping Sarah by the hair and yanking her back, flinging her back across the floor as he shoved his right foot brutally hard against Gabrielle's left thigh, stepped on her right foot where it rested on the floor, then thrust a thick cattle prod deep into the groaning woman's

138

sopping opening and jammed his thumb down on the button.

Gabrielle howled in a strange, warbling tone, her body thrashing madly on the sofa as Jubal kept the electricity flowing. Then she gave a final shudder and went still.

He pulled back with a snarl, and whipped around, staring at Sarah where she crouched on the floor.

"Filthy Jew!" he snarled. "You'll be punished for this!"

"But you said only the one who came would be punished," Paul said mildly.

Jubal stared at him, bug-eyed. "She obviously enjoyed it, the filthy Jew slut!"

"I think you are right. That is what these Jew girls do best, fucking people."

"The bitch should be raped to death! To death!!" he snarled.

"An interesting thought. I wonder if it's possible to rape someone to death?"

"We shall find out!" Jubal snarled, glowering at Sarah.

He stomped over to her and backhanded her, sending her flying back onto the floor, then hurried after, grabbing her hair and roughly throwing her over onto her belly. He gripped her by hair and crotch, forcing her up onto all fours, then moved his robes aside, pulling out an erection gained from watching the lewd, lesbian perversion on the couch, and thrust it deep into her quivering body.

Sarah gasped, looking up at Paul as he stood back watching. She felt embarrassed in front of him, yet an undeniable sexual heat was spreading through her body. She wanted to deny it, both because of Paul and to deny this filthy Arab scum any idea he might cause her pleasure, yet her body had already decided on its own and there seemed nothing she could do to fight it.

So she gave herself to the pleasure, groaning like the slut both men called her as the Arab pig's cock rammed into her again and again. Her insides caught fire and her mind was churned and boiled in the swirling waves of sensory pleasure that enfolded her.

She thrust herself back onto Jubal's lance as he cursed her and savagely rode her, his hands clawing at her hips, tearing at her hair, slapping at her breasts. The tight halter had made her sex so intensely sensitive, her pouting lips wrapped around the Arab's pounding meat with delight and sent waves of pleasure through her body.

Even as Sarah cried out in pain she felt the pleasure rising like a hovering wall of water, like a tidal wave that grew greater and more powerful as it rose. She felt the quivering tension in her body, the pressure building up in her mind as she grunted and moaned and whimpered under Jubal's violent rutting onslaught.

Then the orgasm swept down about her, the tidal wave swamping her mind and flinging it up and down like a cork bobbing in a flood tide. She cried out in release even as Jubal yanked back on her hair, screamed in pleasure even as he slapped furiously at her dangling, swinging, jiggling breasts.

And as Jubal emptied his seed into her she felt her spasming pussy sucking it down lustily, drawing at his tube of flesh, greedily demanding more.

She barely kept from collapsing as Jubal pulled away, raining curses on her. She knelt there shakily, eyes glazed, head hanging so low her hair touched the floor.

Then Paul/Achmed was behind her, his hardness against her. She felt herself pierced anally, felt Paul slowly working his hardness down into her rectum as she groaned and slumped to her elbows on the floor.

"Filthy Jew whore!" he snarled, slapping at her behind. His prong lurched deeper with each slap as the sharp pain distracted her. Then he was buried inside her and rutting almost as hard as Jubal had. His balls slapped against her wet, pouting pussy lips and she whined in heated pleasure, straightening her arms, pushing herself up, then flinging her head back as she threw her hips back onto his tool.

Glory! It was glorious! She had never felt like such a whore! And her mind revelled in it! To be used! To be ridden like a bitch dog!

She felt another orgasm rising then sweep around her. Her head jerked up and down like a wild filly and she drove herself back against Paul with terrible need, grunting and groaning and whining in feverish heat, the orgasm rolling up and down like an out of control roller coaster.

But even as Paul was spending himself within her bowels Jubal was making arrangements, angrily watching Sarah as she howled in delight.

Shortly thereafter, though Paul expressed some doubts about the wisdom of it, she was bent over a strange machine in one of the private rooms of torment. It was a table of sorts, low to the ground. It had two deep round cups lined with rubber suction cups, and her breasts were forced down into them.

A rounded metal bar was brought down across the small of her back and locked into place even as her arms were pulled straight down on either side of the table and locked into place by metal restraints.

Likewise her legs were spread wide, metal restraints locking about her ankles and thighs. Then a long, thick metal tube shaped much like a male phallus was pulled out from under the table. It was on a swing arm, and it swung out, then up, then around against her sex before Jubal rammed it home.

A second phallus came swinging up around the first, and Jubal pushed that into her rectum, locking both swing arms in place.

Then he threw a switch and the table began to hum with power. Sarah felt the suction cups begin to move, felt them closing in around her tender breasts. They moved in waves, kneading and squeezing her soft orbs, even as the small metal plate at the centre of each cup began to slowly rotate and give off tiny sparkles of electricity.

The two large metal dildos inside her began to hum as well, then the one in her pussy began to move, slowly easing back, then pushing in, pumping in a slow steady stroke that increased as Jubal turned a dial.

The second one began to move then, moving in counterpoint to the first, thrusting up into her rectum even as the other slid down out of her belly.

Then the men left, turning off the lights and closing the door, leaving her alone and helpless with her metal lover.

Edward sighed as Amanda tongued his nipple. He smiled benignly and reached up to grope one of her round breasts.

She kissed his throat then the side of his face before bringing her mouth against his.

He turned his face aside.

"Not on the lips," he said impatiently.

"I'm sorry, master," she said, kissing her way back down his body.

She licked at his balls and he brought his hands behind his head, watching her, thinking of how wonderful money and power were, how they could buy him anything, even the utter, abject surrender of the sluttish, snobbish, oh so superior Amanda Graham!

"Dance for me, slut," he ordered.

"Yes, master," she said in her low, breathy voice.

She moved off the bed and stood next to it, letting her body slowly undulate in time to the music, grinding her pelvis as her head rolled in slow, erotic circles and her hands moved over her body.

He picked up the remote and changes stations, bringing a faster one and setting a faster pace, watching her swing her hips and thrust her pelvis out lewdly, watching her slide her tongue over her lower lip and look seductively at him.

"Enough. Into bed, dog."

She crawled back into bed, embracing him, her lush breasts flattening against his chest as he brought a hand around to cup and fondle her round behind.

She snuggled in against him, her softness delightful against his skin. He pushed her down, however, down towards his crotch, and she moved willingly, eagerly, or so it seemed, her lips trailing over her belly and back to his cock, engulfing it and taking it deep, then bobbing up and down as she caressed his testicles.

Oddly, her surrender annoyed him, in a way, for it deprived him of an excuse to further torture her. Not that he really needed an excuse of course, and not that he couldn't make her life difficult in other ways.

He gripped the back of her head and rolled over, rolling her with him so she was now under him. Holding her head he began to thrust down into her mouth, feeling a mixture of fear and hope that she would dare to bite him again.

She didn't, even as he tilted her head and savagely forced his entire erection down into her throat she did nothing but shudder and tremble and push feebly at his belly.

He held himself deep, grinding his crotch into her face as she lay beneath him. When he did raise himself it was only to thrust back again as he used her throat like it was her pussy, rutting wildly, bouncing atop her face as her movements became more and more frantic, then less so.

He spent himself inside her throat and rolled off with a groan, and the white faced girl gulped in air in between coughs.

"You'd better learn to do that better," he said calmly. "I'll expect you to deep throat me every day now, and if you can't, well...we'll just have to take the whip to you again!"

He reached down and entangled his fist in her long, silky

143

hair, then literally dragged her up the length of his body until she lay on her back next to him. He idly twisted and pinched her nipples as he admired her body, smugly content.

16

Meghan and Victoria were kneeling on all fours, naked, on a small pedestal. A number of men sat around watching or chatting idly as she and Victoria slapped their behinds together and ground their hips in lewd lesbian gratification.

They had been shocked to discover each other. Meghan knew the other woman only slightly, but had passed on what she knew about the alleged slave ring to someone in Victoria's office, and Victoria had then come to speak to her about the inactivity of Lord Andrew.

Both of them now deeply regretted ever hearing of the white slavery club. Both had now been 'guests' of it for almost two weeks. Victoria had been captured earlier, but was delayed by her time with Lisette.

Her first day with Lisette was spent largely serving her sexual needs. The next day she had been a sexual servant at a small cocktail party the girl had thrown. Humiliated, she had been forced to crawl among half a dozen beautifully dressed women, enduring their scornful comments and contemptuous looks.

Then, while the woman had sat, fanning themselves against the heat, sipping fruit drinks, and giggling, Victoria had been placed on all fours on the floor before them and taken by a large Asian man from behind.

The humiliation had been even more intense than anything she had previously undergone, for these women were obviously intelligent, sophisticated, well to do, and members of the ruling class - wherever they were. To be so used by a man in front of them was horrifying. He had rutted into her like a cheap whore as the women laughed and made jokes about how much she must be enjoying it.

When the first man was done a second had sodomized her, then a third had made her perform oral sex on him. Afterwards she was ordered to place herself across Lisette's lap, and then spanked.

Another shock to her system, another indignity that could not be born. The ignorant little chit ten years her junior had smacked her hands down so hard that each had stung terribly, all while the others had watched and giggled. And to her further humiliation she had begun to cry, sobbing and begging her to stop as her backside had burned in pain.

She was allowed to perform oral sex on Lisette then, and then must crawl to each of the other woman for a spanking before eating them as well. By the end her pride was almost completely obliterated, and she meekly licked Lisette's feet at the woman's command, then crawled back to the little room where she'd lain the previous night.

Now, two gigantic double-headed dildos were buried within her rectum and vagina, the other halves inside Meghan's, and as they slapped their behinds together and pulled them back the men watching could see the twin tubes of rubber glistening before they were engulfed once again.

Meghan's left ankle was strapped to Victoria's right, and vice versa, and her arms were pulled straight back down her body and her wrists strapped to Victoria's wrists. Each girl had long hair, Meghan's blonde, Victoria's brown, and it was wound and tied together, forcing their heads back.

Under the circumstances, the easiest, and least painful thing to do would be to remain still. But neither woman did. They knew the watchful overseers would respond with far more pain if they did not do as they were told, and they had been told to continue to grind their hips and slap their buttocks together around the thick dildos that had been forced deep inside them.

Not being 'special' girls, neither had been introduced to the complex with a special rape. Instead they were routinely abused, both physically and sexually, as the servitors and overseers 'trained' them to please their new masters.

Their days were long and hectic. They got very little sleep and very little in the way of nourishment. Whenever they were alone soft, persuasive voices told them how much they loved the masters and how they must obey them and please them.

They were put through their paces like dogs, whips slashing instantly across their tender flesh at the slightest hesitation in obeying an order. Their wrists were constantly bound behind their backs wherever they went to reinforce their sense of helplessness.

Much of their time was spent in 'class', where instructors gave lessons on deep throating and fellatio, on anilingus, massage, and every possible known sexual position, the pipes gave off a soft, pleasant vibration which, after the first few days of shock, had most women in a constant state of sexual arousal no matter what they did to try and fight it.

The classes which would have been the most boring were actually the most exciting, but not in any sexually pleasant way.

These were the classes in a slave girl's duty to her master. The instructor would often toss questions out rapid fire to individual girls and the girl must answer correctly and instantly to avoid a painful discharge of electricity up into her pussy.

Even most of the demonstration classes - where the girls were not seated, had the same kind of electrical threat. For then there were portable electric prods the girls wore up inside their sheaths, strapped in tightly with a kind of thick, heavy leather G-string that was locked in place. There was a

146

powerful battery attached to the G-string and if an instructor or overseer aimed his remote control her way the prod would make a girl howl with agony.

Meghan had discovered this her second day at the complex, when she'd awakened in her cell after spending the entire previous day on that platform to find a man spreading her legs and beginning to rape her.

Since her hands were restrained behind her back there was nothing she could do but lie there helplessly as he thrust himself into her with violent, brutal motions, then came in her belly.

Immediately afterwards the metal prod was thrust into her, small wires sticking out of the end and attached to the T-shaped leather belt thing. The belt was buckled around her waist, then the lower portion brought down between her thighs and up behind her to snap in place at the back of the belt.

She was led to her first class, where she'd found a half dozen other newly arrived slave girls all similarly clad. As soon as her wrists were unlocked so that she could demonstrate her understanding of how to jerk off a penis she had punched the instructor and ran for the door.

She never got there. A horrific pain had blasted into her and collapsed her before the door clawing at her groin.

The pain had continued, and she'd thought she'd lose her mind as she shrieked in agony, rolling over and over again on the floor as she slapped and pulled and grabbed at her crotch, trying to tear the leather away so she could relieve the agony that was tearing away at her vitals.

That had taught her, yet the stubbornness that had irritated many a teacher in his day, as well as her superiors on the police, had got her into trouble again as she had refused to tongue one of the overseer's anus during a class on that subject.

As a demonstration to the other girls she had been taken to a corner stand none had paid much attention to, and strapped into it.

The stand was a tall metal bar with wide legs and a metal collar on top.

There was also a sharp six inch long spike protruding out of the bar a foot or so below the collar.

With her throat locked into the metal collar she had to thrust her chest out violently to keep from being stabbed by the spike. Of course her wrists were bound to the sides of her collar. Then her feet were lifted and placed into metal restraints which forced them backwards and prevented her from supporting her weight.

All her weight came down on her wrists as the overseer had proceeded, to her shocked horror, to whip her breasts with a riding crop.

Whenever she even thought about that Meghan's hands tried instinctively to cup her breasts, which, even after several days still ached and showed the welts of that beating. She had hardly been able to talk for the next two days because of her shrieking during the whipping.

Yet even so her spirit had not been broken. She had learned a dreadful lesson about just how evil these men were, about just what kind of horrible punishments any disobedience would draw, but inside her head her mind still spun and whirred as she sought a way out, some form of escape that offered a chance.

She was raped regularly, at least a dozen times each day, but after the first day that had become something less than shocking, even at times, boring.

The sodomy was less so, mostly because it was more painful. And walking around more or less nude, being groped and fondled and leered at by strange men was also something she had grown used to and no longer really bothered her.

Amazing, she thought, what one can accustom oneself to.

Dancing classes, acting classes, begging classes, of all things, classes in how to feed their masters, in how to use their breasts - all of them seemed to be quite buxom - to massage their masters feet, classes in how to use ones entire body, coated in soap, to clean the master as he lay beneath.

And then there were the nights, and those voices. Meghan knew what they were doing, knew they were trying to brainwash the girls. The techniques were classic and she'd read about them in psychology class before joining the police department.

And the worst of these, she thought, the one which really showed the depths of depravity of the men here, was the pain and resurrection, a particularly agonizing class each girl was subjected to.

It was a class that, even after only a few days, she could see some of the girls responding to.

Small wonder, for the class was simple in its tone, though varying in application. Vibrators, fingers and mouths were used to rouse the girls into a state of sexual excitement just short of orgasm, then small pains were applied, small at first.

She had not understood the first day, nor even the second, but now she did, and even her own body was beginning to respond to it.

Each of the girls was pared off, then, using lips, tongues, fingers and vibrators, one of the girls worked the other up into a state of high sexual arousal. This was aided by the lack of nourishment they had all received, which kept them all a bit light- headed, their minds not working as well as they otherwise might.

Then pain was applied. Small pins were lightly stabbed into the receiving girl's pubic lips, or thighs or buttocks, depending on how close she was to climax. As the pain lowered her excitement more pleasure would be applied, then stabbing pains again.

This was repeated over and over again, with the pins being stuck in harder and deeper to fight off more powerful arousal. Eventually, of course, even sticking the pin into a girl's clitoris could not deter the orgasm, and she would climax with the pain and pleasure mixed interchangeably.

Ultimately, Meghan knew, the objective was to produce girls who would probably climax even as they were being brutally whipped or tortured, perhaps even with nothing other than the pain to lead their minds into a spiral of sexual oblivion.

Yet even knowing this she had come powerfully that morning, the pleasure unbearable as the girl working on her had stuck a pin directly into her swollen clitoris.

It was hard to think, so very hard. For her mind kept drifting away. She desperately needed to sleep, and to eat something nourishing, not the sugar filled junk the girls were being fed.

Of course, that was the idea behind the diet, and the lack of sleep. None of the girls were thinking straight.

Even as she thought this she recognized the signs of arousal inside her body, gave a half-hearted attempt to fight them down, then gave in, her determination fading from her exhaustion and lack of nourishment.

Each time her tight pussy rode down the dildos and her buttocks slapped solidly into Victoria's her mind felt a swirl of heat and pleasure. Pain and pleasure, pleasure and pain. They were becoming one within her frazzled mind no matter how hard she tried to keep them apart...

She tried to hold back, but then Victoria climaxed, gurgling in helpless pleasure, her bound tongue preventing her from making any other sort of sound. The raven haired beauty slapped her buttocks back even harder, yanking forward again to tear at her own clit as well as Meghan's.

Meghan gurgled herself, tears filling her eyes as her tongue pulled against the clip holding it. Her belly filled with liquid heat and her mind disintegrated as a howling storm of sexual bliss engulfed her.

The two young women shuddered and trembled in the throes of their ecstasy, odd animal noises coming from their mouths as their eyes rolled back dazedly.

Meghan sagged, then straightened weakly. There was still four more hours to go before she and Victoria would be freed from their present task. Then they would be cleaned, fed, watered, and given more classes.

She groaned weakly.

17

Paul looked at the girl and smiled, turning and nodding to his host, Hasaan.

"But you can't see her pretty face," he said with a smile.

"Better for you. She's such an ugly Jew girl," Hasaan said.

They were standing before what he had been told was Miri Gathwenz, one of the missing girls he was looking for. It was quite difficult to tell, however.

The female before them, for female it undeniably was, was encased in thick, gleaming leather from head to toe. The face of the leather hood encasing her head had no features, being a smooth, slightly rounded surface. There was a zipper where a mouth might be, and two small holes where nostrils would be located.

Her arms were pulled behind her back, the leather sleeves which surrounded each limb also masking her hands, with no fingers or thumbs to allow her any manipulation at all. Even if there were her wrists were tightly strapped together. As were her forearms and biceps.

Her legs and feet were likewise tightly encased in gleaming leather, her ankles pulled back and strapped to her thighs.

Her legs were split wide, each tightly bound limb at a wide angle from her hips.

She wore a tight leather corset, much like the one he'd seen Sarah wearing earlier, and which compressed her waist to minute size.

She was hanging from the ceiling in a horizontal position, her large breasts, naked, dangling beneath her body. Chains were locked to the top of her leather hood, holding her head up and back, to the straps about her arms, the back of her corset, and to her heels and thighs.

"How long do you keep her like this?" he asked.

"Oh, a few hours, then we find another position. But the hood remains in place. Two months we have had the slut now, and she has neither seen nor heard anything during all that time."

"She is deaf in there?"

"Yes, heavy padding over the ears."

"But you can't tell her what a filthy little Jewess she is."

"I let her know in other ways," he said with a smile.

He took the cigar from his lips and ground it on at the small of the girl's back, then burst into laughter. Paul quickly followed suit.

"I don't know, though," he said. "I'm thinking of having mine put in with the general population for the training they get. It seems most effective."

"True. The females here learn their place. But I don't want this Jew slut bitch to get pleasure from my punishments. I will break her my own way."

"How will you know when she is broken?"

Hasaan shrugged. "Maybe one day I'll take off the hood and ask," he said, then laughed uproariously again.

He motioned Paul around to the girl's rear and gestured to her bared sex.

"Go ahead. Have some," he said with a smile. "Be my guest."

Paul grinned at him, surprised that he actually was finding himself aroused despite his anger at the man and his indignation at what had been done to the Israeli soldier.

He had found a lot of his beliefs changing over the last week or so, and was undeniably attracted to the life of a male totally in control of beautiful, willing females.

Willing? There was no such word here. They were all his to do with as he chose. They never talked back, never argued, never denied anything, were all gorgeous and big busted, and he could do literally anything he wanted to them without anyone caring.

He raised his hand and cupped the girl's sex, stroking his finger along her pink cleft. The girl was someone's daughter, he told himself. She is an abused prisoner. She deserved his sympathy. And indeed, she had it.

But he still felt himself becoming aroused as he slipped his finger inside her and wriggled it in deep.

"She's tight yet," Hasaan said. "But we'll loosen her up. I aim to impregnate her eventually and have the sow's bitch raised in the slave pens."

Paul ran his hands over her beautiful round behind, feeling the softness of her warm flesh, feeling her body swinging freely on the end of the chains as he kneaded her flesh.

What difference did it make, he asked himself? She'd already been raped by legions, and she would never know anyway.

He undid his trousers and pulled his erection free, feeling ashamed, yet aroused beyond measure. The girl made no sound as he entered her, nor as he began to thrust into her. His movements set her body swinging. It must have hurt, but again, the gag stuffed into her mouth kept her quiet as he used her.

When he was done he slapped her on the behind with a laugh, then he and Hasaan left in comradely fashion, to talk about mutual business interests.

Later in his suite he sat back in his king sized bed pondering his problem. He had now found two of the girls, but both were in difficult to reach areas. If they were part of the general population things would be much easier. But as long as they were in the hands of their fanatical owners they were likely to be killed at the first sign of an assault on the island.

That, of course, was also a problem. He'd been astonished at how well-guarded the island camp was. First off the dictator the Viceroy had bought off had surrounded the island with mines. He also had patrol boats circling it to prevent anyone coming near. He had patrols along the perimeters armed with heavy weapons, and a large response group on the island next door ready to rush over at the first sign of trouble.

The Viceroy's own security was even better. The guards were first rate, and all ex-soldiers from elite forces in the west. They'd been lured to the island with high pay rates and the promise of free women ready for their comfort every night.

An all out assault would be extremely difficult and expensive to mount, and would cost a lot of casualties, including among the girls. And yet a small scale attack would have to sneak past all the guards and the hightech sensor systems then escape without being destroyed.

He looked up and grinned as Sarah came into the room. She was wearing the traditional slave outfit of leather G-string and stiletto heels, as well as leather restraints on wrists ankles and throat. Her wrists were clipped together behind her back, which was also normal. When slave girls weren't needed for some task their wrists were always restrained.

"I see you've been released from your kitchen tasks," he said.

"Yes," she said with a pouty look. "I don't know why you had to offer me to the kitchen anyway. As a private slave I..."

"I needed you to go out there and get information," he

154

said with a frown. "You aren't any good to me if you're at my heels all the time, nor if you're stuck here in my suite watching TV."

"I suppose," she sighed, sitting on the edge of the bed.

"I could, of course, put you back into that machine Jubal locked you to the other day."

She shuddered and her eyes closed briefly.

"You have no idea!" she said, her voice soft and quivering. "I thought I was going to die."

"Well, Jubal did say you could be fucked to death."

"It was, the orgasms were so intense and they drain your energy until, well, until you can hardly breath."

"Of course, that wouldn't work on all women," he said with a smirk, reaching up and pulling her back against him.

"Stop that," she said with little force in her voice. "And you can release my wrists now that we're alone."

"What do you need wrists for?" he murmured, his fingers sliding through her hair, then moving down onto her breast, cupping and squeezing it softly.

"Paaaulll," she moaned.

"Come here, slave slut," he growled, dragging her further into the bed, then rolling her onto her back.

"This... we're supposed to be on... on a mission," she gasped as his lips sought her nipples.

"Shut up or I'll spank you," he growled, bringing his teeth down around her nipple and chewing lightly.

"Paaaulll," she gasped, wriggling beneath him.

"Hot little slut," he panted, his hands digging into her soft breasts. "Did that machine squeeze your breasts as well as I do. Was it better than my lips?"

He sucked her nipple into his mouth and chewed on it as his fingers dug deep furrows in the round mammaries, kneading and massaging them.

"Bastard!" she groaned.

He forced her legs up and apart, running his hands down

her taut belly and along her inner thighs. His thumbs pried her soft lips apart and he gazed down at her revealed hole and the pink flesh around it.

"How many men have fucked you today?" he growled. "How many men have emptied their cocks into your whore belly?"

"Many!" she groaned. "Oooohhhhh! Don't!"

He pinched her pussy lips, pulling them wider and wider as he felt his cock stiffening. This was an assignment he would not have believed, he thought, his mind filling with carnal lust. An assignment where he got to fuck the brains out of his sluttish partner, and it didn't matter if she liked it or not.

"Filthy little whore," he shouted.

He pulled his manhood free of his pants, stroking the swollen head up and down against Sarah's soft moist pussy opening. Then he centred it and thrust in, drawing a gasp, then another gasp as he buried himself within her.

His hands mashed her breasts together as he ground himself into her, twisting his cock around in her snug belly.

"Maybe I'll leave you here when I'm done," he growled. "Leave you here to be a slut slave for the rest of your life."

She moaned and writhed, her head back as she gasped and rolled her eyes.

"I bet you'd love it," he said. "You don't even need any training. You were a slut before you even got here."

He began to pump into her, his hands roaming her nubile body as he grinned down at her glazed eyes. The thought occurred to him that he could actually have her run through the basic training program here, and that he could justify it quite easily if he had to. If she was this much of a playtoy now what would she be like after the brainwashing they gave the girls here?

After all, this assignment wouldn't last forever, and he was going to miss having his own little slut slaves to use as he saw fit. In fact, the idea of returning to the life of a single man, of having to seduce women, wine and romance them in order to convince them to spread their legs, was now beginning to seem more and more repugnant.

He drove himself into her with harder thrusts, feeling his power over her, feeling the excitement of being in total possession of his beautiful partner. Each time he thrust himself into her he felt her pussy flesh giving way before his powerful cock, and each time he pulled himself back her pussy squeezed and sucked on his sensitive flesh as if reluctant to see it go.

He ran his hands up and down her legs, pulling them over his shoulders as he leaned further forward, tilting her pussy up towards him as he continued to thrust into her. Sarah's eyes were tight slits as she whimpered and moaned in pleasure, and he felt a wonder he'd hardly even known her back when they'd worked out of the same building.

He reached back for her ankles, then gripped each tightly and forced her legs back, putting all his weight behind his arms as he slowly jammed her ankles back over her shoulders and behind her head. He rose and fell heavily atop her, his hips slamming her buttocks down into the mattress with each stroke, and the springs throwing her pussy back up at him to meet the next.

She shuddered as she came, her pussy spasming wildly, yet he held himself back, continuing to pound down into her. Another orgasm ripped through her, then a third before he finally spilled his seed within her fiery wet belly.

Only then did he ease up on his strokes, moving slower and slower, then pulling back with a groan, relaxing his hold on her ankles and letting her unbend.

She groaned as her legs flopped down alongside him.

"God! You - you nearly broke my back," she gasped.

"Your back was made for this," he said, giving her pussy a final squeeze before rolling away and laying on his back next to her.

"What did you tell Gabrielle?" he asked after a moment to catch his breath.

"Who?"

"Stupid little cow," he said affectionately. "Gabrielle, the girl, remember?"

"Oh. I didn't tell her anything."

He frowned and sat up. "What?"

"I couldn't," she said defensively. "I mean, we didn't have much time and, well, Jubal was right there."

"You had enough time to whisper something to her," he snapped. "You had your tongue stuck in her ear for several minutes."

"She wasn't in any shape to understand a message. I mean, well, she might have given us away."

"You mean she might have given you away!"

"I didn't think it was safe."

"Who's in charge of this mission?" he demanded.

"You are," she said in a surly tone.

"I gave you an order and you disobeyed it."

"It was a stupid order!"

"Stupid!?"

He sat up abruptly, reaching down and grabbing her by the hair. She cried out in pain as he forced her head back, then forced her up off the bed.

"Stop it! What are you doing! Idiot! Let me go!"

"You forget your place!"

"You forget yours, bastard! You think you are my master!?"

"Maybe I'm not in real life, slut, but here I AM your master!"

He forced her over to the corner, where a series of metal rings with small chains attached ran up the length of the wall. He bent her over sharply, then attached one of the lower chains to a ring on her collar, and lifted the long thin cane off a hook set on the wall nearby.

"What are you doing?! Stop it! You can't do this to me!"

The cane slashed down across her upturned buttocks with a satisfying crack! of noise and she squealed in pain.

"You'll learn your place, girl," he snapped. "I am in charge of this mission and what I say is what you do!"

Crack! Crack! Crack! Crack! Crack!

The cane cut across her soft round flesh as she squealed and whined and cried out in pain, dancing wildly from foot to foot as she tried to twist out of the way. But the collar held her tightly, her face against the wall as he continued to cane her lusciously displayed behind.

18

Amanda smiled down at Sir Edward as she went slowly up and down on his stiff erection. His hands gripped her breasts tightly, his fingers working into the flesh with bruising force that almost made her wince. She continued to smile, however, pretending she loved it, gasping softly as if in pleasure as she rode him.

"Ooooooh," she groaned.

"You love that, don't you, whore?" he sneered.

"Oh yes, master! Oh, Master! You're so good to me, master! oooohhhhh! Ungghghhh!"

She let her head ease back and rolled it slowly from side to side, squeaking softly each time she slapped her round buttocks down against his hips.

He reached up and slipped his hand behind her head, then yanked her down, rolling atop her. In an instant he had her legs jammed back against her chest as he pounded his meaty tool down into her belly, grunting with effort as she continued to moan in pleasure.

She cried out, her eyes going wide, then narrowing to slits as she shook violently. She bucked up against him, her pussy squeezing down hard and fast as she pretended orgasm.

Edward growled in delight, hammering himself against her, drilling his stiff manhood down into her tight depths with all his strength as her spasming pussy sucked the juices directly from his balls, swallowing every powerful spurt of juice.

He groaned as he instantly softened, then rolled off her and lay on his back, chest heaving.

She sighed as if in pleasure, then rolled atop him, pressing her soft round breasts against his chest as she flung an arm over him and buried her face in his shoulder.

"You're so good to me, master," she moaned again.

"Better than you deserve, slut."

"Want me to do you again, master? I can make you hard again if you want." Her hand slid down to cup his balls and flaccid penis.

"Go ahead and try," he said lazily.

He lay back as she slid her pert young lips down his body and began to lick and suckle at his balls and thighs. She was extremely talented, he admitted, and soon she was bobbing her lips up and down on his rising tool, taking it clear down her throat each time.

He was thick, and her jaws were spread wide as her lips rode up and down the full length of his organ. But she was obviously happy, and quite enthusiastic. He was very pleased at how well he had trained her.

The plebeians who ran the club liked to have every girl eventually run through their program, but he saw no need of it. She was as obedient as a well-trained dog, and adored him like a cocker spaniel.

He groaned as he gripped the back of her head, yanking her down fully as he spit wad after wad down her sweet throat.

He relaxed his grip then, his hand dropping back to the bed as she drained the last of his juices then licked his organ clean.

When she was done she crawled up alongside him and lay there with an adoring look on her face. He yawned tiredly, glanced at his watch, then reached over and turned off the light.

Amanda's features underwent a profound change as the lights dimmed, and she glared at Sir Edward in hate. One day, she vowed, she would kill the insufferable pig. She felt like vomiting every time he touched her.

But she was rapidly gaining some control over things. Tonight she'd done such a good job she'd worn him out. And he hadn't wanted to make the effort to put her in her cage like he usually did.

She could kill him tonight, she thought as she stared at his shadowed form. She could take a knife or something and plunge it into him when he slept.

Not that that would do her any good. It would certainly not free her of this place, and who knew what kind of horrible punishment they would mete out for that.

She had little in the way of plans at the moment, beyond convincing Sir Edward, the gullible fool, that she was totally broken and utterly devoted to him. She didn't think even he could be stupid enough to take her back to his residence in England, but there was always a chance, and meanwhile playing the part of the happy slut kept her away form punishments and gave her a slim measure of freedom.

She had already got from him that they were on an island in the South Pacific, and that it was heavily guarded by soldiers. Every day she heard helicopters landing and taking off from the heliport, so that seemed like the most logical way of escaping.

But how?

In the last day she'd been able to speak to a few of the other prisoners, and found them frighteningly insensible, their minds filled with girlish thoughts of make-up and pretty lingerie and making this or that master happy.

None seemed to harbour any resentment towards the men who had imprisoned and abused them. They seemed devoted to their pleasure.

Amanda shuddered at the blankness in their eyes, and wondered if she would someday become like them. She knew there was a regular program they ran most new girls through. She had avoided it because she was a 'special' prisoner, brought here at Sir Edward's orders and for his use.

But if they put her through that program... she didn't like to think about what would emerge on the other side. She had already been through so much, she didn't know if she could go through more and still emerge with any strength of will.

When she was sure he was asleep she crept out of bed and out of the aptly named master bedroom. She went into the main bathe and closed the door, then stared at herself in the mirror, wondering at the things she'd been through in such a short time.

Most of the whip marks had faded from her body now, and she still looked like the same girl she'd always been. She'd lost weight, of course. Unfortunately, it that had only served to accentuate her high cheekbones and full breasts. She seemed, at least by his reaction and the reaction of other men, to be more desirable now than she'd been before.

She plastered a stupid smile on her face, then grimaced. What kind of men were these that only wanted a brainless fuck bunny for their tools? She thought of the long conversations she'd had with Neil, and how much he appreciated her keen wit, and wondered that these evil, cruel men were of the same species.

She sighed and left the bathroom, going to the kitchen for a snack. Then she settled in at the edge of the bed, as far from him as she could get.

Morning came, and she woke the instant he started moving. She crawled between his legs and took him into her mouth, sucking softly as his tool inflated. It didn't last long, and she swallowed his semen before sliding her body up alongside his so he could fondle her breasts.

After a minute she slipped out of bed and ordered his morning juice, then ran his bath. After washing him she dried him and brushed out his hair, noting as she did that he was going prematurely bald.

She helped him dress, giggling as she pulled on his shoes, tied the laces, then kissed his foot.

She had a cold shiver as she did, though, wondering whether she was worse off or better than the other similar fuck slaves. For they performed the same tasks yet without realizing they were degrading, performed them happily and took pleasure in it.

Sir Edward clipped her metal bracelets together behind her back, then started for the door with her following.

Almost all the other slaves wore something, if only a G-string. But Sir Edward kept her totally nude at all times, ready, he said, to be used as she ought.

She followed him down to the elevators, then downstairs and through the corridors to the main dining lounge. There women in tight leather outfits scurried about seeing to the needs of the masters who arrived for breakfast.

She studied the girls as they moved around, noting how eager to please they seemed. Were any of them putting on an act like her, or were they all that broken?

One of the men approached their table, trailed by a bright eyed, short haired brunette. The brunette knelt at his feet as the man greeted Edward, then sat down. The two men chatted, and she gazed at the brunette, looking for some spark of intelligence in the wide, adoring eyes.

Then she jerked her eyes around as something the man said caught her attention.

"...haven't sent her through the training program either," he was saying. "But I'm thinking of doing it."

"Well, er, I uhm, find that Amanda here gives fine service without their so-called training. And I'd hate to wake up alone in the morning, if you know what I mean."

"Yes, I do," the man said with a smile. "Still, though we train our dogs we can never do quite as good a job as a professional. Perhaps I'll put this slut through it and let you know if it changes her for the better."

"Yes. Quite. Do," Edward said, nodding his head.

Amanda looked at the girl, and for a moment she thought she saw her give her master a look of reproach and suspicion, then it was gone, replaced by that mindless happiness she saw on so many of the other women.

"I'll see you on the golf course later, my friend," the man said.

"Yes, er, of course, Achmed. After breakfast," Edward said.

Achmed left, the girl following him closely, and Amanda turned her gaze back to Edward, smiling happily.

"What did you mean by that?" Sarah whispered.

"Hmm, oh, well, I heard that our third girl was placed into the training program. The only way to get near her is to go into it yourself."

"Do you know what the program involved?"

"Nothing too serious, my dear. After all, it's designed to teach the new girls how to act, how to please their masters, uhm, how to be obedient little fuck bunnies, basically. You should have no problem with that. I mean, you're already obedient, or at least, acting that way, and you certainly don't need anyone to teach you how to please your man."

He grinned and patted her behind. She winced and gave him a glare.

"How will I contact you if they segregate me with those other girls?"

"Well, you are still my special slave girl. I can visit you any time I want. I can even have you back at my suite each evening, though come to think of it I don't think the girls get a lot of rest."

"I don't know," she said doubtfully.

"You don't have to know. I'm in charge, or have you forgotten so soon?"

"You just wait until we get back!"

"Silence," he snapped. "Maybe you do need the training program. You keep forgetting your place in public and you'll be one dead slut!"

He walked down a flight of stairs to the basement and there met with one of the overseers in charge of training.

"Ah, I'm glad you brought her down, Your Highness. We like to make sure each girl is fully trained, even the private slaves."

"Yes, so I understand. Although I have little doubt she is already in fairly good shape."

They both turned to look at her and she smiled stupidly.

"We'll test her inside, Your Highness, and if she's as far along as you think she won't require much more training. We can put her in advanced mode with the girls who have already been in the program for a while."

"Excellent. She gives good service and I had to be without he for long."

He gave Sarah a pat on the behind, squeezed her, then said goodbye and went back upstairs, leaving her with the overseer.

"Well, slut. How do you like living on the island?" the man asked.

"It's very nice, master," she said. "I don't have to work and I don't have to worry about anything, and I get lots of... I mean, I get to please my master a lot."

"You mean you get lots of cock, you little slut," he said, chuckling.

"Yes, master," she said, bowing her head.

"That's all right, slut girl. We like our slave sluts to want lots of cock. In fact, we make sure they do."

He called someone on the phone and another pair of overseers came to get her. They led her down another flight of stairs and into a small room. There were a number of frightening looking devices scattered around the room, and the walls were lined with whips, crops and canes.

Her wrist restraints were undone and she was given a series of orders that reminded her of dog training. She had to assume various positions, and do it quickly, on all fours, for instance, on her knees with her head back, on her belly with her legs spread or on her back with her knees up and apart.

She crawled across the floor and grovelled for them, licking at their feet and ankles, then held her position, bent over, as they caned her behind.

That was hard, for she'd never actually had to take punishment before without moving. She'd always been forcibly bound somehow.

After that she took a cock down her throat, bobbing her lips up and down its length, then was ridden on all fours, squealing with a pleasure that was only partly feigned.

They decided that she was well-trained, but did not respond fast enough, had not had obedience drummed into her hard enough.

She was placed into one of the classes on obedience. There were five other women in the class. The overseer interrupted the class to bring her in, and she was led to a small low chair and ordered to sit down.

A metal dildo of sorts stuck up from it, and she knew without asking that she was meant to impale herself on it. Bracing herself, she slowly eased down all the way, gasping as it drove deep into her belly. Then her ankles were chained to the sides and she sat there listening to the class.

It sounded ridiculous to her, but she did her best to fake interest as the teacher called out various questions and the women answered them. She noted they answered very quickly. Then one got an answer wrong and cried out in pain. Sarah stared at her, worried.

"You, slut!"

"Me, master?"

"What was your name?"

"Sarah, master."

"Sarah, what is a slave's first duty?"

"To obey her master," she guessed.

Then her insides exploded in pain and she screamed, jerking violently on the chair as she yanked her pussy off the metal probe.

"Sit down!" he snarled icily.

"I... I'm sorry, master," she gulped. "I didn't know we... I mean, that the..."

"Sit!"

She eased down onto the thing again, and when she was firmly down she felt the pain burn into her again. Again she screamed, her fingers digging into the palms of her hands as she squirmed and sobbed, her insides bathed in acid.

But by a supreme effort of will she kept from jerking upwards, knowing it would only lead to more pain.

The pain eased, then went away, and she gasped, going limp.

"Good," he said. "The sparkler is there to help your memory along, but there are far better memory aids if you choose to reject it. We are being tolerant in here, Sarah."

"Thank you, master," she gasped.

"You had better learn the slave's duties quickly. Otherwise we'll start you at the beginning of the program with the next new batch of sluts that arrive."

"Now, Meghan, what is a slave's first duty?"

"To please her master," a lovely blonde girl said quickly.

"Correct. Tammy, what rights has a slave?"

"A slave is not a human being and has no rights!" a black girl exclaimed.

"Correct. Darla, why must a slave angle her throat up when taking a master's cock?"

"So that the underside of the head will rub along the side of her throat wall," a redhead replied quickly.

"Meghan, what is a slave's first duty?"

"To please her master!"

"Yes. When can a slave disobey?"

"A slave can never disobey!"

"Correct."

The questions went on and on, and Meghan was shocked several more times, even though the teacher didn't ask her many.

They went on to their next class, and the girls were all paired off together on low couches. She was paired with the blonde girl named Meghan, a lovely young, bright-eyed girl who smiled happily at her.

She lay back, leaving it up to Meghan to know what was to be done, and saw the girl lean in between her legs, holding a vibrator and a dildo.

This, she thought, could be interesting.

And it was, the girl proved to be quite adept with her tongue and fingers, not using the sex toys immediately. Soon Sarah was grinding her pelvis up into the girl's face and groaning in pleasure. Several time she instinctively tried to grab at her head to jam her face down, only to be reminded that her wrists were tightly bound behind her back.

She was near an orgasm when she felt a sharp pain in her pussy, and gasped, jerking her eyes open. Another pain made her yelp and raise her head to see the blonde holding a little pin in her hand, the end of the pin stuck into Sarah's labia.

She opened her mouth to speak, to protest, but caught

herself in time. She heard another girl yelp, and looked over to see the redhead pulling a pin out of the black girl's pussy.

She laid her head back as Meghan began to lick at her pussy again, her tongue soft and wet and deliciously pleasant. Soon she was grinding her hips up again, and sure enough she got another pin stuck into her, then again, then again.

She wasn't sure what the lesson was here, unless it was that they didn't want the girls to climax, that they wanted them to learn to hold themselves back as long as possible.

She tried, but kept relaxing, and when Meghan turned to the vibrator she was soon yelping away every other minute. Soon the pain wasn't enough to stop her climax and she exploded, bucking wildly up and down on the sofa as pleasure screamed along her nerve endings.

The blonde girl, Meghan, delivered a series of open-handed slaps to her bare little mound as she came, cracking her hand down in hard, rapid spanks even as the climax was rippling through her body.

She came to hate the girl. And then it was her turn.

19

She was not able to go back to see Paul that night. They worked her right up until eleven o'clock. Then she and the other girls were leashed, and forced to crawl on all fours after individual servitors.

She was led into a bathroom of sorts, and ordered into the bathtub. There she knelt on all fours like a dog while the man roughly and thoroughly cleaned her from head to toe.

She was led into another room and strapped to an X-shaped wooden frame. Then a man carefully pierced her nose, nipples and clitoris, ignoring her gasps and squeals of pain as he ran the needle through them. He slipped small golden rings into each, then released her.

She crawled along behind the servitor to the kennel, where she was allowed to drink water from a bowl and eat a pasty kind of substance from a plate on the floor.

There was a metal post in the middle of the floor, with a penis-shaped metal pipe sticking out from the bottom and angling upwards. Likewise there was a large clamp sticking out from near the top of the post.

She was forced to squat with her belly against the post, then sink her pussy down onto the penis. The ring in her clitoris was then snapped to a small chain attached to the post just above the penis thing. She was made to sit down fully, then wrap her legs around the post, where they were quickly shackled.

Her arms were also wrapped around the post, chains attached to her wrists to pull them around towards her opposite side. A small chain was slipped around the post and attached to both nipple rings, holding them tight, pulling her nipples out painfully.

Then the clamp went around her throat, locking it firmly in position even as her nose ring was chained to the post.

"Sleep," she was ordered.

The lights were turned out on her and the other girls, and she thought bleakly of how she was going to get Paul back for this.

She heard a soft whispering sound, and realized it was coming from a speaker set nearby. The words... she could make out some of the words, but not all. They were spoken in a hypnotic voice, and she kept trying to understand but failing.

To make matters worse the metal thing inside her started to hum, and it wasn't too long before she heard soft whimpers and moans coming from the girl next to her, the blonde, she thought.

The post had been cold against her soft flesh, but it quickly warmed, and as she listened to the blonde's soft passion filled voice and the humming metal pipe buzzed against her soft inner flesh she found her own passions rising.

Her breasts were crushed around the post, her arms squeezing them against the now warm metal, and she found herself unconsciously squeezing her thighs against it as well, squeezing in a rhythmic fashion as her breathing grew more ragged.

"God! Oh God!" she heard the blonde gasp "Oooohhhhh!"

Then another sound, another voice, the black girl on her other side, panting for breath, then gurgling in ecstasy.

Sarah fought to suppress moans herself, and tentatively pulled her pussy a little ways up the curved metal cock.

It was very hard to move much because of her position, so her frustration grew even as the sex-heat filled her mind and body.

"Ungh! Ungh! Ungh! Ungh!" she heard from further away.

"Fuck!" she gasped aloud.

She rocked slowly, using the pressure of her arms around the post to pull her a little ways up the metal penis. Even as she did she gasped in pain for the chain locked to her clit ring tugged on it in a way that sent sharp little stinging pains into her body.

But her mind was growing inflamed now, and a little pain was not going to stand in her way. She could feel her juices dribbling down through her pussy lips as they squeezed helplessly around the hard metal cock, could feel the slickness of her milky fluid along every inch of its length as she pulled herself slowly, desperately up and down, an inch, then two, then three, gasping and panting for breath as her insides burned and roiled in agonized pleasure.

Her nipple rings were tugging painfully now as she rocked backwards, and her clit ring was hurting even more. The higher she rode the more it pulled, and she moaned and gasped in pain as much as pleasure.

A small point of her mind told her this was insanity, but her passion could not be controlled, and she fought through the pain as she rocked in place, desperately lurching up and forward against the pull of the chain on her clit, then slapping her buttocks back down onto the cold cement floor.

Then, as before, the pain, the sharp little stinging pain began to meld with the pleasure, the sharp little burst of sensation pushing against the deep, all-encompassing heat of the sexual want within her, elevating it, crackling along its edges as it leant power to it.

She cried out softly, then with more strength, her mind spinning as she slapped her ass down repeatedly, as she tore her pussy up the length of the warm metal prong, her juices trickling down to pool at its base even as her clit stretched painfully.

"God! God! God!" she whimpered.

"Oooohhhhh! Oooohhhhh!" the blonde moaned.

"Ungh! Ungh! Ungh!" the black girl gasped.

The orgasm tore through her and made her and she cried out, her legs and arms crushing her against the post, her body shaking like a leaf as she ground herself against the metal cock. Her mind drifted on a warm sea of wondrous pleasure as all her cares and worries disappeared under the soft heat of sexual bliss.

Then she was still, limp, panting as she sought to regain her breath.

But soon enough the heat started up again, that hot, thick metal buzzing softly within her snug belly, making her clitty vibrate in tune and setting her to once again jerk and shake and moan in the throes of helpless passion.

She lost count of how many times, her mind turning to mush after a while. She, like the other girls, eventually exhausted themselves against the pipes, collapsing and nodding off.

Which was almost when the lights snapped on and their

overseers returned to release them for a new day's training. All of them were groggy and exhausted, both mentally and physically, but as that was pretty much the way their trainers wanted them that presented now great problem.

All were walked on all fours to the bathrooms, then to breakfast, which was cool water and more mush eaten off plates on the floor - without using their hands, of course.

Then they went to close, practising deep-throat technique, on various servitors and overseers. Then came massage, using warm oil on each other's bodies as the trainers looked on and watched their technique.

After that came a jog around the exercise ring, their hands still locked behind their backs, of course.

Following that each girl bent over an overseer's lap for a spanking. This was not considered a disciplinary action but rather a form of sexual foreplay they must learn in order to please their masters.

Then speaking class, where each girl learned how to talk like the slut slave she now was. That meant pitching her voice higher and talking with wide eyes and in a tone which left doubt that there was anything in their heads other than air.

"Would you like to fuck, Sarah, master?" she asked, bright- eyed.

Referring to herself in the third person was also something the masters liked, she came to understand. Now that she noticed, in fact, none of the other women referred to themselves in any other way.

"Ooooooo, please do it to my ass, master," the blonde, Meghan gasped in a throaty, desperate, passion-filled voice that sent a little quiver of excitement through Sarah.

She turned admiringly. Obviously this slut was one of the best trained here. She would have to do her best to imitate the way she acted and the expressions on her face.

After that came the question and answer class. Almost as soon as she slid her pussy down onto the metal pipe she started to feel herself heat up, and as she waited for the first question to be directed at her she felt a mixture of anxiety and anticipation.

It was asked, and she failed it, then cried out, mostly in pain, but partly in something else too as her insides screamed and burned.

Three more times an electric shock was shot up into her tight belly, each one having less effect than the previous, for she was on the verge of orgasm by the last, and desperately trying to suppress it.

She realized she wasn't the only girl in that situation, for all of their faces were flushed as the class ended and they were released to practice class.

Practice Class was where they were given a chance to serve overseers who pretended to be masters, though many of the girls were more than a little confused about the difference by then.

All of them were eager to please by then, and eager to be used. Sarah eagerly licked the toes of the master she was assigned to, begging him to use her any way he desired. She took him into her mouth, then into her throat, groaning in delight as her lips ran up an down his thick erection.

Then she all but squealed in joy as she turned and presented her hot, moist, quivering sex for his enjoyment. He made ready use of it, and a wall of bliss surrounded her as she knelt on all fours, eyes closed and grunting with delight.

Next to her, Meghan was being used in precisely the same fashion, gasping and whining as the pleasure poured through her system. She knew she should be furious, but wasn't. All she cared about was that deliciously hard male organ thrusting into her burning sex hole.

Both girls came simultaneously, their voices rising and falling in blissful melody as the steady slap slap slap of bellies striking buttocks echoed around them.

20

"Harder!"

Victoria felt her chest tighten as she looked at the helpless girl sobbing before her. She appeared little more than a child, barely out of high school, her tear-stained face so sweet, her body so nubile and lush.

She drew back her arm and the bull whip snaked along the floor, then she snapped her arm up and back and the long whip arced out and cracked across the young girl's back, hurling her body forward as she screamed in pain.

Despite herself Victoria felt a wash of heat to her body. She watched in fascination as the young girl shook and trembled, then drew the whip back again.

It had only been a week or so since she had been taken from the common pen to learn something new. That something had been to help the masters punish wayward sluts, or, at least, punish those they wanted to see punished.

Some of the masters were awfully lazy, after all. And if they would have someone pour their tea she supposed it only natural some of them would also have someone else do their punishments for them.

The first time they just showed her a dull-eyed brunette stretched out on the rack and handed her a riding crop. The instructions were simple. If she didn't hit hard enough she'd take the girl's place. Victoria had no intention of risking that and had hit as hard as she could.

She had been surprised at the feel of the whip as it had struck the girl, surprised on how sensuous it felt, on how beautiful and erotic it looked as the welts appeared on her back and buttocks, how powerful the girl's screams made her feel.

After that they had given her her current outfit. She wore

thigh-high leather boots with stiletto heels, a tight leather corset with long dangerous looking cones over her breasts, a dark hooded mask which left her mouth free, but covered everything else, giving her only small eye holes to see out of, long leather gloves that reached past her elbows, and an enormously thick strap-on dildo, black and curved upwards.

Again she had whipped a girl with a crop, this time over her breasts and belly. That had looked and felt even more delicious than whipping the other girl's back, and she'd begun to feel a strange recognition within her.

She'd whipped several girls since then, and raped numerous others. Her favourite time had come when they'd given her a new girl, a petite redhead right off the street. She was exquisitely lovely and large-eyed, but though she had felt a little guilt at her actions Victoria had known she had no choice in them, and had felt a deep excitement stirring inside herself.

Protected by the mask she had torn the girl's clothing off, thrown the sobbing woman onto her hands and knees, and then, surrounded by glistening mirrored walls, raped her good and hard, digging her gloves fingers into her flanks as she rode her for long minutes under the eyes of a crowd of invisible men.

The whip cracked across the centre of the young girl's back, the front whipping around her hip to strike at her lower belly.

Now there was an interesting idea. She looked to the watching masters but saw only approval as she drew her arm back again. This time she whipped down slightly. This time as the whip snaked over the young girl's hip and its tip snapped down against her plump pussy lips.

Her scream was several octaves higher, and the men smiled in approval as Victoria felt her own pussy throb with delight.

This was certainly more fun than being on the other end

of the whip!

Again and again the whip cracked across the young woman's back, until one of the men raised his hand.

She halted at once.

"The other side."

"Yes, master!" she said, not faking her eagerness.

She moved around the sobbing woman, the whip snaking along the floor behind her. She licked her lips as she looked at the exquisite creature and noted her large soft breasts. Her arm rose, drew back, then swung quickly, the whip flying through the air and snapping across the woman's breasts with a soft, meaty impact.

She shrieked in agony, her legs kicking and flailing as the echoes of her scream filled the air. Victoria watched a dark, angry red line appear across her orbs. She shifted to one side, then flicked the whip out. This time just the tip snapped into her left breast, the force strong enough to set the rounded breast jerking as the girl screamed anew.

Annoyed, Victoria snapped the whip out again. This time she smiled and felt her pussy throb as the tip of the bullwhip sliced across the girl's large brown nipple. She could feel the approval of the master watching as she drew her arm back again.

This time the tip cracked violently into the girl's other nipple, and again her screams rent the air, making Victoria wince slightly even as her pussy drooled.

She landed a dozen more blows across the girl's breasts, then went forward. She lifted each of the dazed, sobbing woman's legs up and spread it apart, linking a chain to the leather restraint around each ankle and then raising them so her pussy and buttocks stuck out lewdly and utterly defenceless.

She moved back and the girl's teary eyes looked at her imploringly, knowing what she intended. Victoria averted her eyes guiltily, looking down at the woman's cleft as the whip slashed in.

Victoria moved forward again with smelling salts and the girl moaned and wakened dazedly. When Victoria went back to use the whip the master raised his arm.

"Use her," he ordered.

"Yes, master!"

She moved forward and around the young girl, gripping her curly blonde hair and yanking her head back. She smiled into the girl's tormented eyes, then reached down her own body to the fat strap-on dildo there between her legs. It curved up and she placed the tip against the young teen's shaved and lewdly exposed slit then drove it up inside her.

The girl groaned helplessly as Victoria eagerly pressed her leather covered breasts in against the girl's own plump orbs. She took the girl's hair in one hand and slipped the other down onto her wounded buttocks, digging her fingers into the soft flesh as she plunged her tongue into the girl's mouth.

Her hips moved quickly in and out, the dildo sliding furiously back and forth between the girl's pussy lips as Victoria raped her.

She felt almost light-headed as the rush of shocked pleasure rose within her. The girl was obviously new, almost brand new, and she was raping her. That was an amazing thing, but even though she felt some guilt she couldn't suppress the excitement that caught at her mind and body.

She thrust harder and faster, the little pad at the base of the dildo grinding against her sensitive clitty as she raped the girl. Behind her she felt one of the men slide his hands over her back, then spread her legs as she felt his cock push against her anus.

Soon she was sandwiched between him and the girl, gasping in pleasure, shaking with excitement as she raped the younger girl and was in turn sodomized by the master. Then the orgasm crashed down around her and she cried out in pleasure, jamming her soft breasts into the other girl's as she chewed on her throat.

"There are no other Jewish girls there," Sarah said anxiously.

"You're sure?"

"Yes, master. I mean...uhm, yes."

"I'm afraid that only leaves one possibility," Paul sighed.

He sat in a large, stuffed chair in his suite while Sarah knelt beside him, her wrists chained together behind her back.

"You mean she's dead, Paul?"

"You can call me master, slut."

She pouted unhappily and he smiled and stroked her head.

"That too, though perhaps I should have said two possibilities."

"What's the other?"

"The barn."

Her eyes widened and she bit her lip.

"I uh - you don't want me to go there, do you, master?"

"Hmm? No, I don't think so."

Sarah heaved a sigh of relief.

"What's the matter, little slut? Don't you think you'd make a nice cow?" he teased, reaching out and pinching her nipple.

"I heard things about it," she gulped, fighting a sudden rising tide of sexual heat within her groin.

"So have I. Well, I'll see if I can pay a visit. Unfortunately, they don't let even the members be alone around the cows. They're kept for strictly regimented breeding programs and they don't want some horny guy like me mucking things up by planting the wrong seeds."

"Does that mean we have to leave her here, master?"

"No, what I need to do is get someone in there," he said in annoyance. "You'd be ideal but they'd never breed a Jew, and you're not pretty enough anyway."

She pouted again and he pinched her nipple and slid a

hand down her belly and between her legs. Sarah mewed helplessly, arching her back and grinding her pussy down on his finger as he stroked it along her cleft.

"You're a lovely young thing, Sarah," he said tolerantly. "But they have exceptional standards for their breeding program. Only the most perfect looking women are accepted, with magnificent bodies as well."

He pulled his finger away and she shuddered and caught her breath. "I might know a girl, master," she gulped.

"What girl? Where? Here? Don't be absurd, little slut."

He eased his finger back down against the now moist slit and she groaned anew, her legs trembling.

"She was a... a polisssssss..."

He pulled his finger back and frowned. "What?"

She swallowed repeatedly then licked her lips.

"She was a policewoman in England."

"Glory be! Now that is interesting. How did she get here?"

"She found out about this place and told her superior but he was... he is one of them."

"Hmmm. Is she pretty?"

"Very pretty, yes very pretty."

"But how is her mind?"

"I don't know."

"Perhaps we can have her over a few times to judge. Then, possibly we can convince them to take her in there at the barn."

"But don't they drug the girls there?"

"Yes. I'll have to find a way around that, of course."

He slipped his finger back between her legs, thrusting it up inside her then bringing his thumb down against her clitoris. She cried out softly, arching her back, grinding her pelvis against his fingers as he smirked down at her.

The training was only half over but already he saw some very pleasant changes in Sarah's personality. He pinched down on her clit, crushing it against his finger and half collapsed against the chair, jerking spastically as she shuddered violently.

Then she cried out again, her head rocketing backwards as she climaxed, the pain blown away, shredded by a massive short circuit in her nervous system as the pleasure screamed through.

Her orgasms seemed more powerful now, he noted, and she had less inhibitions. She also was obsessed with sex and in constant heat. He could hardly wait until she'd finished the course to see what she was like.

Still, he needed her in some state of capable mind. So he was letting her get some sleep and feeding her high protein food each night, strictly against what he'd been told to do by her trainers. Possibly doing that would help the other one, the English girl, and she, in turn, might be able to help them as well.

Meghan was doing her best to withstand the brainwashing and training, but she knew in her heart she was failing. She was haunted by the knowledge she was slipping away bit by bit, becoming the brainless sex crazed slave girl they were intent on making her.

She tried her best, she was always tired, and always hungry, and her mind wouldn't quite work right. It was so much easier to do as they wanted.

And her body seemed to be constantly in rut now. It took very little to make her entire nervous system thrum with desire, to turn her from a confident, intelligent, independent young woman to a panting, gasping, whimpering slut who would do anything to have her needs seen to.

She had never felt such need in her life before, nor ever felt so much pleasure. The orgasms were more intense and protracted than she would have believed possible before, some lasting well over a minute and leaving her drained and exhausted.

It wasn't that she didn't like this, of course, but in her heart and soul Meghan did not want to be someone's plaything for the rest of her life. Perhaps in bed, perhaps then, but not in her everyday life, not telling her when to rise and when to sleep, what to eat, or even if she could eat, what to wear (or not), and everything else. She didn't want to be a slave!

She was all ready to return to her kennel at the end of the day when one of the overseers led her down a strange hallway and up a flight of stairs. Then he ordered her to stand and handed her leash to a man not wearing the familiar uniforms of the overseers and servitors.

"You will ensure she is properly bound and equipped before going to sleep, sir?" the overseer asked deferentially.

"Of course," the strange man said.

"Very good, sir. She's making excellent progress."

"So I've heard from my little minx. I'll take good care of her, no fear."

Meghan saw one of the other 'students', a dark eyed girl named Sarah, standing next to the strange man.

Then she was led away, Sarah following, and she got to see some of the club. She looked around curiously, eyes wide as she saw the plush, luxurious surroundings she was led through.

They brought her into an elevator eventually, then after that into a lovely, spacious apartment where, she guessed, the man lived.

"My name is Achmed. You will call me master," the man said.

"Yes, master," she replied at once.

He sat down and the two slaves took up their customary position, on their knees, sitting on their heels, knees spread wide. Their wrists, of course, were shackled behind their backs.

"So, little slut. Your name is Meghan?"

"Yes, master. I'll be given a new name when I graduate, master."

"Really? Maybe I should give my little slut a new name too. What do you think of that, Sarah?"

"I like my name as it is," she replied.

Meghan blinked in surprise, waiting for the girl to be beaten, but Achmed only smiled.

"And you, Meghan? What new name would you like?"

"Whatever you want, master," she said.

"What about Hilda?"

Meghan blinked again and frowned slightly. "Uhm, yes, master. that's a lovely name, master."

"No it's not, it's hideous."

"Yes, master," she said in confusion.

"Tell me, Meghan, are you as much a slut as this one?" He pointed at Sarah.

"Yes, master. I'm a filthy, worthless slut. I'm only good for fucking."

He snorted, then reached out and slid his hand through her soft hair. "Come here, slut," he ordered, pulling on her hair and pulling her forward.

She shuffled forward on her knees, then crawled up over his lap, laying on her belly as he released her hair and ran his hand down onto her plump round buttocks, stroking and squeezing them.

"My. What a lovely behind you have for a policewoman," he said. "Do all policewomen have such lovely behinds?"

"I don't know, master," she gulped.

"So your own boss turned you in, hmm? That was very nasty of him. He betrayed your trust."

"Yes, master," she said, squirming a little as his fingers eased in between her thighs and cupped her pubic mound.

"Do you hate him for that?"

She hesitated in confusion. What would it be safe to say?

"Well, there you were a police constable, a respected

183

member of society, a person with some authority, and now you're a filthy little fuck slave who gets spanked if she doesn't please her master. Don't you think it was terrible for him to do that to you?"

"I... yes... I mean no, master."

"Why?" His middle fingers stroked deftly along her cleft, feeling the moisture beginning to seep out now as the girl squirmed in his lap.

"I... I don't know!" she gasped.

"Why?"

"Because... because I'm a filthy slut!" she gulped. "This is what I was meant to do!"

"But you were a police constable, eh?" He eased his fingers up against her clitty for the first time, rubbing in a slow, circular motion.

"I think it was wrong of him to betray you," he said as he stroked. "I think you should feel that way too. I think you should be very upset at him for betraying you to the very people you were hunting, for causing you to be kidnapped and raped and tortured. I think it's wrong for you to forgive him for that. I think you should escape, and then you can inform on him."

"Y-y-yes, m-master," she gasped, pushing her behind up as she ground herself against his fingers, gasping and whimpering as the heat poured through her body. "Oh! Oh! Oh! Oh!" she gasped.

"It's all very well for you to be a good little slut, of course," he continued, his fingers sinking deep into her throbbing sex. "There's nothing wrong with being a fuck hungry little trollop who swallows cock every night. But still, you probably liked being a police constable, didn't you?"

"I-I-yessss," she groaned.

"And after all, you can't fuck all day long and all night too. So instead of being a happy little police person in the day and then fucking your brains out every night, here you'll

184

be serving meals, cleaning floors and doing all sorts of other unpleasant tasks."

He wiggled his fingers around in her sopping depths, pushing against the elastic silk walls of her sheath, then brought his thumb down against her clit as he began to pump his fingers in and out.

She whined in heat, bucking back against him wildly, bouncing on his lap as her head jerked spastically. Her fingers twisted and jerked as she drew in great, ragged breaths of air.

Then she let out a choked cry of pleasure as she came, still writhing and humping feverishly against his fingers as he ground her clit between them.

He smiled as he raised his eyes to Sarah. She gave him a reproachful look, but he wasn't sure if that was because she was jealous or because he thought he oughtn't to be fingering the helpless little police girl like he was.

He motioned to her. "Come here, slut."

She got to her feet and moved closer, and he turned her and unclipped her wrists. "Go and get some of that food I put in the cupboard earlier," he ordered.

She nodded, seemed about to say something, then turned and padded into the kitchen.

He looked down at her, letting his hand coast back and forth over her lusciously rounded rump as he considered. She wasn't too far gone to at least recognize some reality. It might be possible that if he gave her a little sleep and food she'd be able to take the final training and then... And then what? How was he going to get her sent to the barn? She was attractive enough, with her sweet face, and had an excellent body, her breasts fuller and rounder than Sarah, her rear a perfect white apple.

But she was too young for them to want to breed her. That only left disciplinary problems. He could cause a few of those and demand she be sent to the barn. They might or might not agree with that.

Then he had a thought. That degenerate Englishman had a personal slave girl, and seemed easily influenced. Perhaps it would do better to have him send his personal slave to the barn. Now that he recalled his slave hadn't even been through training at all! He was sure he'd trained her but then the man was an imbecile. Surely it wouldn't be too hard for the girl to fool him.

Meghan was still gasping for breath. He smiled and slid a hand down around her ribs to cup and squeeze one of her delightful breasts. One or the other of them would surely be able to get it done, he thought. Maybe he could get both sent to the barn.

So long as he could do something about the drugs, of course.

21

"Yes, I see." Paul nodded as if impressed, looking around the small room.

It was where new breeders were inducted. As he understood it the process involved at least a couple of days of complete isolation in a special chamber where the girl was trained by a combination of pleasure and pain stimulus. Before and after that she was given a combination of drugs to suppress her personality, dull her sense, and make her happy and content.

However, the drugs had to be carefully administered in the precise amounts. First a complete physical would be done, telling them everything about the girl's blood chemistry, weight and fitness, then the correct combination of drugs would be measured out, and finally applied.

More importantly just being here and chatting he had

noted a glaring security lapse on their part. All the girls were locked within the barn each night, and closely monitored each day as they walked around in the fields. However, the lab itself was not alarmed, and only an ordinary lock was on the door. Some of the windows didn't even seem to be closed, let alone locked!

Well, of course, the members wouldn't be expected to want to interfere with the processing of the breeders, or want anything that was in the lab. It should be a simple matter to sneak back and open the chamber each night, and either interfere with her drugs or give her something to counteract their affect.

But first he had to get the girl here.

After her first night's sleep and a dose of high protein food Meghan seemed a lot more alert, and seemed to understand she couldn't tell anyone. The second morning was even better. She almost seemed human when he spoke to her in the morning.

Happily, she ground herself against his fingers like a bitch in heat without any hesitation at all, so he wasn't interfering with that aspect of her training.

He was running out of time, though. He'd already spotted his third target. She was indeed one of the breeders, sent to the barn as punishment by her master, but already she seemed to have lost all sense of purpose or initiative.

She certainly wasn't going to be any help. In fact, none of his targets were, with the possible exception of Gabrielle. So if he could get both those sluts, Meghan and Amanda, to help, that would be a major step forward. They could help the three targets while he covered them.

The only way out was by helicopter, of course. Both he and Sarah were excellent pilots, and the security was low key at the heliport except when helicopters were taking off. There was concern that escapee slaves might sneak aboard a helicopter, but none that they might actually steal one themselves, especially at night. They were too well bound, both mentally and physically.

That night he presented his plan to Sarah, who was less than enthusiastic. Then after another night of good food and some decent sleep - and after fucking her twice and fingering her to multiple orgasms - he approached Meghan with his idea.

"Meghan, honey. Do you want to go home?" he asked.

"Home? Hmmm. I... I don't know," she said warily.

"It's me here. You can tell me the truth," he reminded her.

"I like it here sometimes," she said. "But I would like to go home again."

"I know a way you can do it, but it would involved some pain at first."

"Pain?" She looked wary again.

"Yes."

"How?"

"There's a man I know. He's a nasty, cowardly man and likes to hurt pretty girls. I need him to be very mad at you."

"Why?" she asked worriedly.

"There's a place near the helipad - that's where the helicopters land. I need you to be placed into this place so you can unlock it from the inside and let me in."

"But... I don't understand."

"You don't have to. You only have to do what I tell you. Can you do that?"

"I think so."

He stroked her behind and then patted her head.

Amanda was kneeling obediently at Edward's heels when Achmed showed up with a naked blonde in tow. She saw Edward's interest immediately rise as he admired the girl's figure and face.

"Well, well," he said. "What a nice pretty pretty you have

188

there, Achmed."

"Yes. She is lovely, isn't she? She's in training. She's new here."

"Ah, yes, I believe I saw her earlier. In training, you say? How is you got hold of her?"

"I like mine before they're fully broken," Achmed said with a leer. "They're more spirited."

Edward nodded and chuckled knowingly, then gripped Amanda's hair suddenly and yanked her head up and back, forcing her to arch her back tightly.

"Know what you mean, old boy," he said with a grin. "I prefer them the same way."

"Yours is quite lovely, I must say." Achmed looked at Amanda closely and she lowered her eyes.

"Built for long hard rides," Edward said, relaxing his grip.

"She looks obedient," Achmed said.

"She, er, she knows not to disobey me," Edward said proudly. "Besides, she's got a big crush on me. Haven't you, pet?"

"Yes, master," Amanda said in an eager, breathy voice.

Meghan snickered, and both Amanda and Edward stared at her in surprise.

"What was that, slut?" Edward demanded, glaring at her.

"Nothing master," the blonde replied meekly.

Edward rose to his feet and gripped her by the collar, yanking her forward, and the girl suddenly lifted her knee and slammed it into his crotch. Amanda's jaw dropped in astonishment as Edward staggered backwards and fell into his chair, his eyes bulging as he held himself. Achmed gripped the girl's tousled blonde hair and yanked it up and back, forcing her to her toes as she moaned in pain.

"Sorry about that, old boy," he said. "As I said, she's only in the training program. She hasn't actually, well, completed it yet, you see."

Amanda watched curiously as Edward's face turned a

variety of interesting colours before settling back to his normal pasty white.

"I... I want her..."

"I'll see that she's soundly thrashed for that, old boy," Achmed said.

"She should be... be..."

Amanda wondered if he was going to have a heart attack. She certainly hoped so.

"Calm yourself, my friend," Achmed said. "I will make you a deal. I will trade you girls for the night. You may do with this one as you choose, provided she is able to take part in her courses in the morning. I will borrow your girl here and make use of her before I sleep."

"Yessss," Edward hissed. "I'll take the filthy little whore and show her some manners!"

Amanda felt sorry for the blonde, who, in fact, looked quite sorry for herself too, but she was glad to be taken with Achmed and leave them behind. He was another pig like Edward, but perhaps she would learn something new about this place from him, and every bit she learned made it more likely she would find a way out some day.

Soon they were upstairs, with another girl who looked somewhat Arabic like Achmed.

"You have not been here long, Amanda?" Achmed asked.

"No, master," she replied, kneeling before him.

"Come here and sit on my lap," he ordered.

She obeyed and had her lay back. His hand moved slowly over her body, and she squirmed lightly. Edward had not loaned her out to anyone yet. So he and those two silent black giants had been the only ones who had raped her. He had been too pompous and proud of his possession. Each man who asked only made him feel even more pompous.

Still, she had long known that eventually she would have to have sex with many men. All the slave girls did. And she,

she thought bitterly, was a slave girl now.

He ran his fingers through her long hair with a wistful look in his eyes. "Such lovely hair," he said.

Then his hand moved down to her chest, cupping and squeezing her breast before easing in between her legs. He was far gentler than Edward, and far more knowledgeable about the female body. Despite herself Amanda started to feel a faint pleasure within her as he fingered her bare cleft.

"Sarah. Come here," he said.

The other girl rose and shuffled forward on her knees, and then, to her surprise, Amanda saw him reach forward and undo her shackles. The girl then turned around and looked at her.

"Spread your legs, Amanda," Achmed whispered.

Amanda hesitated, staring at the girl, feeling a sudden anxious worry. Then she shifted her knees apart slowly.

"Further. Wide apart," he ordered.

She winced but obeyed, swallowing nervously as the girl smiled up at her and leaned in, pushing her mouth against her sex.

Amanda gasped as the girl's tongue slipped between her tight pussy lips. She felt a sudden instinctive desire to kick out at her, even though she knew the girl was only obeying the filthy Arab's orders.

This too she had anticipated, for she'd seen some of the displays put on in the common areas where the slave sluts performed disgusting acts on each other for the amusement of the members.

Still, she'd never experienced any kind of sexual contact with a woman before, and was not anxious to feel it now.

She laid her head back and closed her eyes, then started to moan softly, pretending to be aroused as the girl's fingers stroked her soft pussy mound, then eased her pubic lips aside for her tongue.

It wasn't that bad, she told herself. She was certainly better off than that foolish blonde girl. God only knew what that swine Edward was doing to the poor girl now.

Meghan's eyes bulged and she let out a choked cry of agony as his knee slammed up into her soft pussy pad again, then again.

She was bent over a table, and each time he jerked her legs apart and slammed his knee up into her crotch the force was so great she was actually lifted off her feet. Again and again he pounded his knee into her as her mind swirled with nausea and agony and dizziness.

Then, his face still scarlet with rage, he dragged her off the table by the hair and led her to a round padded bench of some sort. He led her over it and made her straddle it, the rounded padding forcing her legs wide like a saddle.

Instead of sitting her down on it, however, he bent her far over, pressing her chest down against a wider, flatter area next to the saddle.

He gripped her hips and jerked her backwards, and she winced as she felt herself slide an inch or so back onto a narrow, rising lump, a hard lump that pressed up sharply against her pussy, especially against her clit. Unlike the rest of the saddle there was no padding on the lump, which was about three inches long and two wide. Instead it was covered in sandpaper.

And that was pressed up directly against her soft pussy flesh, directly against her clitoris.

In fact, as she groaned and shifted her weight, she realized that her breasts were also pressing down into sandpaper now.

A strap went over her waist to hold her down, then her ankles were lifted up and bound back behind her.

She gasped as she felt herself pierced, felt something hard and thick and round pushing down her pussy tunnel. It started to buzz and shake and she realized it was a vibrator.

Then he left, after giving her behind a smack.

She stared wonderingly at the door. Surely he was going to punish her more than that. Achmed, who's real name was Paul, if she got it right, said he was a nasty pervert and liked to hurt girls.

She felt relieved, though she wondered if he mightn't soon return with some kind of instrument of torture.

She let out a sigh and squirmed a little as her juices started to flow, and she felt the familiar heat between her legs. She made no effort to fight it. If he did return she had come to realize that being heavily aroused could help act as a shield to pain, so it would be helpful to...

"Ow," she gasped.

She had instinctively ground her pussy against the wedge pushing up into it, a wedge covered in sandpaper.

She would have to stop.... stop... she would have to not do... that.

"Oww," she gasped, squirming helplessly, the pleasure rising, the heat and lust foaming and swirling through her body, growing greater and more powerful with each passing minute.

"Oww! God!" she gasped, slapping herself mentally.

Perhaps just a little bit.

She tentatively rubbed back... just a bit. She winced, but it wasn't... wasn't too terrible...

She groaned as her hard nipples mashed down against the sandpaper beneath, then moaned louder as she jabbed her clitty back onto the sandpaper too hard.

"Stupid!" she gasped to herself.

She tried to hold still, then, her mind filled with lust, she told herself it would be all right if she just did it gently.

She moaned as she scraped her pussy and clit back against the wedge again and again. The pleasure was rising like gusher, but so was the pain. But the pleasure had her in its control, and she felt an orgasm building. She bucked back, thinking, not that she was thinking clearly, that the orgasm would relieve the pressure and let her stop.

She shuddered violently, forgetting her decision to rub only very gently, mashing her wet pussy back hard, gasping and moaning as she jammed her sex back against the sandpaper, as it ground back and forth furiously against her eager clit and drooling pink pussy opening.

She went still, gasping, moaning. Her pussy felt sore... raw, and she berated herself for doing that to herself.

But the vibrator continued to buzz away inside her, and the burning continued to rise, and she moaned as she jammed herself back softly against the wedge.

22

"God! I... Oh! Oooohhhhh!"

Amanda jerked helplessly, eyes wide as an orgasm rushed over her. Her legs bounced in mid-air as the girl buried her face between her legs and sucked furiously on her sparkling clitty.

She wanted to scream in denial, but couldn't control her voice as she came in helpless wanton carnal bliss, gasping and whining as she jammed her sex against the girl's hungry mouth.

Then she slumped back against him, panting for breath as he chuckled, his arms around her, his hands cupping and squeezing her breasts as the girl's tongue lapped softly at her overheated sex.

"Bastard!" she whispered.

"What was that?" he demanded, pulling back on her hair.

"Nothing, master," she gasped.

"I think you called me a bastard."

"I heard her," the girl said.

Amanda glowered at her and the girl smiled back.

"No, master," she said in a breathy voice.

"Lying to me?" he said. "I think you need a beating."

With that he turned her and then rolled her onto her belly. Amanda gulped as his hand caressed her backside. She felt a fury rising inside her at this lewd, casual, patronizing treatment. Bad enough when that slime Edward did it, but now every ignorant, drooling male she came into contact with would treat her like a mindless little sex toy!

"Ouch!" she yelped as his hand slapped down on her rear. He slapped her again, harder, then again, admiring the pink flush appearing on her white behind, then again and again, motioning Sarah to come to the side of the chair. She gripped the brunette's thighs and parted them, then pushed her face in between, licking and sucking on her pussy cleft as the other girl gasped and squirmed helplessly.

He let Sarah lick for a minute, then motioned her back and cupped her mound, his fingers sliding into her and pumping steadily as they caressed her clit. He moved his other hand under her and kneaded one of her breasts as he chuckled tolerantly.

"Silly little thing," he murmured. "You know this is what you want. Your hot little pussy is what you live for."

He eased his hand back and let Sarah lick at her again, then smacked his hand down on her buttocks to make her jump and yelp. He slapped her again, then thrust his fingers into her, feeling the moisture and the heat within her body as he pumped them in and out. She started to grind herself back, then halted, shuddering.

He motioned to Sarah, pointing at one of the vibrators sitting nearby and she fetched it for him. He turned it on then carefully stroked the buzzing tool across the gorgeous brunette's aroused clitoris.

"You women," he sighed. "You're all slaves to your voracious sex organs anyway. Why can't you all understand that? You should all be delighted we've brought you here where you can be free to indulge your lovely bodies the way you always wanted to."

He eased the vibrator into her slick tunnel and then buried it inside her. She gasped and chewed on her lip, trying to resist the pleasure rising within her, then yelped as he gave her three swift slaps on the behind.

"But you need a stern hand," he said. "You girls need discipline or you'd be out rutting anything that moves all day long. You're all such complete slaves to your pussies!"

He jammed her clit up against the vibrator, rubbed it for a few seconds, the motioned Sarah forward once again. As Sarah licked away at the woman's clit he slapped her behind again. It was now a bright red, and the skin was quite warm to the touch.

Amanda clenched her teeth as the orgasm hit, then she rutted back against the girl's mouth, whimpering and moaning in delight and wonder at the force of it, her head rolling and jerkin fitfully as he squeezed one of her breasts and slapped her behind repeatedly.

"Climaxing again?" he scowled. "My, my, what a filthy little thing you are!"

Amanda gave a final buck and then collapsed, gulping in air as he snickered and pinched her nipple.

He lifted her up on his leg then, smirking at her as he tugged on her nipple.

"Now is the weedle geerl going to be nicer," he said in a babyish voice.

She glared at him indignantly. "Listen, you condescending little assho..."

She shut up abruptly, her eyes widening, and he laughed and released her nipple.

"So. Not quite so broken and trained as Sir Edward would believe, hmmm?"

"I... I don't know what you mean, master," she said cautiously.

"Tell me, lovely Amanda, do you like it here?"

"Of course, master," she gulped.

"And you want to spend the rest of your life here as a mindless fuck doll?" he demanded harshly.

She stared at him anxiously, then at Sarah.

"We want to leave," Sarah said. "Do you?"

"You can leave whenever you want," Amanda said.

"Yes, but you can't, nor can three other girls I came here to get."

"Who are you?" she whispered.

"A friend, if you're willing to have one."

"What do you want me to do?"

"Something... well... I need you to get into a certain place. And unlock it from the inside so I can get in."

"Me? I can't get anywhere. Edward keeps me under lock and key," she said bitterly, "or haven't you noticed these things don't even come off?"

She kicked one of her feet off, showing the manacle locked around her ankle.

"They'll come off with the proper tools." He reached behind her back and unclipped her wrist restraints, letting her pull her arms apart. "You can do something that will help us all escape."

"I told you Edward keeps me at his side constantly!"

"Yes, but if you make him mad he'll send you somewhere else to punish him, provided someone puts the suggestion into his head first."

"Where?"

"The barn."

"No way! I've heard about that place! They turn you into an animal!"

"I can make sure that doesn't happen. I can interfere with the drugs and isolation. It will cost you your hair, but in a couple of days we'll be out of here and you'll be back home."

She stared at him fearfully, then looked at Sarah, who

nodded.

"What do I have to do?" she gulped.

"The same thing Meghan did."

"The blonde? You made her do that!? Do you have any idea what he's probably doing to her now?"

"Yes, but she's willing to go through it to get into the barn. Are you willing to go through far less for your freedom?"

"I'll do whatever I have to," she said after a moment. "If I get killed well... I'm probably better off."

"Good girl," he said, smiling.

"Stop treating me like a child," she demanded.

"Certainly, if you wish. In the meantime..."

His hand slipped between her legs and cupped her mound.

"I'm not one of your helpless fuck toys," she said, pushing his hand back warily.

"But you are a woman, no? I'm sure it's been a while since you had a real man between your legs."

She gave him a cold look.

"Look at it this way, my dear. The only recent lovers you've had were those two rapists and Sir Edward. Wouldn't you like something more pleasant to remember sex by? And then there's Sarah. Sarah, you see is one of those mindless fuck toys you were referring to, and she can be quite entertaining. Can't you, my dear?"

He took Amanda's hand and pulled it down between Sarah's thighs, then brought it up against her sex. Sarah shuddered and pushed herself helplessly against it as Amanda watched in fascination.

"Bastard!" she groaned again, rolling her head back as Amanda's hand rubbed over her.

"You see?" Paul said with a smile.

He removed his hand and Amanda continued stroking against the girl's cleft.

"She isn't faking that? She gets that hot so easily?"

198

"Again and again and again," he said.

Amanda was simultaneously aroused and repelled. She'd never seen anyone that much a prisoner of their genitals before.

She stroked her fingers against the girl's clit, feeling a rush of superiority and conquest when the girl clasped her wrist and came, bucking and grinding herself against her fingers.

She continued to rub even as she felt Paul's fingers slip down to her own cleft. She licked her lips as she ran one of her hands up under Sarah's breast and squeezed experimentally.

"She's really hot," she whispered.

"As hot as they come," he whispered back. "Helpless to resist the pleasure you give her."

They drew Sarah up onto the bed and Amanda knelt between her legs, staring at her dripping sex opening. Then, with only a brief hesitation, she pushed her tongue forward and began to work it up and down against her clit.

She groaned as Paul entered her from behind, feeling a hot gush of liquid heat within her as he started to fuck her.

The girl writhed and whined under her, and Amanda felt a sense of power over her as she lapped at her clitoris. She pulled Sarah's pussy open and plunged her tongue down into her hole, wriggling it around experimentally, then thrust two fingers up the* small, tight opening, rewarded by a groan as the girl humped up against her.

Her own juices were flowing, she realized, and that made Paul's penetration painless and smooth. His pumping felt far more natural than what she'd had lately, and she was only a little surprised to feel the sexual pressure building up so rapidly inside her head.

Sarah gasped and bucked up against her face as she sucked on her clitty, then let out a long, drawn-out wail of pleasure that made Amanda's insides churn with heat.

It had been forever, she thought, since she'd really had sex. She didn't count anything that scumbag Sir Edward did, nor her shocking rape at the hands of those two monsters.

It felt so good to be giving pleasure to someone who wasn't evil, and so gooood to be getting it back.

23

Tears poured from Meghan's eyes as she shuddered again. Her groin was afire now, but not with pleasure. She had rubbed herself raw against the sandpaper. Her breasts ached as well, and yet she couldn't stop herself from doing it. The programming had taken too deeply already, and the pain simply melted into the pleasure.

But oh how it hurt!

Her sex felt like it was a raw, aching wound, and her mind, that part that functioned on anything but the most carnal level, was frantic that she would permanently harm herself, perhaps even grind her entire clitty off!

Or her nipples. Oh how they ached!

The vibrator continued to buzz, and she sobbed anew as she drove her aching pussy back against the sandpaper wedge, screaming now as the pain tore through her.

"Well, little slut," a voice said beside her. "Having a good time?"

"Please master! Please master! Please! I'm sorry, master! I'm sorry! Please! I'll fuck you, master! Please fuck me! Please! Please fuck my ass! Anything, master!"

He chuckled and slipped his hand down against her breast, then ground it harshly across the sandpaper below, making her scream in pain.

"So you're tired of jerking yourself off, hmm?"

"Please!" she gasped. "Anything! Anything!"

He pulled the strap off, then untied her ankles and lifted her off the saddle. Tears continued to stream down her face as she kissed his chest, then his belly and legs and crotch in desperate relief.

"Get your face down and your behind up, slut," he ordered.

"Yes, master! Yes, master!" she gasped, turning and bending over, then letting herself drop her shoulders against the floor.

He entered her harshly, cruelly, but the sodomy was actually a relief, for she had feared he would do her in the pussy and that would surely ache terribly. Instead all she received was a brutal sodomy.

She was almost smiling in gratitude when he was finished and yanked her to her feet.

"I'll never do it again, master! I promise!" she gasped. "I'm so sorry!"

"I'm sure you are," he said, leading her over to where a two by four sat propped between two wooden braces. It was on an edge, with the edge sticking up, and before Meghan understood what he intended he lifted her up and dropped her down straddling the two by four.

She screamed in shock and agony, her legs and body shaking as she tried to twist away, but he held her easily in place, laughing at her tears and pain.

"You'll be even sorrier when this night is over, you little bitch," he sneered.

He pushed her forward, letting her grind along the corner of the two by four, then dragged her back again. He repeated this several times, laughing as the wood dug up into her aching, raw pussy meat. Then he pulled her back to one side and drew a chain down from the ceiling. He undid the restraints around her wrists and then redid them quickly, after pulling them up high behind her back. He then attached the chain to them to lock them in place.

She certainly couldn't support any of her weight on her arms in that position, nor could she climb off the two by four.

"Have a nice sleep," he said with a sneer.

Then he left and turned off the lights.

He had not pulled the vibrator out of her tight pussy when he sodomized her It was still there, driven up painfully deep, grinding against her cervix now even as it continued to buzz.

She sobbed in misery even as the pleasure began to burn inside her once more, and, unconsciously, she started to grind herself down against the wood below.

She was dazed when the light came on next. She hardly saw him as he moved up next to her and reached down between her legs. He pressed his long middle finger against her clit, jamming it down even harder against the corner of the two by four, and she convulsed in another orgasm, whimpering and shaking.

He grinned in delight, then lifted two heavy weights, each about twenty five pounds, and locked them to her ankle restraints by short chains.

With another fifty pounds of weight jammed down on her cleft, he left her again, this time until morning.

"Sir, it was our understanding the slave would be ready to resume her lessons in the morning," the overseer said in annoyance.

"She kicked me in the balls," Edward said peevishly. "So I punished her."

"Well?" the man demanded of another.

The man was examining her closely. He looked up with a sigh.

"Nothing permanent," he said. "But I don't think she ought to even sit down for a couple of days, much less undergo any further treatment."

The first man tsked in annoyance. "She's such a good

prospect too," he muttered.

Meghan swayed weakly before him, dazed and filled with pain. She bent over and groaned as one of the men sprayed an anaesthetic over her crotch, then rubbed in a lotion to help her skin heal.

Her mind caught at something she was supposed to do, but she was so bleary she could hardly remember, could hardly think.

"Give her a few days of rest and she can re-enter the program," the man said.

"Rest? We can't let her rest at this point in the training! That could ruin everything. The mental preparation..."

Meghan remembered what she was supposed to do then. She moaned and turned towards Sir Edward, then as he frowned down at her, kicked him as hard as she could in the crotch.

The two overseers gaped at her, and she kicked one of them in the crotch too. The second one grabbed her then, flinging her against the wall.

Both were angry and surprised. She had seemed much more biddable, and certainly should have been by now. Her violence said she was still resisting her treatments, and something stronger needed to be done.

Of course, they'd had stubborn girls before, and the final treatment always worked. The blonde girl would go to the barn and see how she liked living life as a breeder. After that she'd no doubt be far more biddable.

Sir Edward was infuriated that the little blonde slut had gone through his clever punishment and then turned right around and defied him by attacking him. Again! What was it with these little sluts that they continued to attack him there?

He was glad to see meek, beautiful Amanda when he left the blonde slut with the overseers and went to breakfast.

"I hope the blonde was properly chastised for her disrespect," Achmed said.

"She's been sent to the barn," Sir Edward snarled. "That will teach the little slut."

Which was when Amanda kicked him in the groin. Hard.

In fact, she kicked him several times, even kicking him when he was rolling on the floor and sobbing in pain. It wasn't until Achmed restrained her that several of the servitors who had rushed up were able to help him off the floor.

"Amazing," Achmed said. "But... I think I know just the punishment for this one. Send her to the barn with that blonde."

"Yes!" Sir Edward growled. "Yes. The barn! Take her to the barn!"

"Yes, sir," the servitors said.

They grabbed her and dragged her away.

Shortly after she found herself in the lab, anxiously looking around at all the equipment. Paul's idea had sounded like it might work, but there was no telling. She might lose her mind here.

She underwent a long physical examination, then lay strapped to a table for more hours while the results of tests came through.

Late that evening a doctor injected her with something that raised a haze of confusion around her mind.

They laid her back on the examination table with her head hanging over the edge, then an electric razor they cut off her long, beautiful hair, leaving only an ugly stubble behind. A coating of an oily substances was slathered over her head, and after a few moments she began to moan in discomfort.

They ignored her, and after a few minutes wiped off the jell to find her head clean and bare, without a trace of hair.

She was lifted onto a small bench inside a metal container, her wrists and ankles tightly bound. Her eyes rolled glassily as electrodes were taped to her head, breasts, and clitoris. Then her head was pulled down over the edge of the table. A tube was pushed forward and inserted in her mouth, then taped there. A catheter was pushed into her bladder, and the box was closed.

Paul was clad in black, and moved silently but quickly through the night, flitting from shadow to shadow as he made his way towards the barn. Once there it was child's play to unlock the laboratory and make his way inside.

Both boxes were closed and locked tightly with padlocks. He hadn't anticipated the locks but it was only a brief delay. Within ten minutes he had the first open and looked in to see Meghan, head shaved and pulled back over the end of the table, throat taut, breasts thrust upwards.

He licked his head appreciatively at the sight of her, watching as she quivered and jerked to some unknown stimuli. He slid a hand along her body, cupping a round breast, then moving his hand between her legs to stroke her clitty.

There wasn't a lot he could do here that wouldn't be noticed. However, taking a small chance he followed the wires leading from her headphones to a small tape recorder. He removed the tape, then went to a larger tape recorder sitting on a desk and played it.

It was quite obvious what they were looking to accomplish, and quite obvious how to short-circuit that. He started to speak into the machine, his message a different one.

She would pretend to obey, she would not speak except around him, but she would remember to unlock the barn door each night at midnight to see if he was there. If he wasn't, she would close and lock it again then go to sleep.

It took more time than he'd expected because of the lock and tape. And once he'd done it he cursed himself for being unable to copy the tape to use it for the other girl. He just didn't have the equipment on him, however.

He slipped the tape back into its continuous play machine then pressed play. Meghan was senseless from the drugs they'd given her, so he made no attempt to communicate with her. He closed and locked the box again, then moved to the shelves of vials and bottles. It took little time to find hers since it was numbered the same as a tattoo on her head.

He poured out most of what he found, replacing it with water. He had foreseen this, of course, and brought some food dyes from the kitchen. They hadn't even asked him what he wanted them for. He was a member, and if he wanted blue or red dye that was his business.

With the vials replaced he moved to the second box, sat beside it, and started to pick the lock. He was on the verge of success when the door opened and a man stood there looking at him in shock.

He cursed and jumped up, but the man slammed the door and ran away screaming at the top of his lungs. Paul ran out, but he could already hear shouting coming from nearby. He turned and raced away towards the beach, his mind working furiously.

The man had had too clear a sight of him to go back to his rooms. It wouldn't take long before they had him identified and then it would be a quick end.

He made his way to the beach and dove in. He knew the waters were mined further out, with small, sensitive anti-personnel mines designed to activate at a particular kind of splashing sound or motion.

In his pocket was a hand grenade, and when he had gone out far enough he surfaced.

Behind him he could see flashlight beams moving everywhere as the guard force searched for the intruder. He had to judge things carefully, and this was a desperation move, one likely to backfire if he didn't have luck on his side. He pulled the pin on the grenade then heaved it towards the mines before diving and swimming back towards the land as rapidly as possible.

He didn't get far, of course, before the grenade hit the

water and went off. The concussion set off several nearby mines.

Too near by.

The underwater concussion slammed into him with tremendous force, hurling him end over end and almost knocking the breath out of him. Stunned and gasping he splashed awkwardly away as new shouts rose from the land, coming closer.

He barely made it to a thick bush that jutted out over the water before collapsing, gasping in pain. His head ached and blood flowed freely from his nose. His chest felt like he'd cracked a few ribs, and he fought desperately to keep silent as the men looked out over the water, speculating on who had died.

Amanda heard soft voices in her ears, gentle, reassuring voices telling her that she must love the masters. That she must obey the masters. They told her of how shameful it was to disobey or to fail to please the masters. And they told her she must never speak. That she must only make a soft sound like that of a cow. Any spoken words would be punished, the voices said harshly, and sharp little crackles of electricity bit into her.

Several times a day a soft mush was pushed out of the tube and into the back of her mouth. When she failed to swallow a small plunger came in behind it, forcing the stuff ahead of it as it moved straight down her throat.

Hour after hour the voices continued to speak, continued to tell her how much she loved the master, how much she ached for their touch, how she lived to please them, how her body was theirs for their use, how she was created to serve the masters.

After the first couple of days the voices demanding love and obedience trailed off, replaced by the soft mooing of female voices. Whenever she heard the mooing a soft buzz of electricity made her clitoris and nipples tingle. In fact, she had several orgasms. Then she would hear a woman speak, and the tingle would turn into jagged aching pain.

She came to dread the sound of women's voices, to fear them, to cringe from them.

Several days later she was lifted out of the box, and given another injection. The haze around her mind grew more firm. A second injection made her smile stupidly, happy for no reason she could discern.

Odd booties were strapped and locked to her feet, and when they ordered her to stand she screamed in pain as the soles bit into her feet.

That lesson learned they slipped a very large ring through her pierced nose, attached a leash, and led her on all fours behind them and out into a field. They walked her around to the back of the barn, then inside and over to a small stall. There the chain was removed, but her ring was attached to a small hook over a nozzle which was forced into her mouth.

Her wrists were locked down to bolts in the floor, and her knees pulled apart and chained. Then two small clear plastic cones attached to hoses were pushed up against her breasts directly over her nipples. They sucked, the suction holding them in place.

They left her there like that for much of the day. She was fed through the tube, and was able to swallow on her own. The suction hoses on her breasts sucked with a strong, rhythmic pattern that soon had her nipples burning and aching. She whimpered unhappily, though she wasn't certain why.

They removed her and set her to wander in the field for the remainder of the day with the other breeders.

The next morning she was placed in the stall again, and once again the tubes sucked on her aching nipples for hours before she was turned loose into the field.

24

Meghan smiled stupidly as they set her out into the fields. She longed to rub her aching breasts but worried about whether she ought to have that reaction... or any reaction. She was outraged at the way she'd been treated, stunned at the enormity of what she understood they were doing to the women here.

All around her women walked around naked, some with heavy bellies indicating pregnancy. Several times that first day she reached up to pat her bald head, amazed and furious at her loss of hair, and worried that it would never grow back.

Her time in the box had been a nightmare, and she shuddered ever time she remembered it. At first she'd been so skunked on whatever they'd given her that she hadn't even realized the passage of time. But as the chemicals had worn off and were replaced by ones she guessed Paul had fooled around with her awareness began to return.

And with it her situation, her tight bondage and aching head, the never ending words, most of them Paul's, and the electrical shocks and tremors which had alternately burned into her or set her insides to burning themselves.

And that mush she'd had to eat, which was disgusting and tasteless. She had no idea how long she'd been held helpless but it seemed like forever. She thought she'd go mad if it hadn't stopped.

Then being placed in that stall and having those cups hooked to her breasts. It was obvious what those were for, and she found that another stunning outrage.

She had met that other girl, Amanda, the one who was also supposed to be helping, but for some reason she didn't seem to have resisted their treatment.

Now any time she tried to come closer the wary woman

hurriedly walked away. There was no way Meghan could approach her without drawing the attention of the 'cowboys' as their keepers called themselves.

That night she was led into the barn and placed in a stall with her nose ring hooked up to a small chain. She was allowed to lie on her side, but her wrists were strapped behind her and her ankles were strapped together.

This frightened her, for it meant, she thought, that she wouldn't be able to do as Paul wanted and unlock the doors. She noticed that none of the other women she could see were strapped in that manner and wondered why she had been singled out.

The next day and the next and the next she was strapped tightly every night, but then they stopped, apparently satisfied she was now a safe little creature and would not try to escape. All they did was chain her nose ring to a ring set in the end of her stall, as they did with the others.

After dark fell the women were herded into the barn and an hour or so later the barn door was locked, leaving them alone in the dark. At that point Meghan would rise and go into one of the nearby offices, which were never locked. She'd sit down and listen to the radio for a while, and poke through the papers there as she waited for midnight.

Just before midnight each night she crawled to the doors, then unlocked them and peered out, hoping Paul would show up. When he didn't, she closed and locked the doors, then returned to her stall, put the nose chain back in her ring and fell asleep.

Time passed, day after day. Each morning she endured the milking process, and after weeks she noted her breasts were starting to swell and were becoming increasingly tender, the nipples more and more sensitive. One day she was startled to feel small drops of liquid squirting out of her enlarged nipples.

Each day after that produced larger amounts, until they,

like the other cows' breasts squirted small thin streams down the tubes during each milking. Oddly enough she found this arousing. Now that her breasts were accustomed to the milking cups they didn't ache any more, or at least, did not ache in the same way.

Instead her tender breasts throbbed and pulsed with pleasure during and after each milking, so much so that she had to cup and stroke them when nobody was looking, and several times once released she crawled rapidly to a far corner of the field, lay on her side and masturbated with as little movement as possible, gasping and moaning through a wonderful orgasm.

She had to keep such behaviour discrete, however. None of the other cows seemed to possess any kind of sex drive, nor much in the way of intelligence.

One day, a good month after she had been there, she and several others, including Amanda, were singled out and herded over to the far side of the field, then made to line up and go into a small fenced-in enclosure.

There were a half dozen of the cowboys there, and most of them were holding tightly to ropes that were locked to the collars of naked men.

Meghan's eyes widened at that, though none of the others seemed to take any notice. The men were wild-eyed, almost crazed as they stared at the women. They lunged towards them, trying desperately to get at them, and the men holding their ropes had to yank them back and whip at them with large sticks to keep them back.

It was dreadfully obvious that both men had erections, immense, monstrous erections that jutted down from their loins. Though both men were extremely handsome to the point of prettiness to look on, Meghan had no desire to make either of their acquaintance.

She watched nervously as the first two women, including the Amanda girl she noted, were led placidly forward.

Two low posts were sunk into the ground, and atop each post was a kind of rounded leather saddle. Meghan watched Amanda as she was led to the saddle, placed across it, then had her wrists chained down on the one side while her knees were pulled wide and chained apart on the other.

Still the woman just knelt there, unaware of what was going on.

One of the men bent over behind her holding a squeeze bottle with a long plastic hose. He inserted the hose into her pussy cleft and squeezed the bottle several times before slowly withdrawing the tube. Meghan saw a gooey substance oozing out of Amanda's pussy.

One of the men was led over, and the tube was pointed at his shockingly large penis, then more goo was poured over it.

It was, she assumed, lubrication of some sort.

There were three men clinging to him by now as he hurled himself against the ropes, trying madly to get at the lewdly displayed rear of the cow now firmly locked down.

Amanda turned around and eyed him nervously for the first time.

Then the man was released and he hurled himself atop her with a howl of exultation. Meghan stared, mouth wide as he mounted her, ramming his cock into her without a second's hesitation, producing a long howl of pain from Amanda.

The man rutted at her frenziedly, hammering his loins into her shapely rear. Meghan winced as he heard the solid pounding of his body against her buttocks and felt her guts churning as she watched, knowing they intended the same for her.

She wondered if she could stand it, if she could possibly go through that without revealing herself. The woman next to Amanda was also being ridden furiously, and like Amanda was sobbing and mooing desperately.

The rutting at least did not last long. The men signalled

their climax with howls of pleasure, then were yanked free and dragged away. Meghan could see the gaping pussy openings of the two sobbing, mooing women and felt an odd twinge of heat along with her fear.

She fought it, but she did not have the same mindless state as the other cows, and had been conditioned before coming here to be a nymphomaniacal tramp. After her initial shock at the brutal breeding program she witnessed the next set of coupling with more of a jaded eye.

It had been a while, more than a month, she thought, since she'd last had a cock inside her, and though she was not eager for the kind of wild screwing the cows were being subjected to she did miss being taken herself.

The two women were done and released with slaps on their rounded behinds, then Meghan and another woman were led forward. She desperately tried to appear unconcerned, like the others, as they led her over the padded saddle then strapped her wrists and legs into place, her rear up and out and terribly vulnerable.

Two new bulls were led in, growling and gnashing their teeth as they stared at the cows placed before them. Meghan tried to keep her eyes from showing her alarm as she looked at them.

The nozzle was slipped up deep into her pussy and slowly pulled back as an oily substance was pumped into her. She felt her pussy warm slightly as it tingled inside her.

Then the bulls were released. She braced herself, breathless and filled with terror at what would happen to her if she gave herself away.

The man made incomprehensible animal sounds as he slammed against her. His cock thrust at her thigh, then found her sex and rammed up with brutal fury.

She screamed, even as the other woman did, the sound one of pure pain, instinctive and helpless. His mighty cock tore her pussy wide and thrust up into her like a spear, impaling her in a heartbeat as his powerful fingers dug into her flanks and ground himself against her.

Her pussy was in agony, at first, and her mind reeled. She sobbed at the pain, pulling instinctively at the bonds holding her. Barely, she remembered to moo, the sound exploding from her as the pain tore across her nervous system.

He started rutting almost instantly, his thick prong rasping across her aching pussy lips, tearing in and out, pistoning like a frenzied machine inside her belly.

She came very close to cursing and pleading with them to stop several times. Only the fact that she knew, absolutely and utterly, that it would do not the slightest good stopped her. She mooed despairingly like the woman beside her until the pain began to slowly ease.

As that happened and her well-lubricated pussy began to cope with the furious drilling it was receiving her mind settled down somewhat. She grunted in time to his pounding, her buttocks soon bruised and aching and her insides numbed.

His long tool was pounding against her cervix, jarring her insides, making her orgasm shake and quiver, bruising her kidneys as it remorselessly hammered up deep into her belly.

It continued to be painful, yet the pain was little compared to what she had endured on the island, and she soon began to feel a lewd excitement at being pounded like that. It was almost like a wild animal was raping her instead of a man, and his big cock was sawing fiercely across her clitty with every motion.

She felt little quivers of pleasure beginning to roll through her, and closed her eyes, whimpering as she feared another kind of revelation for the men. They would be deeply suspicious of a cow having an orgasm during her breeding. For obvious reasons cows weren't supposed to enjoy breeding.

Meghan's body jerked and shuddered as her insides quivered and ached. She felt like she was being punched in the

214

guts again and again and again, yet even so there was the lewd sensation of pleasure mixed with her outrage.

They were attempting to breed her, she realized. That was both a compliment and a shocking indignity, yet all she could think about was how raw and carnal it was to be like this, being mounted like an animal, by an animal.

She felt the heat pouring through her, sizzling up and down her spine and seeping through into her nervous system. She found herself instinctively rutting back, or trying to. Her bonds kept her from most motion.

The pounding of his cock left her breathless, and the sounds she made, gasping, groaning, sobbing, were consistent with that of the other cow being mounted. But the reason for those sounds began to shift, just as the sounds themselves shifted subtly.

Soon, Meghan knew she would not be able to stop herself from climaxing. Her body was tensed and filled with sexual pressure as the brutal raping continued, as the man growled and slobbered onto her back, his hips blurred as he rammed himself into her aching behind.

Then it hit, and she cried out, the sound, luckily, easily interpreted as pain. She tried to keep her mouth shut, and gurgled in mindless ecstasy as the orgasm tore though her.

Her head jerked back again and again in what was an obvious signal had the men been watching. But they had grown bored with the sight and were gathered in a corner chatting.

She shuddered violently, jerking spastically in her bonds for long, long seconds, then collapsed as the man spewed what felt like gallons of his semen up into her aching, weary body.

The men came and pulled him off, then unstrapped her and slapped her on the behind. She crawled away weakly, moaning, her insides and buttocks raw and sore.

She was released back into the main pasture, where she

rubbed her aching behind and cupped her burning, swollen sex.

For seven straight days she and the others were brutally raped by the bulls, then they were set free to wander for another week before being tested for pregnancy.

25

Gabrielle did not look up as Jubal opened the door of her cage. She could not have even if she had wanted to. The cage was small, barely large enough to contain her kneeling body, and she was tightly bound.

"You are enjoying yourself too much in there, Jewess," Jubal said with a sneer. "I have come to bring you a pleasurable companion."

A servant came in and unfastened the wires that bound her, then dragged the exhausted woman out of the cage and massaged some life back into her cramped legs as Jubal looked on.

"Since you enjoyed your time with that little Jew lesbian so much I have brought you another one. Even better. This one is not a Jew. Still, she has much experience with perverted sluts like you, so I'm sure she will have you squirming in no time."

He pushed the servant aside and grabbed her by the arm, yanking her to her feet, then half dragged her out of the room and flung her across the floor. She landed in a tumble, fetching up against the legs of someone with a gasp of pain.

She looked up and her eyes widened. It was a woman. She wore stiletto heeled leather boots that rose almost to her thighs and elbow length matching gloves. A kind of halter pressed in under her large breasts, lifting them up. The sides of the halter pulled in on either side of her chest, pressing her breasts together. The straps then curved in around the tops of her breasts, criss crossed her chest, and went over her shoulders.

But it was her groin that drew her attention, for she wore a strange assembly of straps, and protruding from them was an enormous black leather cock of sorts, curving slightly upwards.

The woman was attractive, with her dark hair pulled back behind her tightly. She smiled, but it was not the soft smile Gabrielle remembered from Sarah. This smile was cold and hungry.

"Isn't she beautiful, little slut?" Jubal said.

Gabrielle moaned softly.

The woman reached down, gripping the sides of Gabrielle's head, pulling her up to her feet. Gabrielle stood there, staring, gulping in air as the woman smiled. Then she yanked her head forward and crushed her lips down, her tongue driving into her mouth.

Gabrielle recoiled as her breasts made contact with the other woman's but the woman's fingers dug into her skull, keeping her in position. The woman twisted her around and jammed her back hard against the wall, pressing her own body against her, grinding her flesh against Gabrielle as her tongue flittered around in her mouth.

The woman reached down, cupping Gabrielle's breast, squeezing it roughly, twisting the soft flesh as Gabrielle gasped in pain. She bent then, chewing on her breast, her teeth digging into the soft flesh, biting her nipples.

She straightened and reached down to the leather dildo, one hand sliding down to squeeze Gabrielle's buttocks, jerking leg apart as she pushed the dildo against her bare crack and shoved it inside.

"Please," Gabrielle gasped, the sound barely audible.

The woman thrust in deeply, and Gabrielle cried out, thrown up and back hard, the pain intense as the thing punched deep inside her. The woman bit down on her throat, grinding her hips against her, grinding her breasts against her as Jubal looked on and snickered.

Gabrielle whimpered and gasped as the woman gripped her bruised bottom with both hands, the leather covered fingers digging in bruisingly hard. Her hips bucked forward again and again, thrusting the thick leather cock up into Gabrielle's belly with powerful pumping motions.

She tried to pull her head aside, but the woman's mouth followed her, her lips and tongue ravenous as she ground herself against her, jamming her back against the wall.

Suddenly she pulled back, the dildo tearing free from Gabrielle's aching sex. She flung the startled girl forward so she fell onto her knees, then put a foot against her backside and pushed hard so she was flung forward onto her belly.

When Gabrielle rolled over the woman had ripped the dildo thing off her and her loins were now bare and as shaved as Gabrielle's own. She straddled the prone woman, and Gabrielle looked up into her sex as the woman dropped to her knees above her face.

"Eat me," the woman said in English.

She lowered her sex, pinning Gabrielle's arms back with her knees, jamming her sex into Gabrielle's mouth. Gabrielle clamped her mouth shut, frantically trying to twist her head away. But the woman just ground her moist sex back and forth over her lips as Gabrielle was filled with disgust and horror.

"Lick her, you Jewess slut!" Jubal ordered.

She refused, keeping eyes and mouth closed as the woman continued to grind her sex against her mouth.

Jubal snarled a command and the woman dragged her up to her feet. Gabrielle made no effort to resist as her arms were bound up above her head to chains hanging from the ceiling, then her legs spread wide and locked to the floor.

The woman raped her with the dildo once more, then

sodomized her while Jubal watched.

"I will return. I have something special for this whore," Jubal snarled.

He left, and Gabrielle's head sagged. Her legs were so weak she all but hung by her wrists as the woman looked on.

"You look so hot like that," the woman whispered.

Her hands cupped her breasts, but much more softly than before, fingers gently following the round contours, avoiding the black marks of bruises. She bent, gently mouthing one aching nipple, her tongue soft and slowly as she licked and caressed it with her lips.

She kissed her throat, and shoulder, then gently on the forehead and cheeks before licking her way down her body. Gabrielle moaned as she felt the soft pink tongue sliding along her slit, then easing up between.

She remembered Sarah, and how lovely her tongue had felt there, remembered the only person who had been gentle with her since this nightmare began, and she felt a shudder run through her body. She let her head fall back, trying to ignore the woman, trying to ignore the sensations as her tongue slipped back and forth between her pussy lips, then rode up to gently stroke against her clitoris.

Yet this woman was, if anything, more adept at such perverted work than Sarah had been. Her tongue expertly teased and awakened the heat within her, setting her legs to trembling and her insides to steaming and twisting.

Her breaths became ragged and her mind began to float on a soft wave of pleasure as her hips ground forward into the woman's mouth. Pleasure swept up around her and folded it's arms around her, and she came, for the second time in her life, trembling violently in her chains, sobbing aloud as her nervous system burned with unfamiliar sensations.

She went limp, moaning. The woman continued to lick her, her hands sliding up her body to gently tweak nipples that now burned with pleasure, then around to caress soft buttocks. Her tongue pushed into her and wriggled around inside, then slipped upwards to tease her clitoris.

Her hips began a lewd grinding motion again as the pleasure rose within her. And suddenly the woman rose, moving to one side. She returned with a strange metal tube and pressed a button. It began to buzz, and the woman smiled, rubbing and rolling it against Gabrielle's soft, wet sex, then easing it gently up inside her.

Gabrielle felt her insides begin to shake in tune to the vibrations of the thing, felt the pleasure soaring, her mind bathing in it.

The woman moved behind her, picking up a riding crop, then she heard the family hiss as it cut through the air. An instant later it bit into her buttocks and she cried out in pain.

Yet this time the pain was mixed with pleasure, and when the crop landed again she felt a hard blast of sexual heat that all but quashed the pain.

Again and again the crop landed, rising up her body, cracking against her lower back, then her shoulders. The pain whirled around her but the pleasure was the hotter, and another orgasm tore through her dazed body as she pushed herself back, arching her back to raise her backside, sobbing in pleasure as the crop bit into it.

Paul looked out into the hall carefully, licking his lips worriedly. He was fairly sure they'd stopped looking for him, given him up for dead, but he didn't know that.

"What a bloody disaster," he muttered to himself.

The mine had been more powerful than he'd thought and the underwater explosion had stunned and nearly drowned him. He'd also taken a chunk of shrapnel in the leg that had forced him to lie up in hiding in a basement storeroom.

Fortunately, a slave girl had been sent down to fetch something. Naturally the girl was trained to obey any master, and that meant any male. She'd obediently fetched him a first aid kit, and kept him supplied with water and food while he hid out.

And, well, he was a man, wasn't he? Why shouldn't he make use of the lovely young brunette's willingly offered body? The girl, Lisa, was delighted to have him mount her each time she delivered his food.

In fact, he was going to make use of her in his plan for tonight. It was going to be hard. God only knew what had happened to Sarah during his absence, to say nothing of the two he'd sent to the cow barn. He was going to have to take his chances and hope luck helped out. Otherwise he was going to have to leave one girl behind, along with those two who had meant to help him.

"Here I am, master," Lisa whispered as she hurried up to him.

"About time," he muttered. "All right. You remember what I told you?"

"Yes, master. I think so."

He put on the clothes she'd brought then took her hand and hurried down the hall, sprinting towards the entrance to the public areas.

Once there he settled down and walked more sedately, with Lisa following behind. No one took much notice as they moved through the corridors.

He went downstairs to the private torture chambers. Miri was still hooded, and followed meekly along behind as Sarah held her leash. But Gabrielle was in use. She was standing, spread-eagled, chained in place as another woman used a riding crop on her naked body.

At first he assumed someone was there to watch the performance, but it soon became obvious the two were alone. The second woman was clad in thigh high stiletto-heeled boots, a tight leather corset that thrust her breasts up and out without concealing a single inch, a leather collar, and long black leather gloves. An enormous strap-on dildo stuck up and out from her loins as she drew her arm back and slashed the crop across Gabrielle's well-marked back.

There was obvious excitement in the strange woman's eyes, and for a moment he thought she might be the French girl he had heard was involved with the club, but when he pushed open the door she halted, dropped to her knees, and smiled at them.

"How may I serve you, master!?" she asked happily.

"That's Vicky," Lisa whispered. "She's from the pens, but they use her to punish other girls."

Paul moved forward, ignoring the kneeling girl and unlocked Gabrielle's chains. The girl slumped in his arms and he cursed softly.

He glared down at Vicky, thinking quickly. "You, girl, stand up. Lisa, help her lift Gabrielle."

The two slaves hurriedly obeyed, then followed behind as he took Miri's leash, leading them back down the hall.

Suddenly Jubal came around a corner. He started to smile at the sight of him, then saw Gabrielle and frowned. He held a cattle prod in one hand and swung it down angrily.

Paul's fist caught him under the chin and he fell back against the wall, the prod falling from his fingers. Paul snatched up the prod, activating it with the flick of a thumb, and as Jubal rose he grabbed his head, yanked it back and stabbed the prod down straight through his open mouth and into his throat.

He left it there as Jubal began to thrash wildly on the floor, nodding to the wide-eyed women to follow as he took up Miri's leash again and led them away. Jubal continued to thrash on the floor until finally going still.

Five minutes later he had led his little group to the main slave pens. Sarah had been sent to the pens after he'd been caught, and he merely had to go down there and request her services to have her turned over to him. She smiled prettily when he arrived, but made no other reaction.

"I'm glad you're still alive," he whispered when they were alone.

"Thank you, master," she said brightly.

He frowned and looked her up and down.

"Do you remember me, Sarah?"

"Yes, master," she said.

"You've been through the full program, haven't you?"

"Yes, master," she said perkily.

"Did they take you there after I left that night?"

"No master."

"Well then what did they do to you?" he demanded impatiently.

"They tortured me for a week, master, to find out if I knew who you were and what you had been doing."

"And what did you tell them?"

"Everything, master," she said happily.

"Everything?" he demanded.

"Of course master."

He thought furiously. Sarah knew he meant to have the two girls in the barn help him, but he had been caught while trying to pick the lock of the Amanda girl's box, so they may have assumed he didn't have the time to do anything. In any case, since he was dead they had no reason to worry about security until someone else managed to infiltrate their way in.

No doubt they were being extra choosy about who they allowed into the club these days, but that should not affect his intentions tonight.

He looked at the smiling girl and muttered a curse under his breath.

Still, she would obey his orders and that was all he needed at the moment.

He took a carriage from the stables, hooking up two bland-eyed 'horses' as Sarah, Vicky, and Lisa put Miri aboard. Then drove to the barn.

It was just before midnight. He had no real belief the blonde girl - formerly blonde girl - would have been able to sustain her cow-like masquerade for this long, or that if she had she would still be checking the door every might, but he decided to wait and see. His plan, such as it was, was to ransack the lab in hopes someone had left a key behind. That probably wouldn't work either, in which case he'd have to leave the three girls there and go with the ones he had.

Then, much to his surprise, he saw the door sliding open and a small face peer out. He scurried forward as she crawled back, wide-eyed.

"I bet you thought you'd seen the last of me!" he said jovially, rubbing her bald head.

"I... I was... what happened?" she stuttered.

"Things went wrong, and I almost got killed, but I'm here now getting the hell out of here."

He and and Sarah hurried inside and he closed the door behind him.

He flicked on the lights then hurried to the nearby office. A quick blow shattered the glass and he went inside and checked the dockets listing the location of various breeders.

And there was his final girl!

"I found Amanda, master!" Sarah piped up from across the barn.

"Fine. Bring her," he called.

She wasn't one of those he'd been sent for but he felt an obligation to her and the Meghan girl. He hurried through the ranks of mostly sleeping cows until he got to the right pen. Then he opened it, woke the girl there with a slap on her behind, and unhooked her ring from it's chain, leading her out.

"Here. Take her leash," he ordered Meghan.

Meghan stood up shakily, holding a post at first. Her legs had got exercise, of course, and they had been straight whenever she laid down, but she had not walked on them in well over a month.

"Where have you been, you bastard!?" she demanded, glowering.

"I told you, I was delayed."

"Delayed? Delayed!? Do you have any idea what it feels like to be mounted by a bull?"

"A bull?"

"Might as well be! Bulls are men, well-endowed men driven utterly mad by drugs!"

"Oh, well. I'm sorry you didn't enjoy yourself. Then again, you seem to have come through things all right. I did manage to get your drugs substituted before you received them. So I guess you just spent the time out in the sun getting a tan."

"That almost made it worse. That other girl, Amanda, she just crawled around and slept all the time happy as hell. I almost wished I'd had the drugs sometimes."

"Well it's not too late. If you like, just stick around here gabbing and you'll get them for real!"

He turned and hurried back to the others. Meghan followed more slowly, still massaging her aching legs.

Amanda, without her beautiful hair, was kneeling on all fours next to Faleis, the third Jewish girl. They both had wide, empty eyes.

"Come on. Get them to their feet and let's go," he ordered.

The strange procession moved out of the barn. To speed things up the two cows were loaded on the cart with Miri. Meghan couldn't walk very well so she got up beside Paul. While the other three trotted along next to them as they headed for the helipad.

There were two guards there, but one was asleep. Paul dealt with them both easily, then loaded all the girls into a big American made CH-53 helicopter and started the en-

225

gine.

He kept looking for people to come running, guns blazing, but the rotor moved faster and faster, and he took off without incident. He flew low, almost at wavetop level, heading straight south towards Australia.

http://www.silvermoonbooks.com
http://www.Thebookshops.com/erotic

<u>Don't miss our web site!</u>
Free first chapters of all titles
Mail order purchase
Credit card purchase and downloads
Future information
etc etc etc

Next month we bring you PLEASE SAVE ME! another fine novel by Dr Gerald Rochelle:

The man with the pony-tail sprawled lazily across the back seat. Barbara squeezed herself against the door, trying to keep as far away from him as she could. Her heart was beating fast and she felt her cheeks flushing with fear. The man looked across at her.

"Nice tits, really nice tits."

He leant across and pushed his hand into the top of her blouse. She could not believe what was happening. She was terrified and tried to push him away.

"Get away! What are you doing?"

"Feeling your tits, what do you think I'm doing you fucking bitch!"

He pushed his hand further inside her blouse and cupped one of her breasts in his palm. He lifted its weight then squeezed it hard. She cried out and tried again to push him back but he was too strong.

"Very nice. Now let's feel the other one shall we?"

He drew his hand roughly under her other breast and squeezed that even harder, then he reached his fingers up and pinched her nipple. She cried out again but as she tried to pull away he squeezed it harder. It hurt terribly, sending a deep stinging pain into her breast and causing her to gasp for breath. She could not pull away.

"Very nice," he said pushing his face in front of hers, "very nice indeed."

He pressed his mouth against hers and started to lick around her lips with his tongue. She pulled back and turned her face away but he stared at her angrily and, pulling his hand out of her blouse, grabbed her face and turned it back to him.

"Don't turn away from me you bitch!"

He started to kiss her again and this time, no matter how much she tried to turn away she could not. He ran his tongue around her lips and then probed it inside her mouth, licking her tongue and the insides of her cheeks. She could not stop him and let him probe her mouth until it was wet and sore.

Then the front passenger turned around to see what was going on.

"Leave her Ramon, you fucking Spanish animal! We've had no instructions about her yet. You'd better not spoil the goods!"

"It's only a bit of fun Carlo."

Ramon pulled back and Barbara gasped. Her blouse was undone and her bra was pulled down on one side exposing her breast. She reached down to button it up but Ramon grabbed her hands and laughed as she fought against him. She started to scream.

"Keep the bitch quiet can't you?" said Carlo.

Ramon clasped his hand across her face but she twisted away and screamed even louder.

"For fuck's sake Ramon, keep the bitch quiet!"

Ramon sat back for a second then grabbed the front of her white blouse and tore it. It ripped easily and he took the panel of material, wound it up like a rope and pulled it across Barbara's screaming mouth, forcing the sides of her cheeks back as he pulled it tightly. Then he stretched the two ends behind her head and tied them firmly. Some of her long hair caught in the knot and she snorted and gasped in pain but because of the tight-pulled gag she could no longer scream.

Her eyes widened in fear and she started to throw herself about frantically. Her tongue pressed against the back of the gag and she thought she was going to be sick. Ramon grabbed her blouse again and this time ripped the front of it completely apart. Her left breast stood out nakedly from her exposed bra. Its pale flesh was reddened by his rough handling and the nipple that he had squeezed so hard stood out prominently. Then he rolled her over on her front across the back seat and pulled her arms behind her. She gasped and fought for breath but he took no notice as he wound the material from the blouse tightly around her wrists, forcing her facedown and almost sitting on her.

Barbara stared into the leather of the seat and felt the hot pressure of Ramon's body on top of her as she bit into the gag terrified and ashamed. Her hot breath condensed against the shiny surface of the seat and she felt its wetness against her burning cheeks. She did not know what was happening. She could not believe it. She was being abducted but she did not know by whom. All she knew was that they had mentioned Portman. But how could that be? He was a client at the office. What was going on? She felt faint and wanted to cry but she was too terrified to make a noise.

Here is the extract from Victorian Scrapbook, vignettes from a sterner age, by Stephen Rawlings, author of *Jane and Her Master:*

MASTURBATION IN VICTORIAN ENGLAND

The Victorians had an almost pathological fear of masturbation or 'the shameful act', as it was often referred to. For boys who indulged, blindness was prophesied. Boys caught massaging their erect penises were savagely whipped and many curious restraints were used to deny them access to their genitals, ranging from arrangements of straps and sheaths, to leather drawers with padlocked belts. Even involuntary emissions were considered disgraceful and injurious to body and soul, based on a misinterpretation of the story of Onan in the Old Testament, and the ravings of the more manic Early Christian Fathers.

To prevent this latter disaster boys and men, sometimes under coercion but often of their own free will, so burdened were they with guilt, would wear special sheaths at night, lined with small sharp pins. The flaccid penis could be easily inserted, without too much discomfort but, if an erection occurred, presaging lewd dreams and nocturnal emissions, the pins pierced the delicate skin of the engorged organ and the pain involved woke the sleeper and saved him from sin, if not from agony.

Girls were treated as least as severely. It is a mistake to think that the Victorians did not understand the sources of sexual pleasure in women. The clitoris is not a late twentieth century invention and our forefathers and foremothers understood its capabilities very well. However the morbid fear among the middle and intellectual classes of any thing that smacked of joy in sex led them to condemn female masturbation as roundly as that in the male.

If they had no biblical authority for this condemnation, medical science was willing to fill the gap. Eminent doctor after eminent doctor filled the pages of the medical journals with warnings to mothers to prevent such unnatural vice in their daughters. The most notorious was Baker-Brown, who summed up the findings of his colleagues in declaring that masturbation in the female was the source of hysteria and madness, that the practice was a disease that, if unchecked, would otherwise 'proceed inexorably from hysteria to spinal irritation and thence to idiocy, mania, and death'.

The first symptoms of the disease, he thought, manifested themselves at puberty, when girls became 'restless and excited and indifferent to the social influences of domestic life.' There might he depression, loss of appetite, or a quivering of the eyelids, and an inability to look one in the face!

One clue was that such girls often wanted to work, to escape from home and become nurses or sisters of charity; we can easily imagine how Baker-Brown would have reacted to Florence Nightingale and, in his own terms, he would have been entirely justified. Miss Nightingale, according to her own diaries, was 'a martyr to the shameful act.' Night after night she would seek solace between her thighs, unable to resist the temptation to frot her bud until passionate convulsions overcame her, only to writhe in mental agony afterwards, as inbred guilt took the place of evaporating erotic emotion.

To guard against these ever present dangers, parents of daughters were advised to watch them closely for the tell-tale signs, to examine their underwear and night-gowns for the shameful stains of vulval lubricity and to curb their blood with cold showers and loose drawers, removing stimulants such as red meat and French novels. Mechanical devices, chastity belts and leather drawers were employed, similar to those imposed on the boys, but girls also faced another more drastic cure, such as their brothers never endured. In the ultimate, the medics advised, if the girl persisted in this dangerous course, there was nothing for it, for her own good, but to surgically remove her clitoris, so that the practice could be put p[permanently beyond her reach!

Letter from Dorinda, Countess of Batewell, to her sister, Lady Camilla Travaise:

My Dear Sister,

How wise of you to write concerning your eldest. It is, I know, a very trying time, when daughters reach a state of bud, and yet are not yet ripe to plant. As you say, when seeking my help, I have travelled this path before you, and with more than one fair flower, and will impart to you what words of wisdom I may.

In the first place you must harden your resolve, and not let pity for a tender plant impair your duty to her, for her ultimate welfare, no matter that it may be painful for you both in the short term. she has her whole lifetime before her, and it may be blighted, or even cut short, if you fail in your duty at this time, and take no action over the dreadful discovery you described to me. I must emphasis as strongly as I can that what you found, her stimulation of her woman's parts, the frotting of the pubic nerve, is a matter filled with terrible danger. The most eminent of physicians have given public warnings of the inevitable progress to madness and death if unchecked.

Now to matters practical. In the first place she must, of course, be severely punished, to drive home to her the seriousness of what she has done. I recommend at least a good birching; several dozens of strokes at least, and well laid on. Indeed, for my own daughters, I preferred to use a whalebone rod. Like myself you have more than one chick to consider and I heartily recommend to you that she should be whipped before her sisters, bare-arsed to heighten both her humiliation and the impact of the lesson on the younger girls, since they will see so much more clearly how her bottom so scorched by the rod if there are no drawers to draw a veil across the seat of her punishment.

Once the girl is well thrashed and penitent (You must not hesitate for her own sake to repeat the dose if you do not detect an adequate humility in the girl after) you will need to exercise a constant vigilance. These young things are wilful and devious, and quite capable of backsliding, however genuine their repentance may seem at the time. Ensure she is watched carefully by her governess to check on repetition. Have her look out especially for erection or inflammation of the pubic nerve, excessive wetness between the legs, or stains in her drawers, which should be inspected every time they are discarded. If necessary appoint one of the maids to collect the used garments and bring them to governess. Listlessness, inattention and lack of respect for authority, an inability to look one in the eye, these too are all symptoms of the same fatal malady

If this occurs, there must, naturally, be a more severe flogging, again in front of siblings to shame her and deter them, but you must also consider practical methods of deterrence, or restriction of opportunity for sin. Chastity belts can be obtained from several reputable sources, you will find their advertisements in the better class of family journal. but be careful. Even the best may be circumvented by a vicious child. If these measures fail, there is nothing for it but to ablate the pubic nerve. If you baulk at that, though you would be mistaken in your care for her, then try, as an intermediate step, raising such a blister on the spot that she would have no pleasure in touching herself there. A spoon heated in her bedside candle will probably be enough to start with. Otherwise consider rubbing with wire wool or emery cloth, until raw.

Pumice will suffice, if used vigorously enough, but be sure the governess or maid is not distracted by tears or pleading, and continues until the blood flows freely. Have a close eye kept on the wound as it heals, and make sure the process is repeated before the bud has become touchable again. In my experience repeated applications at intervals of fourteen days will often suffice, but do not flinch from weekly abrasion if you have any suspicion that the minx is setting her wicked fingers to her bud earlier. Young women of that age and nature are notoriously sensual, and will brave considerable discomfort if they can thereby stimulate themselves to erotic indulgence.

Above all, my dear sister, you must steel yourself to be cruel to be kind. Better the girl should suffer now than go mad later and then have to face her maker on the last day, with her brain destroyed, and her soul irredeemably soiled. Believe me, I too have known the pain of having to treat a beloved daughter harshly, but I do not regret it nor, I believe, does she. You must not hesitate to write me further, should these measures prove unavailing, and I will try and help you from my own experience,

Yours loving sister,
DORINDA

On the next page we continue Rex Saviour's *Erica* - only we now we are going beyond what was in the book:-

"Well how do you like that? Uses the belt on you most days, eh? Bare assed?"

She nodded, blushing.

"Wowee!" He licked his lips, but evidently thought it best to change the subject. "I like the jewellery, all those snakes, but aren't they a bit - well, nasty?"

As well as the medallion he could see the snake bangles at wrists and ankles. The bands round her arms above the elbow were hidden by the jersey. They all have inconspicuous rings and hooks that snap together as required, but the miniature padlocks are symbolic only.

We were both silent, and he glanced at me enquiringly. "Is there something I missed here? Does she go for snakes, then?" He turned to Erica. "Fond of snakes, are you, girlie?"

"NO!"

"No?"

"No, I -"

"Yes, girlie? Go on?"

"Oh God, I'm so scared of them, they're horrible, horrible, I hate wearing them, it makes me think real ones are creeping all over me, slimy -"

"Snakes aren't slimy," I said. I was always pointing that out to her, but she never seemed to take it in.

"Slimy and slithery. Slither slither slither!"

The very thought of it was making a squirm more than the dildo was. "It's a hang-over from an unfortunate childhood," I explained. "A very unfortunate childhood ... hush dear, you're getting too excited."

"Sorry, Uncle Rex," she said meekly, but I saw tears in those bright blue eyes of hers.

"You'd better tell Hank about systematic desensitising."

"Uncle believes in this systematic desensitisation therapy - it's very scientific, he's shown me books about it, it means if I wear more and more snakes it will cure me of my fear of snakes. In the end. So being with snakes is good for me, just like being dressed like this will make me less shy. He believes."

I do believe that. "We!" I said. "We believe!"

She hesitated. "We believe."

"And about beating? I wouldn't want him to think I am unkind to you."

"And - and - and so, you see, if I don't accept the desensitisation gracefully - well then Uncle Rex has to beat me till I do."

"Great stuff," he said. "And is all this, er, this therapy stuff, is it working?"

"Well no, no not very well, not yet. I think I'm worse." She glanced at me. "But Uncle says we have to keep trying."

"Another thing is, she doesn't like being touched by a man," I said.

"So being touched is good for her? It will cure her if it is done enough?"

"That's right," I said encouragingly. "She wriggles a bit, which proves it must be doing good."

The man winked at me, and Erica shrank back as he reached out to lay a hand on her knee. I didn't object. It must be good for her. She didn't seem to be any better, but the method surely can't be wrong. Indeed, I know it isn't. An Aunt of mine was cured of a fear of spiders by looking at a little one from a long way off, then coming closer and closer, and then doing the same with a bigger one, until at last she could even touch it.

Hank finished his beer then raised a hand to her chest. "Is it my imagination, or does the little lady have rings in her nipples?"

"Ask her," I said.

"Well, angel?"

"Yes," she said. "But there aren't any bells of them today."

"And no bra?"

234

She wriggled. "No!"

He glanced round to be sure nobody was watching, then reached out and pinched the left nipple through her jersey. We both noticed how she flinched away.

"God, it's true! I like that, very sexy. Er -" For the first time he seemed a little embarrassed. "Do you mind if I ask - is she wearing knickers?"

"No," she said, "no, because Uncle considers them unnecessary."

He whistled. "And does she have labial rings too as well as nipple rings? Do you, girlie?"

Erica glanced at me, but I didn't help her out.

"Uncle did put some on me, but I don't have them on now, because -'"

"Because what?"

She hesitated. "Because - they got in the way of the chain -'"

"Chain? What chain?" His eyes were glistening.

"To keep the snake in -'"

"Snake? What snake, for God's sake?"

"It's her name for a special dildo," I explained. "I made it look as much like a snake as possible."

"Jesus! A snake dildo - she wears it all the time?"

I nudged her into speech. "Well, you see, that's what the chain is for, it comes between my legs from one round my waist. It's locked by a padlock at the back."

"My God! And no, eh? Considers them unnecessary, does he?"

She was blushing furiously as she nodded. "Unnecessary, yes, well, actually, it's more than that I suppose, he burned the ones I had and - well, actually, I don't think I'm allowed -'"

"Come now," I said. "Not allowed? That's not true, Erica dear. I got some special ones for you when you first came to me, don't you remember?"

"Oh!"

"Of course you remember!"

"Yes, Uncle, you did get some for me -"

"Yes, go on, tell him."

"They had snakes embroidered on them. I just couldn't wear them, he tried to make me, he beat me every day for ages because I wouldn't but it was no good, ugh, snakes crawling over me down there - oh God, I couldn't, I couldn't, not down there -"

"You still have them, my dear," I said mildly. "They were quite expensive. You could wear them if you wanted."

"I can't, I can't, not more snakes down there!"

"But the dildo?"

"He put it in. I can't get it out because of the chain. It's horrible, it's getting warm and that will wake it up!" She was nearly in tears.

"No knickers under that apology for a mini-skirt! Wowee! This I must see!"

"Well," I said, "her chain is certainly something we're proud of, aren't we dear?"

"Yes Uncle Rex." She sounded very reluctant, but I decided to speak to her about that later.

"So you'll be glad to show our friend Hank?"

"Yes, Uncle, I suppose so." Even more reluctant, almost mutinous. I would not forget that, and she saw the prospect of the belt in my face. She would not aggravate me any further, I knew. I looked round the lounge. It would be somewhat embarrassing to do it here in the cafeteria, and we mustn't miss the flight by causing a disturbance.

"Come on," I said. "Over by the wall." I could see that a few men were curious as we walked over, but not enough to matter. "That's right, you two face each other. Now, Erica dear, lift your skirt, come on, right up, don't worry about that lot over there, I'll stand behind you to block them out."

Ever so reluctantly the little skirt inched up, and Hank

whistled.

"God sakes, look at that!"

"Turn round for him, dear," I said, "and you'd better damn well stop blushing or I'll change that chain for the snake one." She knows I have a chain made of little gold snakes: I have never made her wear it, but the threat certainly bothers her.

In the meanwhile, Hank's eyes were almost popping out. "God, what a neat little bottom. But isn't that chain too tight?"

She turned back to face him, and glanced at me. "Uncle doesn't think so!" That was as near to a complaint as she dare go.

"And he keeps you shaved?"

Just a little whisper. "Yes!"

She was still blushing, but she was also still holding her skirt up. She was doing quite well. He tore his gaze away and looked at me.

"I have to touch, OK?"

At that moment the flight was called.

"Maybe on the plane," I said.

We had to walk from the terminal building to the bus that would take us to the plane. It was quite windy outside, and Erica was glad enough to get on the bus, jostled amongst strange men though she was.

The steps up to the plane were quite steep and she was blushing even before we got out of the bus. I wasn't sure whether she would prefer to wait in the wind or go up ahead, so in the end we were about in the middle.

The side seats were in blocks of three, so I gave Erica a window. I prefer a gangway seat myself, so Hank was next to her. He raised the seat rest between them so he could lean over and see out of the window.

"Don't squeal, girl!" I said to Erica. "What will people think!"

The refuelling stop at Bahrain was good fun. The plane docked at the terminal - more civilised than Heathrow. Well, to be fair, there were so many fewer planes, in fact ours was the only big one in - it was already quite late at night.

The soldiers looked at Erica in a very peculiar way. I think she had every right to blush in Bahrain airport, she was such a contrast to most of the other women there, Arab ladies with their voluminous robes and hidden faces.

Hank tanked up with more beers: he was the first off the plane to discover that the bar took English money! He was in great form, and stayed close to Erica all the time. The air-conditioning made it rather cold, so she must have felt a little under-dressed as we strolled round. He gave her a hug or two, which the locals didn't seem to approve of. There wasn't a lot to see, though the duty free area was excellent.

Erica seemed on edge.

"What's the matter, dear?"

"Uncle, the snake is getting really warm. Couldn't you get the control thing back straight away, now we've arrived?"

"Arrived?" Hank laughed, a raucus sort of guffaw. "Don't you know where we are, Girlie?" It was Hank giving forth in his usual brash way. "Doesn't she know where she's going, for God's sake? This is a stopover to refuel, girlie."

"Oh God! We aren't there yet?"

"Maybe half way", I said encouragingly.

She was very quiet for a while, nursing her drink as she tried hard not to squirm. "And how long - how long do we have to wait here?"

"It should only be an hour," I said. "But - see that board - there's a delay of some sort. We might be here quite a while if they have to send for spare parts."

At one time we thought we might have to stay all night, but they sorted the problem out, whatever it was, in about four hours.

Back on the plane, I noticed that Hank took his seat first, so that Erica had to clamber over him, which he didn't make easy, though she made a gallant effort not to squeal. I think the beer was unravelling his inhibitions, not that he had started with a lot. And after the meal and a film, she annoyed me by yelping as she scrambled back over him to get out to the toilet. Coming back she was rather reluctant to take her seat: she wanted to swop with me, but, as I said, I prefer the gang-way.

I took the trouble to get a couple of rugs from the racks, one for me and one for them, but, when the lights were dimmed for an hour or two's sleep, she was quite restless until I leant over Hank and told her to settle down and stop disturbing me.

TITLES IN PRINT

Silver Moon

Silver Mink

*UK £4.99 except *£5.99 --USA $8.95 except *$9.95*